HAND MADE MAGE

By

James A. Haddock III

WEBSITE:

Jameshaddock.us
Haddockpublishing.com

Ghost, a young Criminal Guild thief, is ordered to rob the ancient crypt of a long dead Duke. He is caught grave robbing by an undead insane Mage with a twisted sense of humor. The Mage burns a set of rune engraved rings into Ghost's hand, and fingers. Unknown to Ghost, these rings allow him to manipulate the four elements — earth, wind, fire, and water.

When he returns to the Guild to report his failure, everyone thinks he has riches from the crypt, and they want them. While being held captive, Ghost meets Prince Kade, the fourth son of the King, who has troubles of his own. Ghost uses his newfound powers to escape from the Guild, saving the Prince in the process.

Spies from a foreign kingdom are trying to kill Prince Kade, and Ghost must keep them both alive, while helping the prince raise an army to stop an invasion. Ghost finds out trust too soon given is unwise and dangerous. He is learning people will do anything for gold and power. As Ghost's power grows, his enemies learn he is a far more deadly enemy than any they have ever faced.

CHAPTER 1

It was almost dawn, and I needed to be out of the graveyard before sunrise. Putting the night's harvest in the coin purse around my neck, I hid my tools. I left the crypt through the hole I had made in the wall behind a column. Once outside, I replaced the marble facade covering the hole. I looked around and saw no one.

Anyone seeing me leave would assume I was just one of many who slept among the dead. The graveyard was one of the safer places to sleep, and I had done so frequently. Most people had a fear of the places of the dead, but I did not. The dead wouldn't bother you, but the living, on the other hand...

I walked through the wet grass and pre-dawn fog to the nearest gap in the cemetery's iron picket fence, then turned toward the river. The city watch was supposed to patrol the graveyard, but no one cared, least of all the old watchman. I walked at a steady pace down the cobblestoned street, just another early morning figure going about his daily life. I wanted to wash the cobwebs, dust and musty smell of the dead off of me. I liked to keep a neat appearance. People asked fewer questions if you kept yourself clean, and the city watch didn't look as closely at you. I didn't like to draw attention to myself. Attracting attention was attracting trouble, and beatings were sure to follow.

Don't get me wrong, I can hold my own with one or two attackers, with fists or blades. But when the city watch gets involved, you don't fight back. That was a sure way to be found floating face down in the river. You could recover from a beating, the other was more permanent.

The smell of fresh bread from the bakery on the corner reminded me of how hungry I was. That would be my next stop, after I got cleaned up. This area of the river front was already busy with the workmen who loaded and unloaded the barges heading up and down the river, moving cargo all the time.

There were already a few women at the river's edge, washing clothes. "Grandmother, what will you charge me to wash my pants and shirt?" I asked one.

She looked at me and my clothes, "a two-penny." I nodded, taking off my shoes, shirt and pants. "Your small clothes too." I nodded, stripped down, and laid them in the pile. I walked into the cold water of the river. "Here, use this too," and tossed me a bar of soap.

I caught it smiling, "yes ma'am." I washed my hair, and scrubbed myself clean until my skin was red from the strong soap. I rinsed myself well, so it left no soap behind to burn me. I returned her soap, and she handed my small clothes to me. They were damp but clean. I re-wrapped them and waited for her to finish my other things.

She finished, and I gave her a five-penny. "Thank you, Grandmother." I had learned courteousness and generosity paid better dividends than just coin.

"Bless you son, I'm here most mornings when you have need again." She turned back to her work. Clean and damp, I made my way to the bakery. There were a few people in line and I took my place behind them, admiring the smells.

"Next! " I stepped forward, "what'll you have?" the man asked.

"Bread, cheese, ham."

"Five-penny." I paid a girl, probably his daughter, she gave me my food, and I was on my way. I ate as I walked.

I had to report in to Tall-man and pay his part on my night's take. It wasn't good for your health to not pay him his share. "Dues," he called it, for letting you work in his area.

I made my way through dirty, dark alleys and backstreet-

s. The "Den" for this area was under the back of an off-street warehouse. Two toughs were watching the door.

"He's in a foul mood this morning, Ghost."

"Thanks, Dane," I replied as I entered. I heard the shouting as I walked down the musty dark hall toward the back room. The door was open, but I waited.

"You holding back on me, boy?" Tall-man shouted as he put boots to one of the street urchins. "You holding back from me?" The boy never had time to answer before he passed out from the kicking. Tall-man kicked him a few more times, for good measure. "Get him out of here." Two toughs grabbed him and dragged him out.

Tall-man stepped back to his scarred three legged desk — the fourth leg was a rock. Picking up his cup, he drank from it. "Examples got to be made, discipline maintained." He said to no one in particular.
Seeing me at the door he motioned me in. I took my purse from my neck and poured its contents out on his desk.

He looked over the take, and then at me. "You spend any this morning?"

I nodded, "ten-penny." He held my gaze seeing if I would flinch or look away. I did not.

"You holding back?"

"No, Tall-man." He held my gaze a moment longer, then looked back at my take. He took the three rings and left me the three coins. He made a shooing motion, and I took my coins and purse from his desk.

"Lead-man wants to see you." He thumbed over his shoulder toward the closed door in the back of the room. I nodded and went to the door and knocked.

"Come," came from the other side of the door. I opened the door, looking inside at Lead-man, a mean-eyed man with a scar across his face.

"Tall-man said you wanted to see me."

"Yes, come in, and close the door." He spoke in a friendly voice, which he only used when he wanted something. I closed the door and turned back to him. He took out a paper with a drawing on it.

"Do you recognize this?" I moved to his desk looking at the dirty paper, some kind of map.

"Yes, that's the graveyard where the oldest crypts are located, some ancient, maybe some of the first ones. They say they are warded against entry by powerful spells."

He nodded, "so they say. I am told there is a way around the wards. They say that if you tunnel in from the side, you will bypass the wards on the doors." I doubted that, but I held my peace. "This particular crypt," he pointed, "belongs to a Duke. I would think it would be a good place to plunder." I looked at the location, nodding. This was his story, and I would not interrupt.

"I want you to take Shorts and Pick with you tonight, find that crypt and start your tunneling. You don't have to report back until you reach the Duke's crypt, or a week from now to report your progress. Questions?"

"Food for the week?"

He put two golds on the desk. "Anything else?"

"No, Lead-man,"

"Good, go make us rich." Which meant go make him rich. I nodded and left his office.

As I passed Tall-Man's Desk, "Shorts and Pick are waiting for you outside, be back in a week." I nodded and left his office. Shorts and Pick were waiting outside talking with Dane. Pick was a big strong man, a miner as you might suspect with a name like Pick. Shorts was, well, short. Not a dwarf but close to it. He was also a strong man that knew how to use a pick and shovel.

I crossed the alley to them, "they tell you anything?" Both of them shook their heads. "The bottom line is, you'll be working with me, and we have some digging to do."

"In the graveyard?" Pick asked, frowning.

"Where else?" I answered smiling.

"I hate that place, gives me the creeps. I don't want to go

there any sooner than I have too." We chuckled at him.

"I need to get some sleep, so meet me at the west entrance at nine o'clock tonight. Bring lanterns and your tools and we'll get started." They nodded and went their way, and I went mine.

***

I was waiting for them when they arrived, a few minutes past nine. I had three days' worth of travel food for the three of us. If we weren't done by then, I figured we'd need a break anyway.

"Ready?" I asked.

"As I'll ever be," Pick answered and Short nodded.

I led them to the gap in the fence and then on to the crypt I used as my entrance to the catacombs. Gathering my tools and lighting a lantern we climbed down into the tunnels below.

We stopped at an intersection of tunnels.

"If we get separated, I mark each tunnel, I pointed at the wall. It's got a cross, a circle, or headstone. The cross-marked tunnel takes you to the graveyard church, the circle is an exit out, and the headstone leads to the catacombs." They nodded.

We continued to follow the tunnel deeper into the catacombs. The flickering lantern light gave the place a creepy feel. I smiled thinking of how Pick felt about the place.

We had walked for a long time, "You know where you're going?" Shorts asked.

"I know about where we're going based on the map Lead-man showed me. I've never been there before. I'm thinking this is a waste of time. I'm guessing that crypt was plundered generations ago. But I didn't tell Lead-man that."

"Smart thinking, that." Pick said.

We walked on a good while longer, finally coming to a large set of double doors with lion statues standing guard. There were scraps of clothing and bones scattered around the room. That was not a good sign, and I took it as a warning.

"I don't like taking chances, let's find another way around to a side tunnel and dig through." They both nodded and followed me back to the last intersection. One tunnel had a downward slope to it while the other did not. We wanted to stay on this level so we took the one that had no slope. We followed the new tunnel until we felt we were well past the door and started digging.

The first three feet of digging was easy, mostly dirt. After that we hit mostly rock. We traded off digging, stopping to rest and eat. I finally called a halt, and we ate and slept. We woke and took care of the morning needful and ate, each caught up in our own thoughts.

"Does it always smell like this?" Shorts asked. I had been doing this so long I didn't notice the smell anymore.

I sniffed, finding nothing unusual, just the normal musty smell of decay. "Sometimes worse after a fresh burial."

"You must love your job," Pick said.

"I like the solitude, no one bothers me down here."

"I wonder why," Pick said chuckling.

I just smiled, taking my pick and standing up. "let's get back to it."

Our tunnel was about ten feet along when we broke through into another passageway. We went slowly, not sure what we would find on the other side. We made the opening large enough to lean in with a lantern to see more of the passageway.

"What do you see?" Shorts asked from the rear.

"Stone-lined passageway, floor, and walls. I can't see the big doors so we must be a good way from them. Let's open the hole a little more."

Shorts came forward to take his turn opening the hole, and made quick work of it. Picking up the lantern, he stepped through the opening into the passageway, with us close behind.

There was a roar, and Shorts screamed. In the dancing lantern light we saw a stone lion had Shorts' arm in its mouth and was shaking him like a rag-doll. We dropped our lanterns and attacked the lion with our picks. Roars and screams filled the passageway. I swung my pick striking the lion in the back. It squalled, released Shorts and turned on me. As it approached me, a pick crashed into its head and it crumpled into dust and rock. We stared down at the pile of rocks that had been a lion a moment ago. We were breathing hard, trying to catch our breath. Shorts sat against the wall holding his ruined arm.

"Where's the other one?" Shorts asked.

I jumped up grabbing my pick putting my back to the wall, moving over to Shorts and Pick. "Good question." We waited, watching and listening.

"How bad?" Pick asked.

"Arm's broken in a couple of places. No blood. Shoulder's probably in bad shape too, but I can't feel it yet."

"Ok, let's back out of here and get you to a healer. We're not going to split up with that other lion still out there somewhere," I said. We picked up our lanterns and moved toward our tunnel.

"Do you have a back-up plan?" Pick asked. I turned, looking at him. He had his lantern held up at our tunnel, or where our tunnel should have been. It was now a solid stone wall.

"Well, that's not good," I said, looking at the wall. A deep growl came from the passageway back toward the doors we had bypassed. "We can't stay here, let's see if there is another way out. I'll take lead, Pick, you watch behind." They nodded, and we moved away from the growling, moving down the passageway. The growling got no closer, but always there.

"Why do I feel we are being herded?" Shorts asked.

"I had the same thought," I answered, "but we have to move or fight. Right now, I'd rather be moving."

My lantern light pierced the darkness with each step we took. It finally showed an open set of double doors. I moved forward slowly, passing through the door. The room on the other side had two doors — one standing open, the other closed. The open one had a cross over it, so it must go up to a chapel. The other door had no symbol on it, but was guarded by two armed and armored stone knight statues.

Once Pick was through the door, we closed it behind us. Hopefully, it would keep the lion from us. We went through the Chapel doors, but we could not close them.

"You two go ahead, I'll guard here for a bit and then follow. Get to the Chapel and out as fast as you can, I'll meet you up top." They nodded and started up the stairs. The sounds of their footsteps faded, I would give them a few more minutes, then I would follow.

Time seemed to move slowly, and the air was a little close, but I knew it was my having to wait that was making it feel that way.

I heard growling at the far door. I watched the door closely, and it seemed to move as if it was being pushed.

I moved to stand behind a column to the side of the room as the doors burst open. When the lion ran past the column I was behind, I made to bury my pick in its back but missed. Instead, I buried my pick in the floor.

The lion disappeared up the stairs toward the chapel. I needed to follow, but I needed my pick first. I was trying to break it loose from the floor when I was grabbed from behind and thrown bodily against the wall. I lay there stunned, then was grabbed again. I tried to see who my attacker was by the flickering lantern light. It was the two stone knights that had been guarding the other door. I tried to break free of their grip but could not. They dragged me toward the closed door. Try as I might, I could not gain my freedom — kicking them was literally like kicking a stone wall.

As the knights dragged me toward the doors, they opened. At the other end of the room on a raised platform was a throne, occupied by a decaying corpse in armor. The corpse looked at me and spoke. "A thief." The knights dragged me before the throne and threw me down. "Have you come to steal from me?" Not normally one at a loss for words, this time I was too stunned to say anything. "Well, we wouldn't want you to leave empty-handed," he said in a crazy hysterical voice.

The corpse rose from his throne, walked over to a chest along the wall and opened it. looking inside. "Yes that one will do, he will do nicely." He reached in and pulled out something I could not make out. He returned to stand in front of me. A knight held my left hand forward, presenting it to the corpse. It worked gold rings onto my fingers and thumb as flesh fell from its decayed hands. Each ring was attached to a gold bracelet by a gold chain. He snapped the bracelet around my wrist, holding my hand in his rotting hands.

He squeezed my hand tightly and began chanting in some arcane language. When he finished, he said, "It is done, now you won't leave empty-handed." He started laughing his crazy laugh again.

My hand burst into flame! I watched in horror as the gold rings and bracelet melted into runes, then sank into my skin. The only thing I could do was scream, on and on, as the pain became unbearable. Eventually I mercifully faded into blackness and knew no more.

CHAPTER 2

Pain pulled me from the blackness of unconsciousness, but the darkness of the crypt was still around me. I was lying on some steps and there was a faint light at, what I assumed, was the top of the stairs.

I don't know how long I had been out. My mouth was dry and gummy. My hand shot pain up my arm every time my heart beat. Cradling it to my chest, I stayed on my right side as I started crawling up the stairs toward the light.

My whole body hurt from the kicking the knights had given me. It seemed to me a beating from stone knights hurt more than a beating from a guild enforcer. I hoped I'd never have the opportunity to make that comparison again.

I don't know what time it was, but it was dark outside. The light I had been following were the lanterns of the Chapel. I made my way to the fountain in the atrium and drank my fill. I knew I would regret it, but I lowered my burnt hand into the water to rinse the dirt and grime from it. The pain was not as bad as expected but worse than I hoped.

I took a prayer cloth from a pew, wet it and wrapped my hand. I walked around the fountain to the door to leave but stopped. I turned back toward the front of the chapel where the crucifix hung. I bowed, "thank you for the water and the bandage." I wasn't a believer, but why take chances? With that I left the chapel.

Outside there was an early morning mist of rain. I made my way through the graveyard and down toward the river. Maybe I could find somewhere dry to rest before I went to the Den.

Every step I took jarred my hand. The pain was such

that I only realized where I was when I stood at the river-bank. I turned and walked back up the street.

From the porch of one shanty came a voice. "They be no need for washing today, son." I staggered to a stop, looking up through blurred eyes.

"Good morning, Grandmother."

She motioned me over. "Are ya hurt, lad?" she asked, looking at my bandaged hand.

I looked down. "A bit."

"Come inside then, out of the rain." I followed her inside. She had a small fire going. "Get out of those wet clothes before ya catch your death." She handed me a blanket, and I started trying to get undressed one-handed. "Here, let me help." She stripped me out of my wet clothes, being careful of my hand. Wrapping me in the blanket she sat me by the fire. "Tea will be ready shortly."

I kept my hand away from the fire — even this small flame hurt. She handed me a cup of tea, weak but hot, and I was thankful.

She pulled her chair close in front of mine. "Can I look to your hand?" I nodded and held it out to her. Luckily the rain had kept the cloth wet. Wrapping a burn in cloth without ointment is not a wise thing to do.

"I'll be as gentle as I can, lad." I nodded, trying to make a brave showing, I was proud that I didn't cry out, but it was a close thing. When my make-do bandage was finally off, I could see how bad it was in full light. It was not a pretty sight.

"I've seen worse, but seldom. I'll do what I can for ya."

As she worked, she talked, sprinkling powder on my hand. "This will take away some pain as I clean it.

"Saw plenty of burns back during the wars. I was a camp follower for a time, in love with a soldier. When he was killed I kind of lost my way in life. To fill the hole it left, I started helping with the wounded. I learned as much as I could from the healers.

"My knowledge is all mundane, since I have no magic

abilities, but I get by."

"I am thankful for your help."

"In all honesty you may lose the hand."

I nodded, "I'm still thankful for your help."

She gave me more tea, "I've put something in it to help you sleep." I drank it and she lay me down on a pallet. Whatever she gave me worked great, and the next thought I had was "morning." I had slept through the day and night. I got up to do the needful, but moved — slowly the beating and bruises were making themselves known.

I slowly got dressed. She made me more tea and a slice of bread. Once finished, I took my purse from my neck. "It's not much, but the best I can do, for now."

I rose to leave, and she said "come back around in a few days so I can look to your hand and keep it dry." I bowed and left.

I limped my way to the Den. As usual, Dane was standing watch outside.

"You sure you want to go in there, Ghost?"

I frowned, "I have no choice, I have to report in."

"True enough, be warned. Trouble is waiting. Shorts and Pick went in two days ago, and I ain't seen them since."

I nodded, "Thanks Dane."

He nodded, "luck."

I went inside, limping down the hall to Tall-man's office. When he saw me, he barked "wait here," and went into Lead-man's office.

He opened the door and motioned, "get in here!" He grabbed me by the back of the neck and slammed me into the chair. Lead-man looked at me from across his desk. "Before you say a word, be warned those other two fools told all. So, where's my gold?"

I sat stunned.

"There was no gold, the only thing we found..." That was a far as I got. Tall-man knocked me out of the chair, making my ears ring. He stomped on my bandaged hand. I screamed.

"Don't even think about telling me that story about stone lions attacking you. The only way I will believe that, is if one walks through that door, and I wish one would."

I wish one would, too!

There came a growl from behind us, and there in the doorway crouched a stone lion.

"Oh God! He followed us!" I yelled, scrambling toward the far wall. The lion roared and leapt over Lead-man's desk, tearing out his throat. This was not the same sort of lion we had met in the catacombs. This one's teeth were long and sharp, and so were its claws. Tall-man didn't shy away from the fight. He drew his knife and leapt on the lion's back, but his knife had no effect on the creature, and he was dead in the next instant.

The lion turned looking around the room, looked at me, turned, and ran roaring out the door. I didn't move for fear he would come back, sitting motionless, listening to the fighting outside. After a while all was quiet. I waited a while longer, still no sounds.

Tall-man was dead. Lead-man was dead. Others of the Guild would come to see what had happened, and with every-one dead but me, I needed to disappear.

Let them think me dead too.

Money would make my disappearance easier, so I eased over to the desk and searched Tall-man and Lead-man's bodies. Both carried coin purses, with gold inside. I searched the desk but found no more. He must have a hiding place to store the Den's money.

I studied the room, thinking where I might put a hiding place.

Suddenly, my left hand started tingling, and I knew where the hiding place was! I pulled out the bottom drawer of the desk and found some loose floorboards, stuffed with cash.

I lifted out four large bags of gold, some banknotes, and two money belts. I knew if I took it all, the Guild's Upper-men would never stop looking for whoever did this. I filled the purses I had taken from Tall-man and Lead-man with as much gold as they would hold, then put the bags and belts back under the floor. I replaced the boards and the desk drawer as I had found them.

I looked up and the stone lion sat in the doorway looking out, as if he was guarding this room. For some reason I was no longer scared of the lion.

If everyone was to think me dead, I could go nowhere I normally went. I definitely could not go back to my sleeping area at the other warehouse.

My clothes were bloody, so I needed new ones. I had money to buy new, but I needed some to get me to where I could buy new ones. I looked in Lead-man's wardrobe, remembering we were of a similar size. I found a pair of pants and a shirt that would fill my needs.

I changed clothes and threw my old bloody set into the other room. It was then I missed the lion. He was gone. It was time for me to be gone too. I headed slowly down the hall. Dead bodies were in every room. The front door was open, and no one was around. There was no sign of Dane, dead or alive. I hoped he escaped alive.

It was now late afternoon, and I was hungry. I went back to "Grandmothers" house. When I arrived she was sitting on her porch.

"I see you survived your meeting."

"Barely. I need a place to stay out of sight for a few days and heal, and I now have money to pay for food and your help."

She looked at me a moment, "I can hardly turn my grandson away!"

We went inside and she made tea. I took out Tall-man's purse and poured it on the table. It was a tidy sum.

"Use this to buy food, and whatever other supplies you need. You need make no accounting to me for it. Get more tea, since you seem to be running short," I said smiling. She took a few of the coins and left for the market.

Alone, I sat thinking, drinking my tea.

***

Someone was shaking me, "Wake up, you." It took a moment for my eyes to focus. There was a man sitting across the table from me, with Grandmother to his left. Looking around the room, I saw another man behind me and one by the door.

"How much did you put in his tea?" The man at the table asked.

"Not much, just enough for a short nap, he'll come out of it shortly." I glanced at the empty tea up in front of me, then at her.

"Why?" I asked.

"For the reward, lad, nothing personal. I like you but you are far too trusting."

My anger cleared my head. "So now you're the only one left that knows where the gold is hidden." Her mouth dropped open.

"What gold?" The man across the table asked.

I looked back at him. "You're an Upper-man?" He nodded. "Me, Shorts and Pick brought back gold from a crypt, and hid it. Lead-man killed Shorts and Pick trying to find it. Now it's just me and her who knows where it is. I guess she got greedy."

"He's lying!"

The Upper-man plunged his knife into her chest. She looked down at the knife, then at me. "There's your reward, Grandmother, nothing personal."

He pulled his knife from her and she fell to the floor dead. He looked at me considering, then smiled.

"There isn't any gold, is there?"

"Only what's on the table. I took it from Tall-man's body."

He chuckled, "well played, lad," he said looking down at the dead woman. He cleaned off his knife and put it away.

"You were there when the Den was attacked?"

I nodded, "I was."

"Then regale us with your tale," he said leaning forward, "leave nothing out or you'll be joining the old woman."

I nodded, "four days ago Lead-man ordered Shorts, Pick, and I to rob a particular crypt..."

I told him my tale, well, most of it. I left out the part about the melted rings and bracelet in my hand, and that I knew where the Den's gold was hidden.

"And why didn't the stone lion kill you as it had everyone else?"

"I don't know, and I wasn't hanging around to give it another chance. I ran."

He nodded, "you're coming with us, Over-man will want to talk to you." He pointed to the money on the table, "take your money, you earned it." I put the money in the purse and put it away.

I followed him out the door, and got into a wagon with his two bruisers. One drove the wagon with the Upper-man beside him. We drove through the city and across the bridge to Upper-City. We followed the river to a warehousing district, where we entered a warehouse and they took me to a back area. I was sat at a table and given food. "Wait here," Upper-Man said. I sat, ate and waited. With-in the hour I found myself in front of Over-man telling my tale again.

When I finished Over-man sat considering me. "Unwrap that hand," he said pointing.

As easily as I could I took off the bandages. It was a blackened swollen mess but showed no signs of infection. At least the old woman had done that right.

"You might keep the hand, but it will be of little use to you. Will you go back to the crypt?"

"If it's all the same to you sir, I'd rather not."
He laughed, "a diplomatic answer if I ever heard one. Draw me a map we'll check your story, then decide what to do with you."

I drew them a map of the way we went in and also of the Chapel exit. Over-man looked at the map nodding.

"Take him to the holding cell."

I followed Upper-man down to the holding cells; he placed me in one in the back away from everyone else.

"I'll be back, if everything checks out, you'll be out in no time."

I went to the back of the cell and sat down on the floor.

I wonder what they really think?

My hand started tingling and I could hear Upper-man, and Over-man talking, even though they were several rooms away, through closed doors.

"Why didn't we kill him? You have the map."

"We will use him to solve a problem."

"What problem is that?"

"Top-man has set me a task, to see it done personally."

"That's unusual."

"Yes, but it's an unusual task. We hold Prince Kade prisoner in the brothel basement next door. He's not to survive the night. We will use our young grave robber as the murderer, and neither will survive."

"You'll want it to happen in front of witnesses. Maybe a knife fight and fall from the second-story balcony?"

"Yes, that will do nicely. See that all is ready for the performance."

I sat stunned. How could I have heard them? They were going to kill me. I felt panicky.

"Calm down, breath. What else is going to happen?

"*Maybe the earth will open up and swallow me.* That would be a great end of the day."

Before I could react, I sank into the ground like a stone dropping into a pond. I fought like a drowning man, to no avail, I was below ground level. I clawed and fought until it exhausted me. I finally gave up. I just floated there in the ground under my cell.

When I calmed down, I realized I was still breathing. "This is crazy, how is this possible?" I realized my hand was tingling. I thought back to each time my hand had tingled, and each time something crazy had happened. What had that talking corpse done to me?

I need to get back up into my cell. I began rising through the dirt and into my cell, where I stopped rising and was once again seated. I sat there digesting all that had happened, trying to understand it. It was obviously magic. The artifact the talking corpse put on me had to be the cause of all of this.

My hand tingled, I knew they were coming for me. I remained seated, the door opened, and Upper-man stepped in.

"No one eats for free, come with me." I got up and followed him, "we need to move a drunk from the brothel next door — you will help." We went out and around by the alley to the back of the brothel, then down through a door into the basement. There was a guard by one of the doors, "open it," barked my jailer. The guard opened the door and stepped back. Upper-man looked in then motioned me inside. "Wait in here and keep an eye on him."

I nodded, "yes sir," and went in the room playing, my part. They closed and locked the door behind me. I didn't know how much time I would have before they came back. My cellmate had a bag over his head and was bound hand and foot.

I sat on the floor and concentrated. Nothing happened. *Show me... The surrounding rooms.* My hand tingled, and I was looking through transparent walls and floors.

I could see the guard outside the door, and the surrounding rooms. Most were storage rooms, but there was a narrow hall on the other side of the back wall of our room. It reminded me of a secret escape passageway.

I got up and moved to the back wall no one was in the passageway. I put my hand on the wall and pushed. Nothing happened. *I want to go through this wall.* I stepped through the wall. I smiled, "this will come in handy!"

I walked to the door I could see at the end of the passageway. There was no one on the other side of the door. I went to see where the other end went. It looked to go under the street, and deeper into the city.

I went back to the wall of the room the man they called a "Prince" was in and stepped through the wall. It was easier this time. I went to the door looking at the guard. I needed to get rid of him. With my wounded hand it would be tricky.

I concentrated and dropped through the floor into the earth. It was a weird feeling. I was under the guard looking up at him like I was swimming in a pool of water. No one else was around. I concentrated, reached up and pulled him under with me. He dropped in like a rock in water. When he was fully under ground I kicked away from him. When I broke contact he was locked solid in dirt and could not move. He was dead moments later, drowned in dirt.

If my hand was whole, I thought, maybe I could have done it differently. My hand began to tingle and the guard's corpse crumpled in on itself. It looked like it had been there for years. My hand suddenly no longer hurt, so I unwrapped it. My hand was totally healed! It looked perfect. Another mystery was how I could see in the earth's darkness. It was a conundrum for another time. I took the guard's keys, knife, and coin purse.

Checking to ensure the hall was still clear, I rose up through the floor, unlocked the storage room door and went back inside, locking the door behind me. Crossing to the so-called Prince, I knelt down and removed the bag from his head. His eyes were open, and he was staring at me. I had my finger over my lips, signaling him to remain quiet. He frowned but nodded his head.

I untied his hands, "we must be quiet if we are to escape." I untied his feet and he took off his gag. "Can you walk?" He nodded, and I helped him up. He was a little wobbly but at least he was on his feet. I unlocked the door and led him to the door to the escape passageway.

"Follow this, it will lead you to an exit closer to the inner city. Be warned, you have enemies. Someone paid big money to have you killed in a fight in the brothel tonight. That much money usually means royalty." I handed him the guard's purse and knife. "Luck."

"Your name?"

"They call me Ghost."

"Who do you work for?"

"Myself."

"Well, Sir Ghost, I'll not forget this ... know you have a friend if you ever need one." With that he trotted off down the passageway. I barred the door, then stepped through it to the other side.

I had a few loose ends to tie up.

CHAPTER 3

I walked across the hall and through the wall. I found I could move through the earth by simply thinking in what direction I wanted to go.

Eventually, I moved under Over-man's office. I had been betrayed three times in the last three days; I was in no mood to be merciful.

There were only two men left alive that knew my story. Those loose ends stood in the office above me. They were in the office alone with the door closed.

"All is ready?" Over-man asked.

"Ready to go on your word, but doing away with a Prince is a risky business," Upper-man said.

"He's a third son, posted at the fort while serving in the army. He's known as a wild one. There will be some stink, but the money they are paying for the job makes it worth the risk. Let's go earn our money."

I concentrated, and without touching them pulled them both down into the earth where they drowned in dirt. When they were almost dead, I reached toward them. *Heal me! * Their bodies crumpled into old corpses, and my body immediately felt better, stronger, with no soreness or bruises. My gums and teeth no longer hurt either.

And I found I knew more. I suddenly understood knew all of Over-man's business — his deals, his contacts, where the money was hidden, the bank accounts kept. I knew what businesses were owned and where Top-man was. I knew guild codes and even how to read and write despite my total lack of schooling. My head hurt ... it was a lot of information to absorb.

I took nothing from their bodies. I wanted nothing of them found anywhere. Let their disappearance be a mystery, with no more loose ends. I did, however, take the gold and banknotes from a safe room. Maybe someone would think that after the Prince got away, he took the money and made his escape. It left more of a mystery for them to worry over.

It had been a long, trying day and my head was throbbing. I needed some sleep. I lay down on the bed in Overman's safe room and slept. I woke after a few hours and got up-. I needed to think about what my next move would be.

I now had money, and few, if any, knew me. Should I stay in the city or go to another one? I needed better clothes. I was in Upper-city now and would look very much out of place unless I could pass for a laborer.

Astonishingly, although I wanted a bath, I wasn't dirty! It seemed that no dirt stuck to me. Examining my body, I found my hand was completely healed, as well as all the other cuts and bruises.

"OK, first order of business, new clothes." As this was Upper-city there was a clothing and tailor shop nearby. I walked through the wall and drifted along under the building until I came to the tailor's shop. I looked up through the floors, making sure no one was in the shop. I rose up through the floor into the main room. This was easier than breaking in, and now I always had an escape route, straight down!

I rummaged through the used clothes until I found what I needed. Pants, shirt, stockings, cloak and hat, and of higher quality than I'd ever owned. Across the street was a leather worker and cobbler's shop. I was pleased to find a pair of little-used knee-high boots that fit me nicely. I also took a purse, a wallet, and a money belt.

I sank through the floor and went back to Over-man's safe room. I filled my purses with gold, and the wallet and money belt with banknotes. In the wardrobe was a cane, which I suspected hid a sword. There were also two swords and four knives. I picked up the cane. I was right; it was a cane sword. It was a fair blade: not great but serviceable. My hand began to tingle. I felt there was more to the swords, or maybe more could be made from the swords? Metal was from the earth and it seemed I could now bend earth to my will.

I didn't try to figure it out, I just did what felt right. I took the two swords and the cane sword in my left hand. My hand closed around them and began to pulse. Gold runes glowed through the skin of my hand and the three swords melded into one. On impulse, I took silver and gold coins and added them to the melding. When my hand stopped pulsing, I laid the cane sword on the table. I took the knives and did the same thing to them. When my hand stopped pulsing, I held only one knife. Both the knife and the cane sword blade were covered in a thick black crust.

As I looked at the knife, the crust turned to black dust and fell away. What was left was a perfect knife with runes along the blade with a beautiful ironwood handle. The cane sword blade and scabbard were now free of the black crust and dust. Its blade, like the knife's, was perfect, with runes along its length. Its handle and scabbard were Ironwood with silver and gold inlay. It, too, was beautiful, just what a gentleman would carry.

They were both incredibly sharp. I slid the cane sword back into its scabbard. One of the leather sheathes fit the knife, but I would have a better one made later, *or make it myself."*

The sun was up, and I was hungry. There was a coffee house nearby that also served meals. I would go there to eat as a gentleman would. I needed to be away from here before I made my public appearance.

I put the remaining bags of money down into the earth, *"no one can get them, but me."* I buckled the money belt on under my clothes. I put my knife in the waistband at the small of my back. I put my purse and wallet away, picked up my cane, donned my hat and stepped through the wall.

***

I exited a blind alley and walked toward the coffeehouse just down the street. A servitor greeted me as I entered the door. "Good morning M'lord."

"Good morning, somewhere out of the way please, I don't wish to be disturbed."

"Of course, sir, step this way." He took me to a booth in the back and to one side.. From there, I could see anyone approaching, not that I expected anyone. "Coffee, eggs, potatoes, ham," I ordered. I felt like I was starving.

"Yes, sir," he said and left to place my order. He returned with coffee. I'd only had coffee a few times, cold leftovers from someone's cup. *"I like it better hot and fresh."* I smiled. My food arrived, and I set to it. It was all good, *"I could get used to eating like this!"*

As I ate, I kept my eyes on the comings and goings at the entrance. The customers were all gentleman and merchants. All looked well-to-do, some more than others. I spotted one man who seemed to watch those around him, like a cat watching birds. He was probably someone's spotter, setting up for a pickpocket.

My meal finished; I was enjoying another cup of coffee. I continued to watch the crowed as I weighed my options. I was starting with a clean slate, more or less. I had money. I had Over-man's memories, or at least some of them. I could stay or go as I pleased.

And I guess that was the real question, what did I really want to do, now that I was free to choose? There was no rush to decide, I'd think it over for a while before I decided.

The waiter led another customer back to the area where I sat. He took a booth closer to the front door. The waiter nodded and left, returning momentarily with coffee. When the waiter left, the spotter brought his cup and joined the new man.

They put their head together and began to talk. I slid my hand to the wall and pushed a few fingers into the wall. I could now hear everything they were saying.

"They assured me this was a done deal. They assured me he would not leave that brothel alive. What happened?"

"They promised you an outcome, and that outcome you shall have. He is being taken to a party tonight, we'll be waiting."

The spotter got up and left. I withdrew my fingers from the wall. The second man finished his coffee and left.

That was about Prince Kade, I'm betting. My, is he popular! Should I get involved? He means nothing to me one way or the other... Of course, having a Prince as a friend offers many possibilities... If I do this, his enemies will be after me too... Should I go to the party? Maybe a note warning of danger would be better. Watch from a distance... Yes, a note then..."

I paid my bill, giving the waiter a nice tip. I left the coffeehouse and went in search of a scribe. When I found one, I paid for paper and use of pen and ink.

I might as well try my new writing ability.

I reached for the pen with my right hand, as I am right-handed. But my left hand started tingling, so instead I took the pen in my left hand.

In a perfect hand I wrote:

The wolves are going in for the kill tonight at a party to which you are to be invited.

-Sir Ghost.

I folded the letter and put it into an envelope. I left the scribe's by carriage, going to the fort. When the carriage stopped a soldier approached. I held the letter out to him with a coin.

"To Prince Kade."

The soldier took the letter and the coin, saluting, "Yes, sir, Thank you, sir."

When the carriage was well away, I told the cabbie to "take me to the closest church."

"Yes M'lord," came the reply, and a few moments later I found myself stopping in front of a small church. I paid the driver and went inside. I wasn't particularly religious; I just wanted a quiet place to think, and a church seemed like a good choice.

I took a seat in the first pew on the far right. It was a small church of some saint or other, perhaps built by a rich family trying to bribe their way into heaven.

They all smell the same, at least the few I've been in. The smell was of burning candles and holy oils. The priest probably made both.

My hand started tingling. I tensed, but nothing happened. *Show me.* I saw through the floor into a crypt. It was a large one for this size church. Part of the skeleton was glowing. I wasn't sure why, but I wanted to know what was down there. One run-in with a mad skeleton a week apparently wasn't enough.

I looked around the church and through the walls, and no one was watching me. I dropped through the floor and landed in the crypt, ready to run if anything came at me. Nothing happened.

I looked through the casket at what my hand was tingling about. I reached through the casket, grasped it and pulled it out. It slid easily, leaving everything else intact.

It was a leather belt with a leather messenger's pouch attached to it.

I opened the pouch, and at the top was a small pocket with a small book in it. taking out the book I read:

No matter how you came into possession of this pouch, I leave this that they may remember me in some small way. I created this blessed pouch of holding and gave it as a gift to be passed down. If you wish, add your name and add Items to the pouch to be passed down as well. The blessed pouch will hold as much four bushel baskets, and ten times that weight before you felt any pull against you carrying it.

A word of caution... don't put a live animal in it, for it will live no longer than half an hour. Other than that, you may put anything in it that will fit through the opening. Whatever you drop in will be held securely. Food and drink will not spoil. When you want to retrieve it, think of what you want, reach your hand in, and the pouch will give it to you.

— Blanchard, the Quiet.

The next few pages had names listed and supplies left. The last name listed was Randolph, servant to the king. The item he listed was a folding backpack of carrying. Which, it said, was much the same as the blessed pouch only more so... whatever that meant. I closed the book and put it back in its place.

Folding backpack. I reached into the pouch. My hand closed around what felt like canvas. I pulled it out. It was indeed a backpack, a brown canvas backpack. I put it back in the pouch and released it. Looking inside I saw it stored to one side. I was shocked at how big the inside of the pouch was.

I fastened the pouch belt around my waist; it lay flat against my left leg and did not move. I took my cane and put it in the pouch's opening and dropped it. The pouch swallowed it. *Cane,* and put my hand in and drew out my cane.

"Magic... Thank you, *Blanchard, the Quiet.* Sir Randolph, servant to the King. Rest in Peace." I bowed, and left, walking through the wall.

I moved through the earth like drifting with a river current. It was still early in the day, but I needed to go to the fort and find Prince Kade.

"Now that I have this wondrous pouch maybe I should go back and get the money I have stashed. I wonder how fast I can get back to Over-man's safe room?"

The earth become a blur to my eyes, and I was suddenly outside Over-man's safe room. Disoriented, it took me a moment to get my bearings, but at least I didn't fall down! I took the money bags and dropped them into my pouch. The pouch swallowed them. It felt no different, no extra weight.

I thought a moment. *to the Den.* The earth blurred past. It didn't bother me this time, as I was expecting it. I was under the Den. I took the money and dropped it in my pouch. It still felt no different.

"Well, me Lad, welcome to your new life." I smiled. *To the Fort.* Again the blur, and I was outside the fort where the carriage had stopped. It seems I have to have been somewhere previously before I can travel back to it. Good to know.

I moved under the fort looking for the Prince. I found him in the officers' quarters, shining his boots. I thought a prince would have someone to do that for him. Perhaps he had fallen out of favor with his family. That would support the fact that a Royal was trying to have him killed.

Two men approached the door and knocked. "Come." They entered." When are you going to get you a manservant to care for you and your things?"

"We aren't all third sons of the rich... oh! That would be you two." They were all smiling.

"But you're a prince."

"A prince to be sure, but a fourth son, and one who has put his family in a bad light. Hence my serving in the army of our king."

"But even so, shining your own boots?"

"According to my old tutor it's supposed to build character." They all laughed. "What time do we leave?"

"As soon as you are ready."

"I'm ready as soon as I get these boots on."

I stayed underground and followed along with the prince and his two friends. This was easier, and far safer for me. I could see everyone, and no one could see me. We travelled farther into Upper-city toward the Royal Castle. The houses became noticeably nicer, then turned into small walled estates. One of these was our destination.

It seemed to be quite an event; a pickpocket's dream come true. And his head, if he were caught! There was lots of food and heady drink. I don't think I have ever seen so much food in one place in my life.

There was also dancing. I tried to keep watch on the prince, but it was hard. So I just stayed in the general area.

I drifted from group to group, listening. Deals being made, horses and cattle being bought and sold. Marriages being arranged. It was all becoming boring, which meant that the assassins would strike soon, either at the party or right after. A tussle broke out on the dance floor over a young lady and two seemingly drunk men.

"There's the distraction." I looked behind the Prince. Two men who had been waiting against the wall made their move. They approached him blades low at their sides. *"And here come the blades."*

As they converged on the Prince, I rose behind them, slicing one's leg open with my knife and pushing the other on top of him. The hurt man screamed, the other appeared to be holding him.

"Knife fight!" I yelled and moved away. As everyone turned to watch the new fight, I moved over behind the prince. At his shoulder I spoke, "Time to go sire, while the wolves snap at each other in their confusion." I turned, he followed without a word.

We went out the side doors, out a patio and headed around the side of the house. As we got to the corner, I was bowled over by two more attackers. I sank into the ground enough for them to continue rolling over and past me.

I looked to the Prince, who was holding his two at bay with his ceremonial sword.

"You've gotten involved in something that wasn't any of your business, too bad for you," one said to me.

I smiled, "No, too bad for you!" I pointed down, and the ground swallowed both of them.

I reached into my pouch, *cane.* I pulled out my cane,

drawing the sword as I walked up behind one of the men attacking the Prince. I slashed him across the back of his neck, severing his spine. He dropped on the spot. His partner turned to me and the Prince ran him through.

"The others?"

"Dead," I said sliding my sword back into my cane. I looked at the right arms of the two dead men. No tattoos.

We walked around the end of the house heading for the front gate at a leisurely pace. Once outside the gate I flagged a carriage.

"Where to M'lord?"

I looked at the prince. "18 Port circle," he answered. The driver nodded. I got in and we were off. The Prince was looking at his left upper chest, where his shirt was bloody. On the off chance I reached my hand into my pouch, *bandage.* My hand closed on a bandage. *"Bless you, Blanchard."* I pulled it out and pressed it to the wound.

"It seems I'm out of practice, he got inside my guard."

"It's not too bad." I put my hand in my pouch. *flask of rum.* I handed him the flask. "Drink some of this, it should take the edge off." I would have to inventory my pouch and restock it.

I sat back in my seat across from him. "Did you get my message?"

"I did, and yes, I went anyway," he said smiling. "I thought no one would try anything at the home of a duke. Well, his brother-in-law's home, actually."

"That says you have made enemies of powerful people. Only someone who thinks the law does not apply to them would do something like this. Or you are caught up in something larger, and it's not really about you."

The Prince took another swallow from my flask. "I don't like either of those options." The carriage slowed and came to a stop.

We got out of the carriage; the Prince went to the gate. I gave the driver five golds. Then I gave him the guild hand sign. "You took two gentlemen to a nice bawdy house and were asked to wait for them. You ate and had a beer while you waited for two hours. They never showed back up, so you left." He never looked at my face.

"Yes sir, took those two gents to 'The Lily,' and I waited and ate at the boarding house nearby. Those gents never showed. Nice gents they were, paid in advance, they did."

I nodded, and he drove off. I joined the prince at the gate.

"Problem?" I shook my head, "no, we're good." He nodded and pulled the bell rope.

A small barred window opened in the gate. Someone looked at us then closed the window and opened the gate.

We stepped inside and he closed the gate behind us. Never saying a word, he ran ahead of us and opened the door to the house. Once we were inside and the door closed. He bowed.

He took our cloaks, "Your highness. I will tell the master you are here. If you would like to wait in here." he showed us to a sitting area, where I gratefully sat. They brought food and wine in while we waited.

An older gentleman came in. The prince didn't rise, so neither did I. He took us both in with a glance that I was sure missed little. They made no introductions.

He walked over and looked at the prince's wound. "Gotten lazy, let him get inside your guard." He went to a cabinet for fresh bandages and powders. As he returned, he looked at me, "What happened?" I looked at the Prince, who nodded.

"They attacked Prince Kade at a party he was attending."

"How many?"

"Eight. Two as a distraction, two attacking inside the house. Four outside. One attacker inside might not have survived and the ones outside did not. No one saw the Prince kill anyone."

"What about you, did they see you kill anyone?"

"No."

He looked back at the Prince, "Is he your man?"

"A friend."

He looked back at me. "What's in it for you?" My hand started tingling. I wanted to tell him everything but stopped. His ring drew my attention.

"You are compelling me to tell the truth. The ring?"

He smiled, "that is the first time in 40 years anyone has resisted it."

"It's good," I said, "I'm just a natural-born liar, and I get suspicious when I feel the need to tell the truth. I will tell you this, I did not do it for personal gain, I just didn't like the stacked deck."

"Were they Assassin's Guild?"

"No, no tattoos. Criminal Guild. Murder for hire on the cheap."

"You'll both stay here tonight; we'll talk more in the morning. I'll have more information by then. I thank you for the aid you gave Prince Kade. I will not forget it. We have prepared a room for you." A servant step into the doorway bowing.

I rose, bowing to the Prince, "Highness." He nodded his head, returning my bow. I turned and followed the servant out of the room.

CHAPTER 4

The servant led me toward the back of the house, and down a hall. I was looking through the walls. Betrayals had given me a new sense of caution that I planned on keeping. No ambush lay in wait... so far.

The door to the last room was open. He showed me in. "Water in the basin. If you will allow, I'll take your boots, and have them cleaned."

I nodded, "thank you." I removed my boots and gave them to him.

"If you need anything someone will be outside. Breakfast is served at 7 o'clock. Do you need anything more at the moment?"

"No, thank you." He bowed and left the room, closing the door behind him. I waited a moment, and saw that at least they didn't lock the door. The "someone will be outside" was not lost on me. Neither was the fact that I had no boots to walk away in. Smooth.

I looked the room over. No windows, a nice bed, furniture, and rugs, I supposed this was one of their nicer cells.

I saw there was a passageway along one wall with peepholes, so they could observe the room. The servant was there watching. I ignored him. I took a chair and placed it under the door handle. They would probably expect that. I arranged the pillows on the bed, turned the lantern out, and lay down. The servant waited a moment longer then left. There was a man posted at the end of the hall.

I dropped through the bed, floor, and into the earth. I drifted back to where the Prince and the master of the house were still talking.

"And you left, coming straight here, did anyone see you?"

"They saw us entering a carriage leaving the party, nothing more."

"How long have you known your friend?"

"A few days. He helped me leave a brothel quietly and warned me that someone was after me."

"Did he work at the brothel?"

"I don't think so, he seemed to have some trouble of his own with them."

"Then he shows up and helps your escape more trouble, that seems convenient."

"Put that way, it seems suspicious."

"I'll have him checked out, what name did he give you?"

"Ghost. Said he works for no one ... well, he said he worked for himself."

"We shall see. I'll send a message to the fort that you will not be there for the week. That should give us enough time to figure out what is going on. Good night, Your Highness," he said bowing.

"Good night Teacher," the prince said, smiling.

I went back under my room. As I stayed in the earth, I felt my strength returning to me. I lay back and closed my eyes. *Warn me if anyone approaches.* I was a light sleeper. Living on the streets teaches you that. I relaxed my mind and slept.

***

My tingling hand woke me. I looked, the servant was coming down the hall toward my room, carrying my now polished boots.

I rose back up onto the bed and waited. He knocked on the door, "Yes?"

"It's 6:30. Sir, we will serve breakfast in 30 minutes, they expect you. Your boots are at the door."

"Thank you, I'll be there." He turned and walked away but returned to the passageway to look in on me. I got up, did my morning needful, washed up, preparing to go to breakfast. Satisfied, he left the passageway. I removed the chair blocking the door and retrieved my boots.

When I was ready, I stepped into the hall where my escort was waiting. I followed him to the dining room. I was the first to arrive and was shown to a chair at the table.

"Coffee, sir?"

"Yes, please." The Prince came in, and I stood. "Good morning, Highness." bowing.

"Good morning," he waved his hand, "please continue with your meal." I took my seat as a plate of food was set before me.

He received his plate, and we began to eat.

The major domo came in, "the master is delayed, but begs you to eat. He will join you as soon as he is able."

The Prince nodded, "Thank you."

We ate and drank our coffee in silence. Cups refilled, "how's the shoulder?"

He flexed it, "stiff, but not as bad as I'd feared." I nodded savoring my coffee.

My hand tingled, I looked through the walls; the Teacher approached. Two men took position just out of sight in the kitchen, two outside the door in the hall.

The Teacher came in, "I'm sorry to be late couldn't be helped, I was receiving some last-minute news." He sat down and they served his breakfast to him. The Prince and I had a sweet pastry with our coffee. We waited for the Teacher to finish his meal or start the conversation.

"You were correct," the Teacher started, "someone wants you dead. They have tried at least twice. Once at the brothel where you and your friend here met, and again last night. I have not found out who wants you dead or why, as yet."

"At the same time, there has been a shake-up in the criminal guild. A takeover attempt, they say. Lots of bodies, missing leadership, quite a mess."

I nodded my head, "and you are wondering what my part

is in all of this. If I were a retired spymaster with a suspicious nature, I would wonder the same thing."

He kept his gaze locked on me.

"I, too, heard of the takeover attempt, but know nothing of who was involved. I was at the Criminal Guild house on another matter. They seemed to think I had not paid a fair tax on my gains. They said if I did them a service, all was forgiven."

"Later I heard them planning to kill the Prince... that is, to have me kill the Prince. They would throw us from a balcony, both dying. When they took me over to the brothel for me to perform the service I had other plans. Since the Prince was being held in the room next to mine, I released him, pointed him to the exit, and wished him luck."

"And the party?"

"That was just dumb luck. I overheard someone talking about the Prince escaping but explaining they would have another chance at the party. I sent the Prince a message warning him."

He looked at the Prince who nodded, "And yes, I went anyway. Maybe not the smartest move." The Teacher shook his head and looked back at me.

"Anyway, I was curious, and went to the Fort to see if the Prince would heed my warning. The rest you know."

"What did you do that required you pay the guild?"

"I'm a thief."

"Do you also hire out as a killer?"

"No, I try not to kill, and do so only when I have no choice."

"Why help the Prince, what did you see in him that would benefit you?"

I shrugged my shoulders, "A kindred spirit perhaps. Someone who, through no fault of their own, got caught up in the cogs of life and was about to be chewed up. We were kind of in the same boat. Everyone needs help now and then."

"You know Prince Kade is a fourth son and has little to offer you in the way of advancement or wealth."

"He has offered me something more valuable, he has offered me his friendship, that is enough."

The teacher nodded, "What's your name?"

"They call me Ghost, it's the only name I've ever known."

"We must think of something better to call you than 'Ghost'. Anyway, I would recommend that you both stay here until I get more information. Feel free to use the library, training yard, and training hall. Hopefully, for only a day or two."

***

I had never been in a library, so I spent most of my time there. I found I enjoyed reading. I felt like a sponge soaking up water.

He had books on military tactics, history, geography, logistics and supplies, and lots of maps. I studied the maps carefully. He also had a few medico books, and a few about magic. Not very in-depth though, just basic things. He also had many other books in different languages.

During the day the Prince and I would spar, practice swords, knives, and staffs. Afternoons and evenings found me in the library. This become our routine.

One evening when I was in the library, Teacher asked, "You are enjoying the library?"

"I am."

"What do you like best?"

"All of them, but military tactics and logistics are the most interesting."

"Yes, there is more to war, any battle really, than just riding in and killing. If you do everything else right, prepare everything, killing is the simple part."

"It seems logistics and planning can save or kill more than any battle."

He nodded his head, "it can for a fact, but few see this pivotal truth."

"You have read all of these?" He nodded. "How many languages do you speak?"

"Several." He walked to the book shelf, took down a book and brought it to me. "A gift."

I took it, "thank you," I read the title, "Sun Tzu, the Art of War."

"It's a favorite of mine. Translated from the original Chinese."

"Thank you, sir." I said bowing.

He bowed and left me.

I read the book, but it took more than one reading. I studied it, hoping to ask Teacher questions at some point.

I found his basement office, and work area. He had another library down there. These books were on alchemy, poisons, magic, and more maps, histories, and family histories. There were also reports from everywhere on the map.

At night the earth cradled me as I slept. Each morning I awoke rested and refreshed.

On our fourth night together, we were in the sitting room enjoying an after-dinner glass of wine.

"The only thing I have found out for sure is that your enemies are rich and powerful. They are also probably Royals, whether ours or another country's, I cannot say. Your friend here checks out. It appears you were both at the same place at the same time for a different reason. So, now that I don't have to kill you, where do you go from here?"

I took a swallow of my wine, thinking. "What would you suggest?"

"They waste your talents as a thief, no matter how good you may be. I may be old, but I have much life left yet. I would teach you my specialty, as you have already surmised, spy craft, with the understanding that you would serve Prince Kade.

"No, he did not know I was going to offer this and would not have asked.

"You two have a bond, and he needs someone he can trust and depend on. Money cannot buy that kind of loyalty.

Bought loyalty can always be bought again by someone else."

I turned to the Prince, "Your thoughts?"

He thought a moment. "I am honored to have you as my friend and would be honored to have you in my service. It will not be easy, I am a fourth son, with little to offer. Neither of us will live the finest life, but I will share with you such as I have."

I nodded and turned to the Teacher. "I accept your offer to train me in spy craft, in the service of Prince Kade." I turned to the Prince, "and to you, Prince Kade, I swear fealty to you, and you alone, until I am released from this oath."

"I accept your oath of fealty and accept you into my service."

The Teacher laid papers on the table. "From this point on, your name is Sir Draugur de Crypta, Baronet of Black Stag Keep, and five thousand acres. The Keep is small and probably needs repairs and up-keep, but a place of refuge none the less. I have recorded all of this with the crown and it is legal under the Kings law. This makes you a suitable companion for a Prince and fourth son of The King." He gave me all the papers of my new title, lands, and a sigil ring of a rampant stag. I put them in my pouch.

"I recognize the 'de Crypta' part of the name but not the 'Draugur' part."

"Draugur is Icelandic for Ghost[TB1]."

I smiled, "Ghost of the crypt, I like it."

"What are our plans?" The Prince asked.

"We will stay here another week, then we depart for Black Stag Keep. That will cut down on the ease with which our enemies can approach us. I'm still getting updates and have made inquiries. I'm waiting for answers."

"Good, because I'm tired of sitting in one place doing nothing. It will be good to be on the road again," the Prince said yawning.

"I think I will call it a night. I will see you in the morning," I said. I walked to my room without an escort. I still set the chair under the doorknob — some paranoia is a good thing. As normal I arranged my pillows and sank through into the earth and drifted off to sleep. I felt safer and more relaxed protected by the earth.

***

I was awakened by the vibration and concussion of an explosion, closely followed by three others. I looked up through the earth into the building above. The second floor was collapsing down on to the first floor. Or at least the room above my room, which was where the Prince slept, was. If had been in the bed, it would have crushed me.

I saw the Prince being buried in the collapse. I rose up, grabbing him and pulling him to me before the debris crushed him. He was unconscious from a head injury, a broken leg, and probably some broken ribs. I took him to the Teacher's secret basement office. He would be safe here, as the entrance had collapsed, along with other parts of the house. Even though I could see in the dark he could not, so I lit a lantern.

I went up through the house; I found the Teacher, dead. His head was crushed and his body was surrounded by four assassins.

"Find the others, no one escapes!" Three of the men moved off, searching the rubble. I concentrated on the leader and the earth swallowed him before he could make a sound.

I moved to the next assassin and dragged him under. I repeated this with each one. I searched and found two archers on roofs, front and back. They were to ensure no one escaped. I went up through the walls of the building to the archers and dragged them both down into the earth. I stripped the bodies of everything, their weapons, equipment, even their clothes, and put it all in my pouch.

I moved along under the building searching for survivors, there were none. All either had their throats cut or were killed by the collapsing building. I pulled all the bodies into the earth, leaving no evidence about who may have escaped. The body I did not find was that of the major-domo.

I went back to check on the Prince. He was still unconscious. I set his broken leg, as best as I could, wrapping his leg in cloth then, reaching into the earth I made a cast from clay, and hardened it. I realized what I was doing was from knowledge I had gained from the books I had read in the library. I finished by wrapping his ribs and cleaning his cuts.

I went through the building getting all the money, valuables, and gold — including the compulsion ring from the Teacher's hand. There was quite a lot, and it all went into my pouch.

Once satisfied I had gathered all I wanted, I pulled all the bodies into the earth. I went back to the lower office, for now there was nothing more I could do for the Prince.

I pulled all the assassin's clothes out of my pouch and put an outfit together for myself.

I pulled all of their weapons out of my pouch, laying them on the floor so I could see them. I held the knives in my hand and the runes on my hand began to glow. Before I was through, I'd combined all the knives, then all the short swords, then darts, then throwing knives, then bows, and then arrows making the finest rune weapons of them all.

I put all my new weapons into the places in my assassins' clothes designed for them. My pouch fit perfectly with everything, hindering nothing.

I put water close to the Prince and left a note saying I'd be back soon I had a debt to pay, and I knew exactly where the Assassins' Guild House was. I don't think gaining entry would be a problem.

I checked on the Prince again; he was still unconscious. Nodding to myself, I stepped through the wall.

CHAPTER 5

I arrived at the Assassins' Guild, located in a large plain stone house. The surrounding houses were wooden, but in good repair. As a precaution I looked up through the surrounding houses. As I suspected, they also belonged to the Guild. They used them to house the assassins and their supplies. There were thirty or forty of them posted throughout the houses keeping watch.

These people had not, and would not, show mercy, so I did not. I picked off the strays first. Like a predator, I used the earth to suck down my prey for the kill. As the first one came down, *strengthen me.* I moved to the second one and pulled him down, *improve me.* After that I was making stuff up as I went. *Faster, quicker, smarter, more endurance.* After that I stayed with, *improve me, make me better.* I don't know if it worked or not, but one could hope.

I cleared the surrounding houses of assassins, then moved on to the main Guild building. I circled under the building and spotted a man in the lower level working alone at a worktable. He was working with jars of liquids and powders, and was probably the resident apothecary.

There was no one else nearby. I waited until he finished what he was mixing and then pulled him down. *Teach me.* His body collapsed in on itself. I now understood apothecary arts. He had also been the one who had made the explosives that were used to attack Teacher's house.

I looked into the dungeon and found there were prisoners being held in the cells. I pulled the dungeon master under. As I looked around, I found the major-domo, or what they left of him, on the torture table. I let his body sink into the earth to his rest. I found their gold vault; I'd take care of that later. I went through the rest of the house pulling everyone I found down into the earth, drowning them in dirt.

I went to all the entrances and walled them over. Once I was sure I would not be disturbed I took my time and searched the Master Assassin's office. Everything was written in code, which I could now read, having learned it from the apothecary. I gathered up all the papers, journals, and every book I could find and put them in my pouch. I also gathered all the money, gold, jewels, and anything of value not in the vault, and stashed them away as well.

In the master's sleeping quarters stood a suit of black of armor, but not the heavy armor of horse-borne knights. This one looked lightweight, close fitting, but cleverly designed to allow the wearer to move without restriction. It was metal, chain mail, and leather, with a helmet and separate face mask.

My hand started tingling. I looked around to ensure I was still alone. I then gathered swords, knives, armor, anything of high quality metal or leather, piled it all in the middle of the floor and lay the black armor on top of it.

I laid my left hand on the armor and the runes began to glow. I watched as the armor absorbed all the metal I had piled in the floor, morphing, twisting and reshaping itself. Finally, the armor that lay before me was pure black, so dull that it did not reflect light. It had a dragon scale design on the interlocking plates, interlaced with black chain mail and black leather. The face mask and helmet also had a dragon scale design on them. The inside of the armor was covered in runes.

I had quite the pile of things by now. Some of it was too big to fit in the pouch's opening, so I reached in, *backpack.* I pulled the backpack out of the pouch. It looked like a common large canvas backpack. The top tied closed but when you untied it and laid it flat, you could unfold it like a large ground cloth.

I started unfolding it and found there was something inside. It looked like lots of canvas paintings or drawings. The pack kept unfolding until it was about twenty feet square. When the last fold was opened, all the "paintings" stood up and became real-life objects!

Lanterns stood in the four corners. There were kegs of wine, a barrel of water, food and cooking supplies, medical supplies, a table surrounded by chairs with maps on it. A full set of armor and weapons stood to one side. It was a heavier set than my hand had made, but it, too, was all black and made in the same dragon scale design. I looked inside the armor; it had runes inside it like my new armor did. I wondered if this was Randolph's armor or belonged to the King he served.

There were boxes and crates stacked around the edges of the ground cloth, forming walls. There was no telling what all was in them, but I didn't want to take time to find out right now. I started moving all the things I wanted to take onto the ground cloth. I also transferred some things I had put in my pouch onto the ground cloth.

I went back to the gold vault and stripped it bare; I placed all I found there on the groundsheet. Once I had placed all I wanted, I folded the one edge over. Everything became a canvas drawing and lay flat. I continued to fold the ground sheet back to form the backpack. It lay flat on the ground; I picked it up. It weighed nothing more than an empty canvas backpack would. I rolled up the backpack and put it back in my pouch. Again, *"Bless you, Randolph."*

I thought of the door openings I had closed and the walls I had built and sent them back to the earth. I dropped through the floor and went to the dungeon. On a whim, when I rose up through the floor, I brought a large stone guard dog up with me. My face was covered like the assassins were. I touched the lock on a cell door and the lock opened. The door opened and the guard dog stepped in; I followed him. A man sat on the floor leaning against the wall. He had long scraggly hair and beard. He looked to have lost a lot of weight.

"What interest are you to the guild?" He looked at the

dog then at me, he said nothing. The dog growled at him.

Drawing his feet in, "Ransom. They are holding me until my family pays. But the sum they have asked is too much. It would destroy my whole family, which is the point, I think. My family will not pay, and I would not want them to."

"What did you and your family do to draw the attention of someone to pay the guild to hold you and destroy your family?"

"We are merchants, we have merchant houses in many cities and countries."

"What is your name?"

"Arthur Williamson."

I took a purse of 50 golds and dropped it on the floor. "My master may need your help someday. He is the Black Stag of Black Stag Keep. Never speak of the Black Stag being here. Your captors are all dead. Go home, Arthur Williamson."

"He shall have it, whatever help we can give, he shall have it!"

Nodding, I turned and left the cell, followed by the dog. Arthur left right behind me. The next two cells held dead men. I left them where they lay.

I came to the last cell and opened it. The dog and I went in. This man looked as though he had not been here long.

He was sitting against the wall, a collar around his neck, chained to the wall. He had the look of a seaman, probably an officer.

"I will not do what you want, so if you are going to torture me to try to change my mind, let's get to it."

I smiled behind my mask. "Well, before we start, tell me what it is you will not do."

"I'll not haul slaves; I'll not turn my ship into a slaver."

"Are you the captain of the ship?"

"I am."

"Are you the owner of the ship to make this decision?"

"I am."

"And that's your last word on it?" He gritted his teeth, "It is."

"And where is your crew?"

"You are holding them on the ship at the docks, as you well know."

"Oh, I'm not part of them," I said pointing over my shoulder with my thumb. "We were at cross purposes, so we killed them."

He frowned looking at me," All of them?"

"All that were here. Anyway, back to this ship at the docks. Seagoing ship?" He blinked his eyes several times trying to understand what he had just learned. "Hey, pay attention, is it a seagoing ship?"

"Um, yes, an armed merchantman." I nodded.

"Do you know Arthur Williamson?"

"I know the Williamson trading house; we've done business with them before."

"Does the ship have a cargo?"

"No, they took it, and all my gold." He said spitting on the floor.

"So, you don't actually have a ship. You used to have a ship." He said nothing. "As it happens, I'm about to come into possession of an armed merchantman. I'm not a captain, so I'd need a partner. I'd supply the ship and gold to buy a cargo. You would captain it and run the business side. I'll be a silent partner. I'll take 40 percent after expenses, and crew shares — Unless you think you'll get a better offer."

"You pay maintenance out of your share."

"We'll split maintenance as an expense."

"Get me out of here and we have a deal."

"Your name, Captain?"

"Jon Wester, captain of the Bonnie M." I reached down and touched the collar, and it opened and fell off. I led him upstairs to the front door and let him out.

"I'll meet you at the ship." He nodded and walked toward the river docks. I went back inside; the dog and I sank into the earth. In just a few moments I was at the docks and found the

Bonnie M.

I concentrated and pictured in my mind what I wanted to do. I had not tried this in water, so I was uneasy about trying it. My hand gave me a reassuring tingle, and I moved toward the ship. I moved from earth, to water, and up through the bottom of the ship.

I was perfectly dry standing there on the ballast stones. I looked up through the ship and found the assassins. There were six of them stationed around the ship. They had locked the crew in the hold.

I drew my knife and raised up behind the one nearest me and drove my blade up through the back of his skull and lay the dead body down quietly. I killed the others the same way and left their bodies where they fell.

I went to the Captain's quarters and touched the lock on the chest, and it fell open. I took the gold from the chest and went up on deck. I waited there for Captain Wester. I didn't have long to wait. He saw me at the gangplank and came aboard.

"The crew?"

I motioned with my head, "In the hold. You'll find six heaps of trash around the ship that need to be put over the side." I handed him the bags of gold, "here is the gold to finance our ship."

"These look like MY bags of gold," he said, his voice raising.

"Odd," I said looking at them, "they all look alike to me." He just shook his head, taking the gold.

"If anyone shows up asking about the guards, tell them someone came for them and they all left. Release your men, make sure the ship is ready to leave on short notice. Buy what you need to that end. I'll be back tomorrow with further instructions." I turned and walked down the gangplank.

I went down an alley and sank into the earth and then fast-traveled back to the Prince. I stopped under the office then moved to the side nearest the stables. I made a passageway from stone that matched the collapsed passageway that went up into the house. The new passageway opened in a stone wall in the stable. I sealed the old passageway off making it look like just a stone floor. Then I lowered the whole office down another ten feet.

I entered the office from the new passageway. I checked on the Prince — there was no change. I was tired, so I sank down into the earth. *Wake me if anyone approaches, or the Prince wakes up.* I went into a deep restful sleep cradled by the earth.

***

The hand woke me, there were people digging through the rubble above. I drifted up to watch. It was the city watch. Two official looking people stood off to one side. They were talking among themselves. "They've found blood, but no bodies."

"Yes, someone went through the trouble of cleaning up the dead and wounded."

"It has the smell of Assassins' Guild to me, sir, but we'll keep looking."

"Send your report to me at the Castle, this has the highest priority." He turned and walked away. The other man nodding, watching him leave.

I followed the official as he headed toward the Royal Castle. He didn't stop anywhere for anything, just went straight there. He was obviously a known man, as no one stopped him as he entered the Castle gate.

I went up inside the walls as he made his through the Castle. Finally stopping at a door, he knocked.

"Come." He entered and approached the man behind the desk. The man never looked up. "What have they found?"

"Sir Edwin's home was attacked. The attackers used explosives, at least four charges. It caused the building to collapse in on itself. They have found no bodies, only blood, and not a lot of that. We also checked Assassins' Guild house. Everyone, or should I say, all bodies were gone." The man behind the desk looked up at that. "There was no blood, but all papers, books, and ledgers were missing, they had searched, and stripped the place bare."

"No bodies?"

"Except some in the dungeon. Prisoners, from their looks."

"So, they attack Sir Edwin, he believes it's the Assassins' Guild, and he what? Goes in and cleans them out? If that's true the old man still has the juice, and powerful allies. You've found nothing of Prince Kade?"

"No sir, that's the strange thing, we found nothing of any-body, literally. No weapons, no bodies, nothing."

"The King will not be happy about this. Let me know when it changes."

"Yes sir." Bowing he left. I waited. He made some notes then got up, headed for the door. I followed. It was a short walk to a set of guarded doors. He entered. Down a short hall-way he stopped at a guarded door and knocked.

"Come in." He opened the door, entered, and closed the door behind.

There was an older man behind a desk dressed in fine clothes. "Sir Godfrey, you have news?"

Sir Godfrey bowed. "I do, Your Highness. We have con-firmed that Sir Edwin's home was the target of the attack last night. They used explosives to get in, causing the building to collapse. I suspect the Assassins' Guild of carrying out the at-tack. We found no bodies in the rubble of Sir Edwin's home, so there is a chance that Sir Edwin may have survived."

"What leads you to believe that?"

"Because the Assassins' Guild did NOT survive. Their Guild house is empty of any living thing. And the only bodies we found were some prisoners in their dungeon."

"And my son, Prince Kade?"

"Nothing sire, the last word I had from Sir Edwin was that

the Prince was at his home, supposedly safe from a second as-sassination attempt. Sir Edwin was trying to find out who was behind it."

"Well, someone's stirred up a hornets' nest, I'll tell you that. Any Idea who is behind it?"

"As much as I hate to admit it sire, I have no clues at this time."

"Well find out ... someone has gone after a Royal. If they have gone after one, they may go after another. If they are still alive, what do you think Sir Edwin will do next?"

"Probably keep the Prince in the city where his resources are, and if need be, bring him into the Castle for protection."

"I pray that Sir Edwin keeps him safe. He may be a fourth Prince, but he's still my son. All right, let me know when any-thing changes, go find who's responsible for these attacks."

"Yes Sire." Bowing he left the King's office. I stayed to watch the King.

Moments later the other door opened and a lady who could only be the Queen came in. "What news of Kade?"

"Little. They were attacked again at Sir Edwin's home, which was destroyed. We think they're still alive."

"Who is behind this?"

"We're not sure. We're still investigating. You can't hide this kind of information forever, someone will talk."

"I don't want to find out who is responsible for this after my son is dead."

"Neither do I... we'll find them."

I fast-traveled back to the Teacher's office and checked on the Prince. When I saw he was awake I took my face cover-ing off. I entered through the door. He tensed until he saw my face, then relaxed.

"How do you feel?"

"Like a building was dropped on me!"

He looked at my clothes, "Assassins did this?" I nodded. "The Teacher?"

I shook my head," no one else survived." I handed him the

Teacher's ring. He took it, nodding.

"They'll be looking for us to finish the job."

"No, they won't, I killed them."

"The Guild will send more."

"They'll have to come from another city if they do." He frowned, looking at me. "After I got you down here and made sure you were safe, I went back looking for the others. I killed the assassins I found searching the ruins of the house. I tracked them back to their guild house and killed them. All of them. We are safe for the moment."

"You killed everyone at the Guild house? By yourself?"

"Not everyone, there were some prisoners that I released. But other than that, yes, I killed every assassin I could find. That house will trouble us no more."

He had cold sweat showing on his face. "I'll fix you something for the pain." I got a cup of water and pulled a small folded paper of pain relief powder from my pouch. I mixed it and gave it to him. I gave him a plate of meat, cheese and bread, sat down with him and started eating my own.

"I did not tell you everything about myself. I am a thief, but also a killer when I have to be. I don't enjoy it. I'd rather just avoid people. But when I must kill, I am very good at it. The Assassins' Guild attacked this house, killed the Teacher and almost got us. Once I was sure of your safety, I repaid them in kind. As I said, we are safe here for now. But we must decide what our next move should be."

I looked over at him for a response, but the pain relief powder had put him to sleep.

"I have an Idea, but let's talk about it tomorrow." I said, smiling.

I went up to what was left of a room above, where clothes were kept and changed from assassin's garb to plain but well-made clothes that would not draw attention.

I fast-traveled to the alley close to the Bonnie M and walked to the ship, stopping at the bottom of the gangplank and addressing a nearby crewman. "Is Captain Wester aboard? I've come on a business matter."

"Aye, he is, come aboard." I went aboard and was shown to the Captain's quarters.

I nodded my head to the Captain, "I've come with further instructions." He looked at me closely. He nodded for me to continue. "We'll not need you for a time, but in six months bring a resupply shipment for a Keep of 50 men to the western shores at Black Stag Keep. There is a cove there where you can unload." I pulled out another bag of gold. "This is to ensure you are fully financed."

He took the gold and locked it in his chest. He went to his chart desk and pulled out a map. "I know of no cove near any Keep on the western shores."

He unrolled the chart. I looked at it. "The Keep is about here," I pointed. "There is a cove there."

"And if no one is there to meet us?"

"Sell the goods and continue our business. I'll leave a message here with the Dockmaster, with other instructions. Until then continue to trade and make money."

"We'll be there."

I bowed and left the ship.

CHAPTER 6

While the Prince slept, I read reports and information gathered by Sir Edwin — reports from all over the realm. There was news from the wars in the east, trade news from the south and odd scraps of information that fit nowhere that I could see.

There were mercenary companies returning to their wintering quarters. They would lick their wounds, hire replacements, and get ready for next year's fighting season.

There were trade caravans moving in every direction, with the biggest going east and west.

There were Kings offering to sell Baronets and land in contested lands in several regions. If you were looking to start or expand a family that was an opportunity, but one that took money and soldiers. Once you bought it, you had to hold it and pay the King's tax.

Everyone was raiding everyone's ships on the open seas. Some Kings had sold letters of marque, taking half of every ship captured, getting the vessel on the cheap, re-crewing it and sending it out again. Maybe owning a ship was not the best investment, but on the other hand the price was right.

"What have you learned?" asked a voice from behind me.

"That you fart in your sleep." I answered.

"True, but they do not stink, it's a Royal gift." We both laughed.

"Some think we are dead. Others think Sir Edwin still lives, because they believe it was he that had the Assassins' Guild wiped out. If we are alive, they think, we will stay in the city because that's where all of Sir Edwin's resources are. The house is being watched to see if anyone returns.

"The poor have been searching the ruins for anything of value. I let them search, since it makes it look like we are gone or dead. The royal spy master feels that Sir Edwin may be alive, again because of the Assassin Guild House killings, and that we will remain in the city."

"How do we know what the Royal spymaster thinks?"

"We spied on him."

"Of course, we did. Did we spy on anyone else?"

"The King is pushing for answers, since he feels that if someone is willing to kill you, they will go after other Royals as well. The Queen is not happy at the lack of progress. They both seemed genuinely concerned about your well-being."

"Anything else?"

"Not on that front, but I have the beginnings of a plan for our next move."

"What's that?"

"I think it best that everyone continues to think we are dead. Sir Edwin was already planning on us moving to Black Stag Keep. Everyone else thinks he would have stayed in the city, which I think is why we were leaving. We'll travel in the open, disguised as one of many mercenary company's wounded returning home to winter and recover. I'll get a wagon for you to ride in and take some supplies. We'll join a group heading west."

"We have money for horses, wagon, and supplies?"

"Oh yes, our treasury is doing quite well, we recently had a large influx from a Guild donation. Money will not be a problem at the moment."

He smiled, nodded, "I agree with your assessment, and think we should follow through on Sir Edwin's plan to go to Black Stag Keep. Let me think on the rest of it for a bit." I nodded and fixed our meal. We tossed ideas back and forth as we ate.

"Maybe we could hire a few men going our way to better sell our disguise, and as guards for our supplies."

"I'll look around the docks tomorrow and see what's

there. Think on what supplies we will want to buy to take with us. Have you ever been to Black Stag Keep?"

"I have not, I had never heard of it until Sir Edwin gave it to you."

"Hmm, I wonder if that's good or bad." We looked at each other and at the same time and said, "Bad!" and both laughed.

"Oh well, hope for the best, plan for the worst." I gave him more pain powder to help him sleep.

***

After breakfast I left the Prince sitting at the desk reading Sir Edwin's notes and reports and went to the docks looking for likely candidates for our little troop.

There was all manner of injured men there, some missing arms, legs, and other wounds and some with no visible wounds at all. Some had money and others were without, but there were more lacking cash. I sat at a side table nursing an ale. listening to the ebb and flow of the crowd.

"So that's it then, Master Sergeant, the company's disbanding?" came the conversation from one of the tables.

"There ain't no company to disband! The captain and half of the men are dead. What is still alive, except for a handful, has been mauled to squeezings.

"I told ya I would get you home. You're home. That's it. If you want to join up with another company, go with my blessings. I'm done."

"You've been saying that for years. We'll see what's what next season." The soldier left, leaving the sergeant drinking alone. He had a hard look about him, not cruel, but hard.

I waited a bit then went over to his table. "Can I buy you a drink, Master Sergeant?"

"I'll drink 'em if you'll buy 'em." I nodded, smiling, and ordered two ales.

"Sounded like your company had a bad fighting season."

He nodded, "the worst in the fifteen years I've been with them."

"Where will you winter?"

He looked at me over his cup, "You have a reason for asking."

I nodded, "I'm looking to hire a few men as supply wagon drivers and escorts. Guards for the winter, and maybe beyond."

"How many wagons?"

"Not sure, two, maybe four, I'm thinking ten men."

"How far we going?"

"Western Coast, Black Stag Keep."

"Get us another ale." I had another brought to him. He was studying me. His ale arrived, and he drank. I waited.

"I have twenty-two men with me. Ten are walking wounded, two will need to ride in the wagons. The company has four wagons for our supplies and equipment. We also have a blacksmith and a Medico. You would have to hire all of us. I won't split them up to be left here alone."

"How many horses do you have?"

"Ten. They are in decent shape."

"Pay?"

"Winter wages, plus food, and supplies."

"Do you still have your quartermaster?"

"Sergeant Birch," He called.

"Yes, Master Sergeant." A man came to the table.

I nodded. "Take a seat."

I kept looking at the Master Sergeant. "I need a count of how many horses we need to mount everyone and some spares." Birch started taking notes.

"I need a supply list of what you'll need for movement to our destination, including medical supplies. I'll also need a list of supplies to feed us an additional two months, and how many more wagons we'll need to haul all the supplies. Anything I've missed, add to the lists. I put a purse of gold on the table, "For your time if we can't come to terms. I'll be back in the morning; we can continue then."

"We'll have your lists."

I nodded and left.

***

I had a taste for a meat pie, and was sure the Prince would be hungry. I stopped at an Inn and bought four meat pies, some bread and cheese. I went into the alley, put the food in my pouch, and dropped into the earth. It was safer and faster to travel this way.

When I got back to the office, there were two thugs waiting in the outer passageway. The office was empty, and the Prince was gone. I pulled the thugs down into the earth to mid-chest. They were screaming and fighting trying to get away. The dog and I walked through the wall in front of them.

They froze. "Where did they take him, and how long have they been gone?" Neither one spoke. "That one," I said pointing. The dog attacked, biting into his shoulder ripping his arm off. The man screamed, blubbered and died. The dog dropped the chewed-up arm in front of the other one. "Where did they take him, and how long have they been gone?"

He was terrified. "I don't know where they took him, we put him in a wagon, and they left not fifteen minutes ago. We were to wait here for whoever showed up." The dog tore his throat out. Both bodies sank into the earth.

I walked up the stairs to the stables. There had been a struggle here. There were pieces of clay from his cast on the ground. I picked up the clay and my hand tingled. I sank into the earth and followed the hand's directions. I didn't have to follow streets, so I caught up with them in moments.

I traveled under the wagon, there was the driver up front, and two people in the back with the Prince. The wagon turned into an alley and traveled on a way, until I sank the wagon wheels into mud and stuck them fast.

The driver looked at the wheels, "You two get out and give us a push." They got out, one going to each side. As they grabbed the wheels, I rose from the ground behind one and stabbed him up through the base of the skull and let him fall. I did the same to the other.

I walked to the front, "You're stuck man, and good," I said pointing to the rear. He leaned over, looking back. I stabbed up through his jaw and into his brain. I let him fall into the mud, took his hat and put it on, climbing up into the driver's seat. The dog joined me, keeping watch.

I started the team moving and opened the flap to the back. "What took you so long?" asked the Prince.

"I stopped to get lunch," handing him the packages.

He took them, "No wine?"

"You are so needy, no wonder they sent you to the army," handing him a flask.

He handed me a meat pie. I ate as I drove.

"Criminal Guild?" He asked.

"Yes, probably from Top-man."

"I wasn't thinking, the walls were closing in. I needed fresh air and sunshine. I was sitting in the stable, when they came. I thought I was out of sight, apparently not."

"Solved a few problems, really. They brought us a wagon and loaded you in it. How's the leg?"

"Hurts. They cracked the cast, but I don't think the leg re-broke. How did you find me?"

"They were kind enough to leave two men to tell me where they were taking you."

"Where to now?"

"Down to the docks, where we have hired a mercenary company, or part of one. They will winter with us a Black Stag Keep. We will hide in plain sight, just another wagon of wounded mercenaries headed home."

"What story did you give them?"

"Not much of one yet. I was thinking of telling them I was The Black Stag, and you were my Captain. Or You could be The Black Stag, and I'd be your Captain."

"Let's go with the first one, I'll remain in the background. You've already hired them, that will fit how they see you."

"When I left them, I told them I'd see them in the morning, this will push the timetable up some."

"They're mercenaries, they're used to orders changing, they'll be fine."

"Your name, Captain?"

"Captain Elias Drake, at your service."

"I like it, it suits you."

We reached the docks with no problems, just another delivery wagon. I drove down the river front where all the returning mercenaries had their camps. I saw the Master Sergeant at a wagon and pulled up.

I stepped down and walked over to him. "I've got one of my wagons and decided to park it down here. Mind if I tie up with yours?"

He nodded, "fine, put it over there on the end. It's good you came back; you may pick up some good deals."

"How so?"

"Some companies are selling off excess equipment, and stock. If you've the cash, they'll take gold in hand now, versus better offers later on."

"If you're satisfied with the equipment, I have cash available. Let's go make some deals."

"Would you be against others traveling with us, maybe even hiring a few more men?"

"If they meet your standards, I'm not against either option. Before we start, my name is Sir Draugur de Crypta. The Black Stag of Black Stag Keep." I said bowing my head.

"Miller, Sir. Master Sergeant Miller." He bowed his head in return.

"Come meet my Captain." We walked over to our wagon. I opened the back, "Captain Elias Drake, this is Master Sergeant Miller, the man in charge of the mercenary company I've hired."

"Good afternoon, Master Sergeant, forgive my not rising, a broken leg."

"Not at all, sir."

"Don't worry about me interfering with your troops, for the time being I'm just along for the ride."

"How'd it happen, Sir, if you don't mind my asking?"

"I learned the hard way that there are bold soldiers, and old soldiers."

"But there are no old bold soldiers," the Master Sergeant finished.

"My horse fell on it."

"Better you learned in peacetime than in war. On the battlefield it would have probably been the end of you."

"For a fact, Master Sergeant, for a fact."

"I'll check back on you in a bit, Captain."

We turned back toward the wagon line, "Thatcher!" the Master Sergeant called.

"Yes, Master Sergeant?"

"That wagon there, Captain Drake is in it, check on him from time to time see he has what he needs."

"Yes, Master Sergeant."

Miller, Sergeant Birch, the blacksmith Sergeant Smith, and I walked the mercenary line making deals.

We stopped at the horses; my hand tingled. A big bay mare came to me and put her nose on my hand.

"Would you look at that!" One of their wranglers said. "She's usually a handful and stand-offish. You must have apple on your hand. She's a good one once you are in the thick of it. She can run with the best of them, and farther than most. She has a mind of her own, though, and most of the men hate to ride her."

I just smiled. "I'll take her." He shrugged his shoulders, "I warned you. But if you're interested in taking chances let me show you another one." We walked over to another area where he had another horse tied in a roped off area. The first thing I thought was, "black beast."

"I took him as a prize after a battle. No one expected him to live. I doubt he'll every ride to battle again. I thought I might stud him. I'd sell him for the right price." My hand tingled again. "I'll warn you he's a mean one, as most of them are."

I walked over to him and put my hand out. Just as the mare had done, he put his nose to it and was calm. I walked around him looking. Then I walked him around watching him move.

"What think you, Sergeant?" The smith looked him over.

"He's taken some hard wounds; I doubt he'll even carry a knight in full armor into battle again. That wound on his flank still looks iffy. If he lives, could be for stud."

"What's your price?"

"Five hundred gold."

I turned away laughing, "Good luck!"

"Two-fifty."

I kept walking.

"One hundred gold, final offer."

I stopped and turned back, "Done, one hundred gold, including his armor and tack."

"That will cost you another fifty."

"Done, one hundred fifty gold."

By the time we were done our mercenary company had fifty horses that were in good shape, but they, like the men, needed a rest. Fifteen wagons, and sixty-five men. Forty of the men were wounded, but only four seriously. They all needed rest and time to recover. I had paid in gold as we took possession from each company.

"Master Sergeant, we'll buy the rest of our supplies in the morning."

"Yes, sir."

I led the mare and the war horse back to our wagon and roped them off.

"Captain Drake" struck his head out. "What have we got here?"

"A mare with a mind of her own, and a war horse that needs time to heal before I stud him out. Besides, people will look at your leg and him and won't even ask."

He laughed, "probably right. People see what they want to see." He looked around, "are you going back to the office tonight?"

"Yes, there are some things there I want to get."

He nodded, "Don't take any unnecessary chances." I just looked at him. "Yeah, yeah, I know," and he pulled his head back inside.

They brought us both plates of beef stew and bread. It was surprisingly good. After we ate, I took our plates back to the mess wagon. "Well done, Mess Sergeant."

"Thank you, sir."

I headed toward the inn. Once around the corner and out of sight I dropped into the earth.

CHAPTER 7

I fast-traveled to the office, checking to ensure no one was waiting. I sealed the door, took out the backpack and opened it. I gathered all of Sir Edwin's books, ledgers, reports, and notes and stacked them all on the map table on the groundsheet. I looked around a final time, making sure I had taken everything I wanted, folded the backpack and put it back in my pouch.

I knew the general area where the Criminal Guild house was located, but not exactly. I walked through the wall and headed that way. I was within a block of the building I suspected when I started noticing the spotters. Their Guild house was a walled mansion. These guys lived like Royalty.

I had made a mistake at the Assassins' Guild house by hiding all the bodies. People needed closure; dead bodies made sense: must have been a guild war, makes sense, end of story. I still would not risk getting hurt, that would be stupid.

I circled the building, learning the layout. I marked the vault, the armory, and the library and found Top-man's office; he was there.

I moved off to the side and made a vault of my own, hollowing out the earth. I laid out the backpack and changed into my Black Dragon armor, including the helmet and face mask.

I moved up into the house walls. No matter the thickness of the wall I could stay encased within it. There were no innocent people in this house. Everyone here was a stone-cold killer, and there would be no mercy.

I drew my sword, and, starting in the attic, I worked my way down, killing everyone I found. My steps made no sounds. My runed hand held sway over wood, as it did earth, and stone. I left a bloody wake as I moved silently through the house. When I arrived in the basement, I sent my stone dog walking through Top-man's office door. While his attention was on the dog, I came through the wall and took off his head. I left bodies lay where they fell.

I eyed the dog: *Guard, kill anyone who approaches.* I searched the office, took all paperwork, reports, ledgers, books and notes. All of it went into my pouch. I emptied the vault of all gold, money, jewels, and all the other papers I found. I moved it all over to the backpack ground sheet. I took the best weapons from the armory and moved them over to the groundsheet as well.

I took travel clothes and plain but good light armor for myself and the Prince. I piled both sets of good light armor in the floor. I gathered swords, shields, leather items, and piled it on top of the light armor. I laid my runed hand on the piles, and the runes made good light armor into high quality protection. I gathered other things that we would need to look the part we were playing. I also took some nice clothes; you never knew when you might need to dress up.

Once I had everything placed on the groundsheet, I changed out of my Dragon Armor and put on the plain clothes and my new runed high quality light armor. I folded the groundsheet and put the backpack back in my pouch. I let the earth refill the vault I created. Taking a last look around, I let the dog go back into the earth.

Satisfied I had accomplished what I had intended, I headed back to our river side camp. I stopped at a produce stall on the way back, took a bushel of apples and poured them in my pouch, leaving money on the table. I made sure no one could see me and came up in the alley. An alert guard nodded to me as I entered our area.

The horses looked at me but made no sound. I pulled my ground sheet and blankets out of my pouch and spread them out on the ground. I sank down into the ground and opened a new vault. I opened the backpack and got the Prince's new light armor out and lay it to the side.

I folded the backpack and put it back in my pouch and filled the vault. I took the Prince's armor up and lay it beside the wagon, then laidback down and slept soundly under the wagon knowing either the horses or my hand would wake me if anyone approached.

***

I rose early with the rest of the camp, putting my blankets and groundsheet back into the pouch. I took care of my morning needful, then took my horses down to the river to drink, giving them each an apple and rubbing them down. I looked at the war horse's flank wound. I pulled out a paper twist of wound powder from my pouch and poured the powder over the wound. Maggots were present, eating the dead flesh. That was a good thing, since they would not eat living flesh. They would leave the wound clean and the powder would help with the healing.

My horses taken care of, I washed myself off in the river. As I was getting dressed, I noticed a large skinny wolfhound sitting beside the war horse. He was watching me. " Friend of yours?" The dog looked at the horse and lay down. My hand tingled, so I shrugged my shoulders and finished dressing. As I walked by, I threw the dog a meat pie, which was about one bite for him. I left the horses grazing and knew they would not stray. I was also sure no one would bother them, as the dog stayed with them.

I stopped at the wagon; the Prince already had a plate of breakfast. "Do you need anything?"

"Not at the moment, Thatcher is seeing to me."

I nodded and went to the mess wagon. I ate what the men ate at the same table. No doubt they took notice. I looked over the troops, checking the state of their clothes and boots. Most were in good repair. The morale seemed good, and why not? They were being fed, and no one was trying to kill them.

I saw the Mess Sergeant, and stepped over to him, "Good morning sergeant."

"Good morning, sir."

"Tell me, could your stores handle a whole beef, or a half?"

"A half easily sir, but if I had the salt, we'd portion out the whole and salt it down."

I nodded, "the men need meat to help their healing, I'll have it delivered to you."

"That they do sir, thank you."

I turned my plate in, knowing that conversation would make the rounds and the men would know I didn't scrimp on food for their wellbeing. I walked over to the Master Sergeant's wagon.

"Good morning Sir Draugur."

"Good morning Master Sergeant."

"We have the lists you asked for, estimates of cost, and our contract cost through the winter." He handed me the list, I read through it. It was a well thought out list. Of course, it would be, they did this for a living.

I nodded my head. "Agreed, add twenty head of cattle to your list, for more meat on the way. Also, for those that need them have new boots, and wool blankets for anyone. I'll not scrimp a few coins on the health of the men."

"Yes, Sir."

"Do you have a merchant house you usually buy from?" I asked.

"It varies, depending on what we need."

"Are you familiar with the Williamson Trading House?"

"We are, they are one of the better ones, competitive prices."

"Let's go see them."

"Very well Sir."

Master Sergeant Miller, Quartermaster Sergeant Birch and I headed to the merchant's warehouse district.

"Tell me Master Sergeant, when must you renew the Mercenary Companies Charter?"

"If not on contract, usually mid-winter."

"Cost?"

"One thousand gold."

I nodded, "you spoke of disbanding this winter. Would you sell the charter to me and divide the money among the survivors of the company?"

He didn't answer right away. As we walked, he chewed his lip thinking. "What would you do with it, sir? Planning to go to war next season?"

"No, at least that is not my plan. The charter would let me keep an armed force without getting everyone around me wound up. When your neighbor builds an army, it makes people nervous."

"Would you keep the company's name?"

"No, I would change the name to The Black Stag Mercenary Company."

"The name change will cost you an additional one thousand golds." I nodded.

"What price would you give us?"

"Name me a fair price."

"Each man gets fifty gold. Each sergeant gets one hundred."

"Agreed, but you will get two hundred gold. Put all of this in our contract."

"Agreed. Let's go see the Provost and Magistrate and make it legal for you."

***

The Provost and Magistrate office gave less trouble than I had thought. I guess as long as you had gold; you had no problems — or at least fewer of them. That seemed the way of the world.

We left with all the correct seals and signatures for the

Black Stag Mercenary Company Charter, Baronet Captain Sir Draugur de Crypta, owner and charter holder. I was also two thousand golds poorer, but it was worth the price. Besides, I could afford it.

Once outside Master Sergeant Miller turned to me, "May I be the first to congratulate you, Captain de Crypta," and saluted me.

I returned his salute, "thank you Master Sergeant, I will lean heavily on your experience to keep me from screwing up to badly."

He gave one of his rare smiles, "That's a given, sir."

***

We entered the Williamson's merchant warehouse, "Good afternoon gentlemen, how may we help you?"

I stepped forward, "I'm looking for Arthur Williamson, is he here today?"

"May I say who's asking, sir?"

"Captain de Crypta, from Black Stag Keep."

"Of course, captain, a moment, please."

Arthur came out straight away, "Captain, how good to see you!" He played it straight, not knowing how to handle the situation. He looked a lot better than the last time I saw him. He was clean shaven, had gotten a haircut and his cheeks were getting their color back.

"And you, as well Arthur."

"What can I do for you?"

"I have just bought my Mercenary Company Charter, and we need supplies. naturally I came to you."

"We are honored that you have."

I gave Arthur the lists and he quickly looked over them. "Yes, we can cover this. If you would come into my office, my clerks will start filling your order with your men."

I looked at the Master Sergeant; he nodded.

I followed Arthur into his office. "How else may I serve?"

I took off my money belt and handed it to him. "I'd like to open an account with you for Black Stag Keep, and the Black Stag Mercenary Company."

He nodded and opened the money belt, pulling out the currency. "There is much more here than what your list will cost, much more."

"We are headed to Black Stag Keep. In all honesty I don't know what I'll find there. In one month, I want a supply caravan to follow us with six months' worth of supplies for a keep of two hundred men. You will want to have plenty of guards to protect it, as winter is coming on. I'll gladly pay the additional cost for the guards. Anything left you will keep on my account, anything less; I will pay your caravan when they arrive at Black Stag Keep."

"There is also a Captain Jon Wester of the Bonnie M. He will be doing business with you. I own a percentage of his ship."

"I know of him and the Bonnie M. A good reputation."

"If there is ever an imbalance with him, I'll cover it."

"Yes, sir."

"Also, send one butchered beef to my Company Mess Sergeant, down by the river, with enough salt to cure what we don't eat before we leave."

He nodded, "we will do it as you say. Please call on me for any service."

We rose, he bowed, I nodded, "Thank you Arthur."

"Thank you, sir."

Master Sergeant Miller was waiting when I came out. "I've sent for the wagons to come to be loaded."

I nodded, "everything is paid for here, I have some other stops to make. I'll see you back at the company area."

"Yes, Captain."

I walked down the street to an apothecary and gave him a list to fill. When I left there, I went around the corner and down an alley. Once out of sight I dropped into the earth.

I fast-traveled to Top-man's Guild house. The gate had

more guards, and inside the walls was an armed camp. Inside was chaos. They would not have time to bother us.

I fast-traveled back to the alley at the dock camp. When clear, I walked out and on to my wagon.

I saw the Prince had gotten a crutch and was limping around. "Let me get some clay and repair that cast." He nodded and sat down. I went to the river and reached into the earth and got a double handful of clay. As I walked back by my horses, "Come on, time to come up." The two horses and the hound followed me back to the wagon.

I knelt by his leg and started repairing the cast. "A lot of activity today."

"I bought the Mercenary Company's Charter and changed its name to the Black Stag Mercenary Company. I'm now Baronet Captain Sir Draugur de Crypta."

"Oh, is that all?" He chuckled.

Well, we bought supplies too," I said smiling.

He turned serious, "I'm guessing your visit was successful?"

"Yes, we'll have no more trouble from them. I don't think there is anyone left that knows about us, or cares."

He nodded.

"Our unknown enemy is still out there, but he'll have more trouble finding us, or anyone to look for us. Hopefully, this move will break all contact with them, at least for a while. I also brought you a set of light armor. It's by the wagon."

The company Medico came up," Where did you learn to do that, Captain?"

"I read about it in a medico book. It's supposed to support the bones better with less pain than splints."

He nodded his head, "Do you have the book?"

"I do, let me finish this and I'll get it and let you read it."

"Thank you, Sir. Oh, the reason I came over was one of the newly arrived companies has a large command wagon they are looking to sell. It would give you more room and be more comfortable as we travel."

"Thank you, I'll go look at it." He nodded and left.

"We could use more room."

"I'll go look at it." I said smiling. "Come on, hound, let's get you fed too." The dog followed me over to the mess wagon. "Mess Sergeant."

"Yes, Captain?" News travels fast.

"If this beggar comes around, would you give him the scraps? He's a bit thin."

He nodded smiling. "Yes, Captain, we've seen him before."

"Thank you, Mess Sergeant."

I went to find the company who had the command wagon for sale. I found them, and they showed me the wagon. It had a work desk inside that folded closed, an outside folding table, and would sleep two. It came with a good two-horse team. After I bought it, they showed me where there was a hidden strong box built into the wagon. They said they had told no one of the strongbox and me only after I bought it.

I drove it back and parked it beside our other one, opening it and putting a sizable bag of gold in the strongbox. As soon as "Captain Drake" saw it, he moved right in. "Now this is more like it!"

"I'm glad you approve. I tossed him a key and showed him the hidden strong box. There is a large bag of gold in there for your expenses, and more if you need it."

He looked serious, "Thank you my friend."

"Don't worry about it, it's coming out of your pay." We both laughed.

"Captain?" The Master Sergeant called.

"Yes?"

He stuck his head in the side door, looking. He nodded, "good buy. It'll serve you well. When did you want to leave, sir?"

"As soon as everything is in order and you are satisfied,

we can move out. We want to get to Black Stag Keep before the rainy season sets in."

He nodded, "sunrise, day after tomorrow then."

I nodded, "sounds good, we'll travel at the pace you set for everyone to recover."

"Right, sir."

The quartermaster's wagon stopped by, "do you want your saddles and tack for the mare in your other wagon sir?"

"That will do nicely sergeant." They unloaded saddles and tack.

"You forgot about saddles, didn't you?" Captain Drake asked chuckling.

"If I did, I'd never admit it," I said laughing.

***

Before sunrise, I led the horses back down to the river. The hound stayed with us.

It turned out to be a busy day. Everyone checking equipment, taking care of last-minute things before the company move-out.

Mid-morning, I saw a mounted cavalry officer talking to Captain Drake. When he rode away, I went over to him.

"Trouble?" I asked looking after the officer.

"I don't think so, not directly anyway. He recognized me. I told him I was traveling incognito and asked him not to say anything. But you know soldiers and rumors."

"Do you want me to make sure he's not a problem?" My face showing no emotion.

He thought a moment, "no, not his fault, let him go. Maybe he'll keep quiet. But this forces an issue, I want you to take a message to the Royal Spymaster."

"You think that wise?"

"maybe not, but... nevertheless."

The Prince wrote his message. "I'm telling him that Sir Edwin is dead, and I'm traveling incognito to Black Stag

Keep. Hopefully, I'll lose my enemy by moving."

"Do I leave the letter or deliver it?"

He thought a moment, "leave it."

He wrote a second one to his father and sealed it. "Leave this one for my father." I nodded. "Be careful."

"Always." I took his letters and left, heading for the Royal Castle.

CHAPTER 8

I fast-traveled to the spymaster's office. There was no one there, so I left the letter in the center of his desk.

I moved over to the King's office, no one was there. I started to leave the letter there but didn't. I went to his bed chambers and found he and the Queen sleeping. I started to leave the letter on table beside the bed, but he woke up and went to his toilet. I placed the letter on his pillow and waited.

When he lay down, his head landed on the letter. He looked at it in the low light, rose and went into his office, turned up the light and opened the letter.

He looked around the room, at every shadow. He read the letter again then burned it. He sat, thinking, then after a while he went back to bed.

I fast-traveled back to my wagon and lay on the ground under the wagon by the horses. Hound came over and lay down beside me.

My mind would not stop trying to think of anything I may have missed.

I sank down into the earth and opened a vault. I took out the backpack and opened it. If there was going to be trouble, we might need our armor. Better to have it where we could get to it.

I would wear the light armor, Captain Drake the heavy — although it actually turned out to be surprisingly light. There was also a dragon scale design shield I had not noticed before. I emptied one of the larger crates of books and put the heavy armor, shield, sword, and dagger in it. I hoped everything fit him well enough. I did the same with the light set of armor, sword and bow. I raised the crate up through the earth and through the bottom of our extra wagon.

I folded the backpack up and put it back in my pouch. I refilled the vault and raised back up through the ground. Hound was still laying there; we both went to sleep.

***

Before sunrise the camp became a beehive of activity. They assigned drivers to our wagons and hitched the teams up. I saddled my mare — the warhorse would follow behind the Command Wagon.

"We need to warn Master Sergeant Miller there may be trouble." The Prince said,

"Are we expecting any?"

"Better to be ready, and it does not happen, than not ready, and it happens."

"How much do we tell him?"

"Just enough for him to prepare."

I nodded. "I'll take care of it." I went to find the Master Sergeant. He was at his wagon issuing orders.

"Good morning, Captain."

"Good morning, Master Sergeant. I need a word."

He nodded, "All right you lot, get to it." They all left on assigned tasks.

"What is it, sir?"

"I wanted you to know of the possibility of trouble."

"What kind, and how bad?"

"I had a disagreement with someone and they sent people to teach me a lesson. Blood was spilled. They took offense that I didn't bow and take my beating. More blood was spilled, quite a lot actually. I thought it was over, now I'm not so sure. I've been followed and watched.

"They know where I am now, but I don't know if they will push it again. I don't want you blindsided. Better to be prepared, just in case."

He nodded thinking. "These people have troops?"

"So far, they have only used the Criminal Guild, but I don't know for sure."

"It's good you are telling me, as you say, just in case. How bad did you bloody their noses?"

I shrugged my shoulders, "I left more than a few bodies on the floor."

He nodded, "right then, we'll be ready." He turned and started shouting orders. From day one we traveled as if we were moving through enemy territory, with scouts ahead and flankers out. We moved slowly, not pushing the men or the horses. Everyone either was in a wagon or mounted. It was an education for me watching how a mercenary company worked. I rode my mare but stayed close to the Command Wagon.

We made five miles the first day. When we stopped for the night, they set pickets, and mounted a guard. I, for one, was ready to stop, never having ridden a horse that far or for that long. Captain Drake was getting around better with his crutch and I saw he had an easy way with the men. Thatcher made sure he was taken care of.

I brushed the horses every night. The war horse, which I started calling Beast, was healing fine. Hound stayed with Beast when we stopped, but he started following me more and more.

I put a blanket and saddle on Beast but didn't cinch it up, making sure it did not touch any of his wounds. He was fine with me working with him, even though everyone had warned me he was a mean one. I slept in the earth for part of the night and let it heal my sore body.

The second day we made another five miles following the same routine. After the third day we started averaging ten miles a day. I now saddled Beast every morning, getting him back to work. He carried just the saddle and his wounds were now completely healed.

One afternoon when we stopped, and before I unsaddled Beast, I stepped into the stirrup and mounted him. He didn't even flinch. I just sat on him, talking to him for a few moments. Having accomplished that, I took both horse's saddles off, brushed them down, and gave each an apple.

I started riding Beast half a day then changed over to the mare. After a few days I alternated horses, Beast one day, the mare the next.

We had been on the road two weeks and Captain Drake was going stir crazy. One morning before we moved out, I asked him. "You've worked with war horses before, haven't you?"

"I have... some can be a handful."

"You think the leg is well enough to sit Beast?"

"I think I'd like to try." He said, smiling from ear to ear.

I saddled the horses, using Beast's heavy war saddle, and brought the big animal around to the side of the Command Wagon. I looked at Beast, "You behave!" He snorted. Slow and easy we got Drake mounted and Beast never moved. With Captain Drake on him and me on my mare, we rode for half a day before Drake said that was enough for his first day back in a saddle. Before the week was out Captain Drake was riding all day. Both horse and rider were doing well.

One day, we were about to stop when a rear scout came galloping in. "That can't be good news," said Drake.

Master Sergeant Miller sent for me, and we met at the Command Wagon. "Your trouble may have found you."

"What's happened?"

"Another company has been closing up on us for the past few days. Today a scout reported 30 light cavalry, closing fast. As soon as we reach the woods ahead, we'll deploy and face them."

"Your call, Master Sergeant, tell us where you want us."

"Stay in the middle and don't get killed!"

I laughed, "I'll do my best to follow those orders." We stayed out of the way and let the company do what it was trained to do.

Two wagons blocked the road. Archers and pike men

took their places on both sides of the road. Our cavalry held position to the rear, armed with short lances and shields.

If they charged, our archers would start picking them off, then our pike men would stop their charge and let the archers work over what was left. That was what I thought, anyway.

I looked around thinking what I could do. Our flanks were our weak spot. I concentrated on my feet on the ground, moving along the sides of the road. I couldn't let them see me raising walls, so I made potholes that looked like tree stump holes, creating a hole every two feet, one hundred yards out and fifty yards back, on both sides of the road.

I looked around, and everyone was watching the road for cavalry. No one noticed what I had done. The other company's cavalry came into sight. When they saw us, they came on at a charge, thinking they had caught us unaware.

"Stupid!" commented Drake.

When they were in range, the archer's sergeant gave the order to fire. They dropped a few. The pike men planted their lances. The charging cavalry split around them and went into the trees. As soon as they entered, horses started falling and screaming. Riders were thrown as horses stepped in the holes and went end over end.

Some were able to pull up in time, but they had lost a third of their force. As soon as the horseless riders started running away our archers stopped firing. While their cavalry was still in disarray, our horsemen charged them. We hurt them, but it was by no means a rout. They withdrew, and we fell back along the road.

The Master Sergeant ordered archers into the woods to dispatch the screaming horses and bring back prisoners.

They also stripped the dead of equipment — both men and horses. A few horses had survived, and five more came back with our cavalry, so we added them to our troop.

We had lost three horses and four men... So far.

Thatcher came up, "The Master Sergeant has three prisoners, sir. Says you may want to talk to them."

"I'll be right there."

I looked at Captain Drake, who advised, "You go, I'll stay out of sight, just in case they name someone." I nodded and left.

When I arrived, the prisoners were sitting on the ground drinking water.

The Master Sergeant looked at me, I nodded. "So, what's this about then?" He asked, looking down at them.

"Captain took a short-term contract, a thousand gold to delay you, and two thousand gold to kill or capture your two captains. He figured it'd be easy, you being walking wounded and all."

"Didn't work out that way, did it lad?"

He shook his head.

I motioned for the Master Sergeant to follow me. When we were out of earshot, "We staying here tonight?"

He nodded, "that's my thinking."

"A delaying action means trouble ahead."

He nodded his head, "probably a much larger force. They mean to finish you and bringing enough men to ensure it's done."

"How far to Black Stag Keep, do you think?"

"At this pace?" he paused thinking, "between four and six days."

"So, our options are, make our stand here, move the company as quickly as we can and hope we make it, or hide the wagons and make a run for it. Did I miss anything?"

He shook his head, "that about covers it."

"Your thoughts?"

"If we stay here it will be bloody, but we may live through it. If we keep moving as a company, they'll probably catch us in the open, and we're done. Our best option is to hide the wagons here, well off the road, leaving the worst of our wounded as guards. Then make for Black Stag Keep and hope to God there is a fortification there to shelter us."

I thought a moment, then nodded, "tell me what happens

to a company whose captain is captured and surrenders?"

"Depends, some buy themselves out. Some disband, some fold in with the capturing company."

"Does that happen a lot?"

"All of those options happen during war. It just depends on their money, backing, and size."

"OK, we keep the prisoners, let them think we are holding in place. Find a place off in the woods to leave the wagons and the guards. Issue rations for four days. We ride as lancers and archers, using our best horses. Tell the wagon guard force, if found by a great force leave the wagons and make their way to Black Stag Keep. I can buy more equipment. We'll send further instructions as soon as we can. Plan to leave at midnight."

He nodded and started giving orders.

I went back to our Command Wagon and told Captain Drake what we had found out, and what the plan was. He listened nodding his head. "That's the best choice of the ones we have."

"I will pay a visit to our neighbors and sow some chaos in their ranks. Hopefully that will keep them busy and off our backs for a while."

"Don't be late."

"If I am, leave without me, I'll catch up."

I stepped into the trees and dropped into the earth. Moments later I was at our enemy's camp. They were in a somber mood.

I found their horses; they had a few guards out with them. I made five stone dogs and told them to chase the horses back down the road away from us, about ten miles, then return to earth.

I created another four to run through their camp snapping and biting at anyone they found, but not to actually injure anyone. I told them to keep it up until dawn, then return into the earth.

I concentrated on the camp, focusing on each campfire. *Go out.* All the fires went out, leaving the camp dark and cold. I thought to the dogs. *Go.* Five ran at the horses barking and howling while the others ran through the camp barking, snapping and howling.

The horses were running down the road as fast as they could. The camp was dark and disordered. I nodded, satisfied, and returned to our camp.

***

I stepped over to our Command Wagon, picked up our lances and rations and put them into in the saddle packs.

I stuck my head in the Command Wagon, "why aren't you changed?"

"Into what?"

"Your armor, it's in the other wagon." I went to the other wagon and he limped along behind me.

"You finished with the neighbors?"

"They weren't that far away and were already in bad shape. I stole their horses and ran them off." At the wagon I opened the crate and started laying out our armor.

He just stared at me a moment. "This thing you have about stealing... you're going to have to work on that."

"It's a hard habit to break, but I'll try."

Thatcher came up, "If you're ready sir, I'll take the wagons."

"As soon as you help Captain Drake into his armor."

I got my armor on and helped Thatcher finish Captain Drake.

We mounted; his shield attached to the war saddle and Beast was excited. "This armor is amazing; it's lighter than any armor I've ever worn. The swords are the best I've ever seen, and it all fits like it was made for me."

"Maybe it was, it's yours, and Beast as well. What's mine is yours."

He looked intently at me, holding out his hand, we clasped wrists. "Thank you, my friend, my brother in arms." I nodded. We rode toward the front of the formation.

They covered the wagon tracks going into the wood as best they could. Everyone was there so there was nothing I could do to help.

We numbered 42. Master Sergeant saw us in full armor and nodded, "Good," a man of few words. We formed up ready to move.

A little before midnight the scouts led us out. We kept a steady pace but did not push. We didn't need for a horse to break a leg stepping into some hole in the dark.

We walked our horses at daybreak, eating on the move. We kept an easy trot going that the horses could hold for a good while. We kept going all day with only short breaks and stopped at sundown to eat, sleep and rest the horses until midnight.

I hoped we were getting close, and I hoped the Keep could shelter us. I needed to know for sure, so when it was full dark I dropped into the earth.

I followed the road as fast as I could. It wasn't like "fast-traveling" it was more like what a bird must feel like flying.

I could feel the ocean was not far away. The Keep was supposed to be on the ocean, when I got to the coast I turned north. I found it, not far along the shore.

I suppose you could call it a Keep, but it had seen better days. The Keep itself was a combination of a Donjon Keep and a Shell Keep. At least it still stood, and the walls were intact. The Donjon was set against the back wall of the Shell, which were joined with steep cliffs. The moat was more of a moist dip.

I looked through the keep and found it abandoned. I came up through the shell wall and stood atop it. It would take years to rebuild this place, but I didn't have years. I sank back into the earth under the Keep... I would need more room.

I pictured in my mind what I wanted. A bigger Donjon with a bigger hall. More rooms and stables for more horses. A better well. Thicker and higher walls. A thicker stronger gate and portcullis.

I kept what I wanted firm in my mind. *Build, rebuild and restore.* The runes on my hand glowed, and the Keep started to move. Walls moved and grew. Everything expanded and grew. Rotten wood was restored to new. Bedrock moved up under the whole Keep, setting a solid foundation.

The moat was now twelve feet deep, twenty feet wide and stone lined. Water began filling it. If it came from the earth, it was being renewed. Of course, everything came from the earth.

I didn't have time to admire the work... I had to get back to the men. I wanted to "fly" the road back to them to see the terrain. The Keep sat at the end of a forested valley with craggy cliffs all around. There was some open farmland, but I saw no people.

The valley narrowed until the road between the crags was not wide enough for two wagons to pass. This narrow section of the pass ran for a hundred yards before opening out onto an open plain. I pictured in my mind what I wanted, *build it.* A thick tall wall grew out of the ground with a heavy gate, guard towers and a portcullis.

I left the gate open and flew back to the company, which by that time wasn't all that far away. I got back in time to sleep in the earth and restore my strength. When everyone started stirring, I rose from the earth and sauntered out into camp.

We moved out within the hour. As usual, the scouts moved out first. We kept our pace slow and easy. An hour before dawn, we came upon one of our scouts waiting just before we entered the forest.

When we got to him, he gave his report. "There's a mix of heavy and light cavalry waiting a mile the other side of this piece of forest. The other scouts are checking along their flanks to see if they are hiding anything. Looks to be about ten heavy and the rest light, maybe fifty in all."

"They're just sitting there?" I asked.

"They know we are coming, I'm sure they have scouts too." The Master Sergeant answered.

I nodded. I knew they could not have been there that long; I would have seen them as I passed. They probably pushed their horses hard to get there ahead of us.

"I think we should dismount and rest our horses. We'll wait for the other scout's report. The sun will be up in an hour, so let's wait until then before we decide what to do. Besides their heavy cavalry will probably stay mounted tiring their mounts even more. I'll take every advantage I can get."

The Master Sergeant nodded, and ordered the men to dismount, eat, and rest their horses.

CHAPTER 9

The other two scouts returned, confirming the original man's report. Captain Drake, Master Sergeant Miller, and I walked to the edge of the wood. We could see them out in the open, still sitting on their horses. There looked to be five knights and their men at arms in heavy armor and the rest appeared to be lancers, roughly fifty in all.

"Can you tell who they are?"

"The main banner belongs to Baronet Sir Gordon Lansford of Port West Gate. It's really a port, more like a cove, but he likes to sound important." Captain Drake answered.

"He is an ambitious, conniving little man. Someone has bought him off with money, or perhaps the promise of a title and power. He dreams of being a peer of the realm. He's not very smart, but ruthless. He will want to talk first, thinking to intimidate us into surrendering. When that does not work, he will threaten us.

"I must admit, though, he can fight and loves a one-on-one challenge."

"I think once the talks fail," I said, "we charge them, lancers in front with archers behind. When we get within one hundred yards the lancers break left, archers right. Archers fire three arrows as they can, circle for another volley, then we all break off and let them chase us. When their horses tire, we do the same thing again. When the time is right, lancers will close and finish them.

"Unless someone has a better idea."

They were both staring at me. "He studies strategies and armed conflict," Captain Drake said looking at Master Sergeant Miller, who was nodding, thinking it over. "I like it."

Captain Drake nodded, "Me too."

"Then let's go talk to Sir Gordon."

We walked back to the men and mounted. We explained our planned tactics so they would be ready upon our return. Master Sergeant tied a white cloth to his lance, and we rode out to meet the enemy.

Sir Gordon and two of his knights came forward under their white flag.

Captain Drake and I left our face masks open, as was the custom under a white flag. Our horses weren't quite nose to nose when we stopped.

I waited until he was about to speak, then spoke first, interrupting him. "Good morning, gentleman!" That put him off his prepared speech.

"You will surrender yourselves to me at once," he snarled.

"Will you at least introduce yourself before making demands?"

"I am Baronet Sir Gordon Lansford of Port West Gate. You will surrender to me or we will take your bodies back. One is as good as the other. You are both imposters."

"Did you hear that, Captain Drake? We are fellow baronets." Drake just smiled, letting me do all the talking.

"You will surrender..." that's as far as I let him get.

"Port West Gate? Port West Gate... What is it about that place that I'm supposed to remember?"

"Pigs, sir." Master Sergeant said.

"Their women?"

"Pig farmers, Sir... I don't know about their women, Sir."

"Ah, yes, pigs."

Sir Gordons face was redder than I'd ever seen anyone's. I must have struck a nerve there.

"Your bodies it is, then." He snatched his horse's head around and rode back to his armsmen.

We looked at the Master Sergeant, "What? I don't know about their women!"

We laughed and rode back.

Captain Drake and Master Sergeant took the head of the column with the lancers. I took the head of the archers, strung my bow and had arrows at hand.

We moved out in columns of two at a walk, then a trot. I could not see the exact distance so I had to trust Captain Drake and Master Sergeant Miller to do their part. Then we were at a gallop. It wouldn't be long now.

I held on with my knees and notched an arrow. Lancers broke left. We broke right. I had bodkin-headed arrows to use on the knight's armor. I fired my three arrows, and we whipped past Sir Gordon's men.

We continued around their rear and circled back toward their front, and I fired three more arrows as we passed their stalled ranks. The rest of the archers followed my lead, firing more arrows. Then we followed the lancers galloping away from Sir Gordon.

In his rage he spurred his horse and men after us. It didn't take long to tell their horses were about done in. We continued on, then followed Captain Drake with a turn and started our second run.

The lancers broke left we broke right, firing arrows as we went by. Men and horses fell, and we were off again. We could tell right away their horses were blown, lathered and hurting.

We turned for a third time. As we approached, they slowed and tried to turn to catch us dividing. The lancers hit them square on, and they could not hold. Archers put their bows on their backs and drew swords, following the lancers in on top of their stumbling cavalry.

Mare hit Sir Gordon's war horse squarely in the side, and they went down. His bannerman went down beside him. I was off Mare and on Sir Gordon before he could recover. I kicked his bannerman in the head, and he was out. I pulled Sir Gordon's helmet off and put my knife to his throat.

"Yield!."

"No!"

"A dead body works for me, too." My blade started to cut.

"Yield!" The rest of his force quickly yielded to us and the fight was over.

I turned to retrieve the banner we had won and saw the point of the banner lance stabbing at my face. I grabbed it, pulling it to me and drove my dagger into the Bannerman's eye. A brave man, he did his duty, dying to protect his banner. Sir Gordon's men, now my prisoners, dropped their weapons and sat down.

I wiped my bloody knife off on the banner, and handed the banner lance to Master Sergeant Miller. He took the banner off and reattached it upside-down, showing our victory over them.

I need a banner. My hand tingled. "I wonder." I reached into my pouch and pulled out a banner. It was a Rampant Black Stag on a blue background. I handed it to the Master Sergeant, and he attached it to the banner lance over the top of the upside-down banner.

He handed our banner to Thatcher, who had taken a wound fighting at Captain Drake's side. He held it high, grinning from ear to ear.

We saw to the men, most of whom had a wound of some kind. We had lost eight men and three horses. Sir Gordon lost twenty-eight men, one of whom was a knight, and twelve horses.

Our archers had devastated them. We also captured their supply train, which drove right up to us before the drivers realized what had happened.

We stripped the dead of their equipment and buried them. Captain Drake allowed them to bury the knight in his armor and with his sword.

We stripped Sir Gordon and his knights of their armor and his men of their equipment.

"Is there any reason to keep all these prisoners, other than the knights, maybe squires, for ransom?"

"Not really, they're not mercenaries so no one will buy

them back. Families can't afford it."

"Captain Drake?"

"Keep the knights, and Sir Gordon of course. Send everyone else home, with messages to send a ransom for the release of the rest."

I nodded, "Master Sergeant mount them on the worst of the horses, one day of rations, water, and send them home. Load the knights and Sir Gordon in a wagon."

He nodded, "Yes, sir." He walked away giving orders.

I now owned six warhorses, five geldings and one mare. I walked among them, my hand tingling. They all stayed calm toward me and gave us no problems.

We loaded everything into the supply wagons. Everyone mounted, and we moved out, heading for our new home.

***

We made Black Stag Pass by mid-afternoon, passing through the fortress gate and stopped. Sir Gordon stared at it.

"Master Sergeant, close the gate and portcullis. Assign a detail to man the tower."

"Yes, sir."

That done, the rest of us moved on. We could see the Keep in the distance but could not make out features. The closer we got the better it looked. I had seen it, but the sight still impressed me.

We rode through the open gates and into the courtyard. "Master Sergeant, close the gate, and take our guest to the dungeon. Barracks are over there."

"Right sir," the Master Sergeant took charge and got things moving.

Captain Drake and I went into the castle proper.

"Shall we have a look around?"

"I think we should," he said looking at everything as we walked. "I don't know what I expected, but it wasn't this."

I nodded, "Sir Edwin put a lot of work into the place. He

must have been planning to come here before our trouble started. Lucky for us."

He said nothing, but nodded.

"I wonder why he didn't leave a caretaker, or someone, or a small guard force to watch over the place." I said, keeping his mind off of me.

"You would think he would have."

"I would have. I hope he's not lying dead around here somewhere." We kept looking around the keep. Even the furniture was all in good repair. I smiled.

The Castle had two living areas on opposite sides of the Great Hall and kitchen. Both were the same. Captain Drake took one master bedchamber, I took the other, snuggled against the cliff.

We went to check on the barracks. The Master Sergeant had everything in hand and the men seemed pleased. There was a mess hall and kitchen attached to the barracks, where they were storing our captured supplies. There was a good bit there, as they had supplies for seventy-five people. "Thank you, Sir Gordon!"

The Master Sergeant came over, "guard mount's set, all secured sir."

"Thank you, Master Sergeant, when do you suggest we go get the rest of the company?"

"With your permission sir, at first light. I'll take a detachment of ten men and escort the rest of the company in."

"I'll not tell you your business, Master Sergeant, but take all you need in supplies, horses, and equipment."

"Yes sir, and you ain't been doing bad handling the business, sir."

"Thank you, Master Sergeant, I take that as a great compliment. It must be the company I keep," I said, smiling.

I left them to their tasks. I walked back into the castle proper. Once out of sight I dropped into the earth and went down into the dungeon walls. I wanted to see what our guests were up to.

Sir Gordon was in a foul mood. "They should feed us better than this. We're not common foot soldiers."

The others said nothing letting him vent.

"I'll have my day as soon as the rest of the forces arrive."

"What forces?" One knight asked.

Sir Gordon said nothing for a moment, then stuttered, " When my people hear I'm captured, they'll raise an army to come for me."

He was lying. The knights looked at each other, saying nothing, but knowing he was lying.

I rose back up to my room, changed out of my heavy armor, and put on the light armor. Then I went to find Captain Drake.

***

"We may have trouble," I said when I found him.

"You see, that's why no one invites you to parties. You're always bringing bad news."

"Not true, what about the time... OK, point taken. Anyway, I was eavesdropping on our guest. It seems Sir Gordon does not like the food. He promised his day would come as soon as the rest of his forces arrive. The knights asked what forces and he lied, saying his people would come for him."

"You know that's not true. His people would never come for him. But what forces could arrive and from where?"

"What's between here and the northern border?" I asked looking at the map.

"Not a lot, as far as I know. My brother, Prince Mathew, Duke of the Northern District, has a Keep on the northern border. But it's on the eastern side of the country."

"So, there is nothing keeping Hinterland from marching an army down the coast. And Prince Mathew could not deploy his army for fear or leaving the center of the country open."

"Essentially, yes."

"And if Sir Gordon has sold us out, they would control the

whole Western Coast."

He nodded.

"What about The Duke of the Western District? Can he help?"

"I'm doing all I can." He said smiling.

I laughed. Then I suddenly made the connections. "That's what all of this has been about! This whole thing! Hinterland is going to invade, so they wanted to get rid of the Duke of the Western District and cause confusion. Maybe Sir Gordon thought they would promote him after you were dead. He could ride in and save the day. Then sell us out to Hinterland."

"I don't see any holes in your thinking."

"How did they know you were here and who hired the mercenary company that attacked us?"

"The spymaster. The message you delivered told him where we were going. The one to my father told him I suspected the spymaster, and that I had told him so we would see if the spymaster reported it to him. Unless you know of anyone else who may be suspect."

"Not that I know of. But did he report your letter to the king? That's the question, and the answer will tell us one way or the other. The question now is what do we do with this information."

"The first thing is for Master Sergeant Miller to get back here with our troops and supplies as soon as possible. Hinterland can't leave this Keep intact along their supply lines. They must take it to secure their supply lines. We'll discuss the matters with Sir Gordon in the morning. Let's sleep on it and see if we think or anything else."

I nodded, bid him good night, and went to my chambers, ostensibly to sleep. But I had other things I needed to do, and it would be a long night.

***

I sank into the earth. I needed to know if the pass guarded by my fortress gate was the only way into my valley. I started at the keep and flew around the cliffs. I found a few animal trails and grew the cliffs to close them. I also found a footpath that wound through the cliffs and crags, so I closed it off.

I also stumbled on some large coal deposits, some silver, and a little gold. I put a few chunks of coal in my pouch. There was a nice slow river that ran through the valley, and I wondered why there were no farms.

I went through the cliffs in back of the keep overlooking the ocean. Captain Wester was right — there was no cove there... yet.

I concentrated on what I wanted, *build it.* Cliffs shifted around and rose to form the protective wall for the cove, which could hold three or four ships. I angled the protective cliffs such that unless you were looking for it, you would never see the entrance.

The sea bottom was deepened. There was now a sandy beach where small boats could land and a stone wharf where a ship could tie up.

A stone roadway led up to a pasture. I made a break in the crag wall that connected the valley to the pasture. It was behind trees so you really couldn't see it from the Keep unless you knew where to look.

I'd "discover" it later.

It was now about midnight. I flew the road an army would have to come down if they invaded the West Coast. A hundred miles north there was a place where the crags funneled down to a pass only fifty feet wide, a route which cut three hundred miles off the trip. I grew crags up and closed off the pass.

There was also no water on the west side of the new crags, and that would hamper any army passing through. It was the best I could do tonight.

I fast-traveled back to the Keep and slept in the earth the

rest of the night to regain my strength.

CHAPTER 10

Drake and I were sitting at the head table in the Great Hall when they brought in our six prisoners and sat them in chairs facing us. We had discussed how we should proceed beforehand.

"Sir Draugur, for the benefit of everyone here, will you introduce me?" I rose and stepped to the end of the table.

"May I introduce His Royal Highness, Prince Kade, Duke of the Western District, Fifth son of His Royal Highness King John."

All five knights, to their credit, took a knee. Sir Gordon didn't move … "he is a fraud!"

"Rise, Sir Knights, you may take your seats." They bowed and sat back down.

"I can understand why you would make such a claim, Sir Gordon. To do otherwise would be to admit that you attempted to murder a Royal Prince at the behest of a foreign government. What you don't know is that the Hinterland invasion has failed."

The color drained from his face.

"Their army was met and trapped on our side at the border as it was headed here. Their defeat was complete. The plans you thought were so secret were known, which was why Black Stag Keep was rebuilt. You were not satisfied with being a baronet with prosperous lands and became greedy. Did you imagine yourself a duke? To kill me and take my place? Is that what they promised you?"

The five knight's heads hung as they contemplated the truth and their part in the plot.

The prince waited while everyone stared at Sir Gordon, who finally found his courage. "Yes, I was to take over as Duke of the Western District."

"Well, at least you didn't sell out cheaply. Do you have any last requests?"

Sir Gordon said nothing.

Prince Kade nodded, "Take him back to his cell."

Soldiers came forward and took him away. The knights awaited their fate. "From what I've seen, you were ignorant participants in Sir Gordon's plans, but one can never be sure, so I have decided to let you redeem your honor on the field of battle. In fact, what I told Sir Gordon was a ruse ... the Hinterland army was not destroyed and is still on the way."

The men gasped as they realized the truth.

"Your armor and horses will be returned to you, and I expect you to prove your loyalty to the crown by going home and raising as many fighting men to our cause as you can. Then, you will return here to serve your new liege lord, Baron, Lord Draugur de Crypta, who now owns Port West Gate, all of Sir Gordon's holding, as well as Black Stag Keep and lands."

I hoped the surprise didn't show on my face.

The prince rose and so did the knights. I bowed, "your highness," and the prince left the room.

I turned to the knights. "Gentlemen, time is our enemy. You must go raise your men and return as quickly as possible. Your horses, armor and equipment await you at the stables."

They bowed, "Yes, my lord," and were escorted out.

The men helped them armor up, and they left within the hour. In their place, I would have done the same, before anyone changed their mind! I watched from the battlements as they rode out, with the escort I'd detailed to get them through the Pass fortress.

The prince joined me on the battlements.

"Not to look a gift horse in the mouth, but will the king

let your decisions stand?"

"Yes, I'm the Duke of the Western District, I rule here, as long as I support the King."

"Now that you've shown me the bait, what is the trap?"

He laughed, "so cynical?"

"It's kept me alive this long."

He nodded, becoming serious. "I need someone I can trust at my back. I don't have the time or the desire to sift through all the courtiers and sycophants to find someone I might trust a little. You, I trust with my life. If we survive, we'll both live comfortably wealthy. In the meantime, Baron, you have to raise an army to support your duke. That will cost money. You also have to go to Port West Gate and tell Sir Gordon's wife that her husband has ruined her. She is no longer the Baroness."

"What will happen to her?"

"Sometimes wives are thrown out with little or nothing. If she is involved with his treason, we will execute her as well. That depends on you, my good baron. Just hope she doesn't look like a pig." He walked away laughing.

I had to chuckle, "Oh, you're funny, maybe you should be a court jester!"

Out of curiosity, I walked down to the dungeon and found Sir Gordon sitting in his cell staring off into the distance.

"Have you come to finish it, then?"

"No, I have no such orders. I came to ask you about your wife."

He swiveled his eyes to me, "what about her?"

"Was she involved?"

He chuckled, "Hardly. Baroness Annette can barely put two sentences together in a conversation. But she is good with numbers, books, and running the household, I'll give her that."

"Do you have children, a son?"

He shook his head, "she was no good in that regard either. I wouldn't worry about her, though. Her conniving father, Bernard, will find another use for her as he has all of her life, treating her like one of his prize pigs. He's the one you should watch out for."

He got a contemplative look and nodded, coming to some decision. "He's the one who put Hinterland in contact with me. He is also the Top-man for the Criminal Guild in Port West Gate. The Prince was right, I was greedy. A lust for power and wealth consumed me.

"Bernard saw it and used it to advance his agenda. I thought once I was duke, I would be free of him, but now I see how wrong I was. He would always be there, with his hand in my purse."

I said nothing ... just listened to him.

"Bernard has three sons. The oldest two, Ben, and Bart, are in the Guild as well. The youngest, Charles, oversees the farms. I should have killed Bernard a long time ago, but he was my path to power. I never realized he was really my jailer, and I was working for HIM."

He said no more, just sat staring at the wall, perhaps at dreams that would never be.

"What would you do for a second chance?"

He looked at me, "who do I have to kill?"

"Whoever is in our way. You would need to change how you attain power. You see how the Criminal Guild works. They have a lot of power and wealth, but don't show off. You would work in the background gaining control and power."

"Where?"

"Hinterland. If you agree, you will go there and start gaining control over the Guild, working your way up to Top-man... lord knows, you're a schemer and brutal enough. If you can get it done, we'll set up a network taking over Guilds everywhere. Do this right and you could eventually run the Guild for the whole of Hinterland."

"You're the Prince's spymaster?"

"In a way, but we might as well get rich while building an

information trade network."

"If I'm caught, they'll kill me."

"Most surely. Do you have any better offers?"

"It seems I have only the one."

"Will you take it?"

He hesitated only a moment, "yes, I'll take it."

I nodded, "there is no going back. There are no other chances. There will be only death if you fail, either by them or by me."

He nodded, "I understand."

I put a purse of gold and a purse of gems on the table. Inside the gold purse was an earth coin that I'd made. As long as he carried it, I could find him. "Your name is now Lane Graves. Make up the rest for yourself. Come with me."

We left the cell and walked to the stables; we saddled horses and rode out. I escorted him to the Pass Fortress and saw him through. "If they don't kill you, send me a message in a year. Good Luck." He nodded and rode away.

When I got back to the stables the Prince was there with Beast. "Sir Gordon?"

"I executed Sir Gordon for treason. That other man was our first spy going into Hinterland." He nodded. "I plan on going to Port West Gate in the morning, did you want to come?"

"No, I'll stay here, in case something happens. I see your new warhorse is a mare. Are you planning on having Beast cover her?"

"I am, the next time she's in season."

"That should make a fine foal."

"I'm hoping so."

***

After the evening meal, I retired to my chambers, then dressed in my black armor with helmet and face shield.

I sank down into the earth and moved rapidly toward

Port West Gate, following the road, which was deserted at that time of the day.

I arrived and decided that calling the place "port" was stretching the point a little. A large cove, a stone quay, a pier, and a small fort overlooking the cove was not really a port. There were two ships moored to the quay, one built to carry cargo, the other an armed merchantman. The merchantman flew Hinterland colors.

I went down through the stone pier to that ship, made a vault in the stone, and crossed over from the pier, through the water, and up through the bottom of the vessel.

I looked up through the hull. There were many people on board, equipped as troops to take the port once the invasion force made its appearance.

The hold held chests of gold and jewels, black powder, cannon balls, and other supplies, so I moved it all into the stone pier vault.

Then I went up through the wood into the wall of the captain's cabin where I found another large chest of valuables, which I moved to join the other chests.

Then I heard loud voices in the outer part of the Captain's cabin: "The fool was captured, and confessed to being a Hinterland conspirator. He is to be executed, if he has not been already."

"No matter, our army is well on its way. They should be here before anyone can do anything to stop them. As long as your Guild keeps the people in line, we will have no problems."

"Me and my boys will do our part. Just remember our bargain."

"He and his boys? This must be Bernard and his two sons. How convenient." I concentrated on the ballast rocks and raised five large stone dogs. *Kill everyone on this ship ... no one escapes.*

The dogs split up and went to work. I swelled the wooden door closed and trapped everyone in the Captain's cabin. The screaming and shrieks of terror started, matched by the growling, barking, and howling of the dogs. While the dogs attacked, I moved all the ship's cannon and their equipment to the pier vault. Then I concentrated on the masts and set them on fire. This made the panic worse.

I moved back into the stone pier and waited. The enemy soldiers and sailors jumped from the burning ship onto the pier and ran, but one by one I pulled them down into the pier. Not one escaped. The ship burned to the waterline and the dogs, their bloody chores done, went back to being ballast stones.

I went deeper under the pier and made another vault. I opened the backpack and placed all the chests from the ship onto the ground sheet, opening each one in turn. They held gold, jewels, and gems, handy for bribes and pay-offs. I changed out of my black armor and into my plain clothes and light armor, folded the ground sheet back into the backpack and put it into my pouch, leaving the cannon and powder vault for later use.

I searched out the local Criminal Guild house and looked it over. It was not as big as the one in the capital, but seemed wealthy ... but not for long. I emptied the vault of everything while raising and loosing stone dogs on them.

I came out in an alley and went into an inn, ordering wine and taking a seat in the back, out of the way. When the servant brought me my wine. "The Lansford house?"

"Back up Main, and north at the crossing. Big house down on the right." I paid her and sipped the wine — not great, but not the worst I've had.

I left the inn and dropped into the earth and moved to the Lansford house, where I found Sir Gordon had installed a vault in the house's basement, evidence he had amassed quite a bit of wealth. I left it alone for now.

There was nothing else I could do that night, so I flew through the earth back up the coast to Black Stag Keep.

***

I ate breakfast with Prince Kade, "I have some documents for you to take with you when you leave," he said. "They are your official seals and the certificates naming you Baron of Port West Gate. People will want to see them before they turn everything over to you. I would suggest you stop by the provost and magistrate and show them first.

"I also have a list of things I need, if you would be so kind."

"Of course."

I dressed in nicer clothes, stopped at the Prince's office and picked up the documents and his list.

"I also have a letter for my father. Do you have a secure way to get it to him?"

"I do." he nodded and handed me the sealed letter.

I rode alone, as I felt we could not spare the men for an escort ... and I didn't need one anyway. I'd hire one for show when I got to Port West Gate.

I let the mare have her head and set her own pace. She set out at a fast pace and kept it up for a good while. I saw no one on the road, or the sign of any recent passing.

I made Port West Gate by mid-afternoon, went straight to the Provost and Magistrate's office and entered. "Good morning, sir," a clerk greeted me.

"Good morning, my name is Baron, Lord Draugur de Crypta. I'd like to see the provost and magistrate."

He stood, "Yes m'lord. One moment, please." He hurried into the inner offices.

The provost came right out. "Good morning Baron, please come in."

"Thank you."

"Please, sit. How may I serve?"

I took out the documents.

"I have been named Baron of Port West Gate. Here are my

seals and certificates ... I thought you should be the first to know."

"We had heard rumors, but you know how rumors are. If I may ask, what of Sir Gordon?"

"Executed by the crown for treason, as well as the attempted murder of Prince Kade."

He sat, stunned, "my God, the rumors are true. And the invasion?"

"Our reports say a Hinterland army is heading this way, so we are raising an army to meet it. We are gathering at Black Stag Keep with a plan to stop them short of Port West Gate."

"What can we do to assist?"

"I don't want to start a panic. I want a smooth transition as I take over as Baron and it will take me a while to see what kind of mess Sir Gordan has left us. If you would let people know who I am, and that all is well, that should calm things."

"Of course, m'lord."

"I'm told there is a mercenary company that winters here. Where can I find them?"

"Usually at Klader's Inn. Shall I send for their captain?"

"I have not eaten; will you join me for a meal, provost? We'll talk to the good captain while we eat."

"Thank you, sir, yes." (Of course he would, officials never turn down a free meal!)

We walked to the inn a few blocks away. "We had some excitement last night at the port."

"How so?"

"A Hinterland ship burned to the waterline and the fire killed everyone on board."

"There were no survivors?"

"None."

"That's odd."

"My thoughts as well."

I let his mind fill in the blanks. We found the mercenary captain at the Inn and the provost introduced me.

"Please Baron, join me," said the captain, whose name

was Chard.

"Thank you." The provost and I ordered our meal.

"To be blunt, captain, I'm sure you've heard the rumors about Hinterland."

"I have."

"I have my own mercenary unit, 'The Black Stag Company' but we need more troops, so I want to hire your group. How many men can you field on this short notice?"

He thought for a moment, "eighty, maybe a hundred."

"How soon can you be ready to march?"

"If we are supplied, three days."

"Provost, can you help with local merchants supplying the captain what he needs?"

"I can."

I put a purse of gold on the table. "This will get you started. Draw up your contract and I'll meet you here in the morning."

"Yes m'lord."

"Now if you gentlemen will excuse me, I have other business."

They rose and bowed, "good afternoon."

I retrieved my horse and rode to the Lansford house.

As I rode up a groomsman met me and took my horse. "You are expected, sir," he said bowing.

CHAPTER 11

The door opened as I approached. "Good morning, Sir, Baronette Annette is in the sitting room. If I may announce you?"

"Yes, please. Baron de Crypta."

He led me to the sitting room. It was a very nice house, well-built and with well-appointed furniture. He opened the door to the sitting room, "Baronette Annette Lansford, may I present Baron de Crypta."

She rose and curtsied, "Baron de Crypta, please, come in."

I bowed in return. "Thank you."

"Some tea perhaps?" She had a soft voice.

"That would be nice, please."

"Tea please, David."

He bowed and left the room, returning quickly with our tea, which she served.

"Thank you, David, that will be all."

He bowed and left, closing the doors behind, but pausing outside. As he left, I noticed that he was armed with a knife.

As we sat, sipping, we looked each other over and I saw something I had seen in street girls. She seemed to be dressing down, as if trying to make herself unattractive. If you were ugly or dirty, those girls learned, people showed less interest in you and fewer men bothered you. Despite that, she was clean and neatly dressed.

"Baron?" She moistened her lips to speak.

"Yes?"

"May we speak plainly?"

I nodded, "If that is your wish."

She nodded, "It is. How bad is it?"

"They found Sir Gordon guilty of treason and the attempted murder of Prince Kade. The crown executed him."

She closed her eyes, gripping the arm of her chair. "Fool, selfish fool!" she whispered. "His holdings?" She asked, tears in her eyes.

"The crown has seized everything, all assets, lands, money, everything. He also implicated your father and two of your brothers, and they confessed before being executed."

Tears ran down her face, but her voice held. "My youngest brother?"

"He was not involved. He will keep the family holdings."

"Thank God for small miracles. You've come to question me as to my involvement? Is there to be a purge?" Her hand still griping the arm of the chair.

I shook my head, "you were not involved." She relaxed a little. I drank more tea and waited.

"I take it I'm not Baronette Lansford any longer?"

I shook my head, "No."

She nodded, "what's to become of me? Will I be sent away with nothing?"

"That depends on you."

She closed her eyes; her face turned red. She sat back and opened her eyes looking at me with fear. I held up my hand.

"What I mean to say is, Sir Gordon said you were very good at keeping accounts, books and records, and that you were a good manager. Perhaps we can help each other."

"Go on," she said.

"I don't think you are as slow and unintelligent as some think, but that you allowed them to believe that because it suited your purposes."

She stared at me, saying nothing.

"I also think you knew more about the things going on here, in your house, and in Port West Gate than anyone ever suspected."

"How do you propose we help each other?"

"I need someone to act as a caretaker, to help me manage

affairs here in Port West Gate. I won't treat you like a fool, please don't treat me like one. When we are alone, as we are now, we will speak plainly to one another. When others are present, we will be actors in the theater of life. Let them think all is well with the world."

"I will remain in this house?"

"Yes. You will lose nothing and will carry on as before, managing the businesses."

"And where will you be staying?"

"The inn for now, I'll split my time between here and Black Stag Keep."

Her eyes widened, "You're the Black Stag?" I nodded.

"Is it a deal, we shall be open and honest with each other?"

"Yes."

She nodded, "then this is your house and you will stay here. I will move my things into the guest room you will have the master's rooms. I will be your guest.

"That will keep the wolves from me, necessary because my husband made many enemies. The local Criminal Guild, which my father and brothers ran, will quickly come to inform you that you owe them a tax."

"The Guild won't be a problem any longer. All were found guilty of treason and executed. Your enemies are now my enemies."

She stared at me absorbing the new information. "Everyone?"

"All we could find, at least the top managers."

She nodded, "good riddance! They hurt my mother and me."

"No longer. There is no need for you to move your things, I'll take a guest room. I'll only be here part time anyway. Do you have a vault?" I knew she did.

"Yes, but there is no key. Gordon gave me operating money and I had to account for every penny," she said harshly. Realizing what she had said, her face reddened.

I pulled the vault key from my pouch and handed it to her. "Shall we go see what we have in our vault?" She took it and led me down to the basement. The servant, David, followed at a discrete distance, but close enough that if she needed him, he could act.

She unlocked the door, and we stepped inside.

I saw her eyes make a quick inventory. "Is it as much as your figures show?"

She smiled, "I was a little short, but not by much."

We left the vault; she locked the door and began to hand me the key.

"You keep it, you're the accountant and manager, we'll go over the books later."

She put the key in her pocket. "Will you stay for dinner?"

"If it's no trouble, thank you. And you can tell David he doesn't have to kill me now." I said smiling.

He eyes grew, "David?"

He stepped from around the corner, bowing. "My lady did not order this, Baron."

"I thought not. Trusted, protective, retainers are more precious than gold, David. I approve of your watchfulness. Continue to watch over the lady."

He bowed, "Yes, Baron. Dinner at the usual time ma'am?"

"Yes, the Baron will join us."

"Yes, ma' am."

David departed. "When we are alone, It's Draugur."

"Annette, My Lord Draugur."

"Pleased to meet you, Annette."

"the pleasure is mine, Draugur."

***

Over dinner we talked of business ... who was doing well and who was not. Who could use capital to expand, and who was about to default on their loans. She explained ideas she had for expansion and for new enterprises. She told me who was extorting whom and who was corrupt, and said she believed the provost was not one of them.

She knew who was smuggling, and who had the best goods.

Sir Gordon, with his bloated view of his own importance, apparently did not realize what a treasure he had. If he had paid attention to her, I thought, he would have been ten times richer.

Her youngest brother managed three hog farms but could easily handle a few more if we financed them. Her mother was still living and stayed on the original family farm with the youngest son.

My hand started tingling. I looked through the wall and saw a group of men forcing their way into the kitchen.

"David, take the lady up to her room. Stay there with her. We are about to have company." David did not hesitate as he ushered Annette out of the dining room quickly and quietly.

Six men came into the dining room. "You must be the new Baron," the leader said.

I nodded, "I am."

"We're with the local Guild, we've come to collect the tax." The others laughed. I laughed with them, to their surprise ... they were used to terrifying people.

"You've moved into Sir Gordon's house quick enough, his wife, too, I'm guessing," said the chief thug.

"That's because he no longer lives. I'm taking over ... is that what you plan on doing?"

"No, we're Guild tax collectors, and you're our golden goose."

"That's not entirely true, is it? There is no one left alive at the Guild house. I took it over because they were trying to steal from me, so I killed them."

"Well, however many men you sent in to do the job, they ain't here now, are they?"

"I didn't say I had them killed, I said I killed them." I

concentrated on the lamps, *Out.* The flames went out and I dropped through the floor.

"Find him." The leader shouted.

I watched them stumble around the room trying to find me in the total darkness. As they spread out, I came up behind one and stabbed him up through the back of the skull. He dropped dead where he stood. I moved to the next one, cutting his throat and letting him fall. The next one I stabbed in the groin, and he started screaming. Two others began fighting each other in the dark, so I waited and killed the victor.

Their leader was the only one left. He had backed into a corner and was waiting. I rose up through the floor across the room.

"Thank you for coming tonight, it saved me the trouble of tracking you down." I walked over to him, grabbed his knife hand, and stabbed him through the eye, letting his body fall to the floor.

Light. I walked over to my place at the table and took a few swallows of wine. *"Killing can be thirsty work."*

Then I looked up through the floor and saw Annette sitting in a chair, with David standing behind, pulling her head back with her hair with his knife to her throat.

"It's always something!" Finishing my wine, I went up through the wall into her room's wall and waited to see what he would do.

"This had better work," she whispered. My jaws tightened as I realized she'd betrayed me.

"It will! Once he's dead we'll take the gold and be gone, Just as we've always planned. This place is about to be overrun with Hinterlanders, anyway. Their army will come from one direction and their navy is here at the Port."

I concentrated on the Lamps. *Out.* The room dropped into darkness; I stepped out of the wall, striking David's elbow and driving his knife through Annette's throat. Before he could react, I slashed his throat.

Light. They were still alive, bleeding out. "You deserve

each other ... Sir Gordon was luckier than he knew." I stonily watched them as they died, their eyes full of disbelief.

Then I dropped all the way down into earth, made a vault and moved everything from the house vault. I got all the records from the office and put them in the new vault, leaving them to go through later.

I came back up through the floor and looked over the scene, then walked out of the house and rode to the provost's office to report the crime. I caused quite a stir, walking in covered in blood, and the clerks quickly rousted the magistrate and the provost.

I said the Criminal Guild had tried to rob us, but a fight had broken out and I was lucky to be alive. Of course, they took me at my word — that of a Baron! — and the provost figured the Guild was behind it all.

They removed the bodies from my house, and everyone had left, I looked through Sir Gordon clothes, choosing something that suited me, since we were similar in size and build.

I slept the rest of the night in the earth and let her restore my strength and calm my mind.

CHAPTER 12

I rose early and well rested, then dressed in my new clothes with my personal equipment clean and polished. I walked to the inn where I had met Captain Chard and had breakfast and tea while I waited for him.

I thought over the events of the last few days ... indeed the last few months. I had changed a lot in a short amount of time, generally improving, but decided I wouldn't mind if things would slow down a bit. I could use some boring time right now!

But Hinterland, it seemed, would not allow that respite. I needed to send as many troops to Black Stag Keep as possible, as well as delivering a letter to the king laying out the situation and my suspicions. I wondered if the comment that David made about the Hinterland Navy was true, or just his speculation.

I saw Captain Chard when he came in and waved him over. "May I offer breakfast, captain?"

"Yes, thank you, sir." He ordered and was brought tea while he awaited his meal.

"What numbers can you field?" I asked.

"Eighty-five," he said handing me a contract. I looked over it and saw it was a standard contract like I had with Master Sergeant Miller. They would buy their own supplies, which was fine by me, and I just had to pay the bottom-line cost.

"You will be ready to move in two days?"

"Yes."

"Agreed, then." I signed the contract. I took a wad of bills from my pouch and gave it to him. After a quick count, he nodded, "Done."

He signed and gave me my copy.

"I'll meet you outside the town in two days."

"We'll be ready."

I paid for our breakfast and left. Outside I turned down the alley, and once out of sight dropped down into the earth. I had a letter to deliver.

I fast-traveled to the Royal Castle and up inside the walls of the king's office. He was sitting at his desk reading through papers. I slid through the walls to the spymaster's office and found he was also reading papers and writing notes, safely out of the way.

I went back to the king's office; he was gone. I stepped out of the wall and placed the letter on his desk, then stepped back into the wall and waited. I needed to make sure he, and no one else, got it.

The king returned from his office, probably from his privy. He sat down, saw the letter and jumped back up, drawing his dagger. I thought he was pretty quick for an old guy. Looking around the room, reassuring himself he was alone, he sat back down, broke the seal on the letter and read it. He sat back, tapping the letter in his hand, then read it again.

He nodded his head with a decision, "guards!"

The door to his office opened. "Yes, sire?"

"Go get the spymaster and bring him to me."

"Yes, sire."

Things were about to get interesting. The guards escorted the spymaster into the king's office.

"What is it, sire?"

"How long?"

"How long what, sire?"

"How long have you been working for my enemies? Your assassination attempts on Prince Kade have failed. Sir Gordon in Port West Gate has been caught, confessed, and executed, messages were intercepted. So, how long, and for what?"

The spymaster said nothing for a moment. "How

long?" He shrugged his shoulders, "a while. For what? For riches and power, of course."

The king shook his head. "You won't be able to spend any of it. Take him to the dungeon."

The guards didn't move. The spymaster chuckled. "Did you think I would not have planned for this if it were to happen? You're getting old and sloppy."

I moved around the wall and got behind the guards and drew my knife.

"You're making my task more difficult; you were supposed to die peacefully in your sleep. Now I must think of something else. Oh well, the king is dead, long live the king!"

The guards drew their daggers, and the king whipped his out, crouching to meet the attack.

I sprang from the wall, stabbing the spymaster in the kidney and slicing up. He passed out from the pain and hit the floor. As the closest guard turned toward me, I slipped my blade under his ribs and into his heart as I pushed him into the other guard. They both fell with me on top of them. I stabbed the last one through the eye, killing him instantly. I rolled off and was on my feet.

The King had not moved, staring at me, waiting to see what I would do.

I bowed, "sire, pardon the interruption. You probably didn't need the help, but I needed the practice."

He chuckled, "Yes, well. He sheathed his dagger. Is he still alive?" He asked, pointing with his chin.

I checked, "he is, for the moment." I cleaned my blade and put it away.

"You stepped through that wall. I haven't heard of that in a long, long time."

"Yes, well, let's keep that between us, shall we?"

"You saved my life, so I never saw a thing. You work for Prince Kade, the one he calls "Ghost." You deliver messages."

"Among other things."

"I can only imagine. He said shaking his head. Is he well?"

"He is."

"He says he is at Black Stag Keep, raising an army to meet the Hinterland forces."

"We are."

"The last time I heard of that place it was almost a ruin."

"We've made some improvements," I said, smiling.

"Sir Edwin?"

"Dead, I'm afraid, killed when the Assassins' Guild blew up his house trying to kill Prince Kade."

He nodded, "I thought so when I heard no more from him."

"The Guild houses?"

"They killed a friend and tried to kill another. I returned the favor."

He nodded, "Yes, a very good friend."

"John?" The queen stepped through the door, sucking in a breath when she saw me, bodies and blood. She drew her dagger — this was a valiant couple!.

"Hold, he's one of ours, well, he's Kade's Ghost, actually."

I bowed, "My Queen."

She bowed her head, "Sir Ghost." I smiled.

"Sire, if you and the queen could be seen elsewhere, I'll take care of this and bring you what information I can."

He nodded, "come my lady, let's go for a walk in your garden." They left. I concentrated and the two dead bodies sank into the floor with all their blood. I took hold of the dying spymaster and we sank into the earth.

The four of us went down under the castle. I concentrated on the spymaster still holding him. *Teach me and show me all.*

As it had when I did this to the alchemist, a lot of information was passed to me, so much that I almost passed out. It took me a few hours of resting in the earth to recover from the strain.

He had four other spies working in the castle, three men and a woman. I found them, and when they were alone pulled them under and left them.

I slid into the spymaster's office and got his ledger from a hidden cache. I could now read and write his code and found he'd been a busy sod. Embezzlement, blackmail, assassinations, the Criminal Guild, it seems everyone had been paying him. He had an estate here in the capital, where he kept his money, and I'd have to visit it to steal the gold and find more information.

***

I found his walled estate easily enough, and evading the servants, I entered his office, swelling the wood to jam the door in place. I took all the papers he had there, then went down to the vault, where I found a wealth of paperwork about blackmail, embezzlement and such. The who, what, where, why, and how, was all documented. I shrugged my shoulders... it was not my job to figure it all out. But I got curious. "On second thought, I'll keep these," I moved out into the earth and opened a vault, opened the backpack and moved the contents of the spymaster's vault into it.

I took all the other papers, ledgers, and books back to the spymasters office in the castle and left everything there. That was someone else's job now, and I had other things to do.

I went through to the king's office. He was there alone, looking out the window. I stepped out of the wall, "Sire." He turned to me and I bowed.

"What have you found out?"

"He had four other spies here in the castle, and I have removed them all. I've put all his papers in his office, but most are in code I can't read. You should be safe now."

"You are returning to Prince Kade?"

"Yes, sire, I have pressing matters to attend to."

He went to his desk, "Take this to him." He handed me a letter.

"And this one from me," the queen said stepping through

the doorway.

"Yes, my queen."

"Take care of my son, Sir Ghost."

"We take care of each other, my queen," I said and stepped through the wall.

She looked at the king, to find him smiling. "We saw nothing."

She shook her head, "Nothing."

***

I fast-traveled back to Port West Gate and slept that night in the earth letting her restore my strength.

I went to the Inn for breakfast, then walked the streets of the port. Most everyone seemed prosperous, and there was a lot of activity at the market. I was pleased to see the stalls well stocked. As it was a port, I would expect that, but there was also plenty of farm produce being sold along with imported items.

Word was getting around that I was the new Baron, and many townspeople greeted me by name. I stopped and talked to a few farmers. They seemed pleased that I didn't intend to raise taxes.

I found cattle drovers on the outskirts of the market.

"Good morning."

"Good morning m'lord," One of the four ventured.

"Good morning! I'm looking to buy one hundred cattle; do you have that many ready this year?"

"Between the four of us we might m'lord, or at any rate close to it."

"I'll want them delivered to Black Stag Keep. Make me a price including the delivery of them there. I'll be paying in gold. Half now, the rest upon delivery."

"It would be a week before we can get them there." I nodded.

We agreed on a price and I paid them. They left straight

away with their cattle. I left it at that to see which one figured out I might need to hire a drover to manage my cattle.

I continued my tour and wound up down at the cove. I walked up to the fort overlooking the cove. There were two guards there, doing nothing.

They both bowed as I approached, "Baron."

I nodded looking over what there was of the fort. Mostly it was just a wall fronting the cove. "She's seen better days."

The older one chuckled, "that she has m'lord. I remember when they built her. She was supposed to be a full fort but they decided it cost too much for such a shallow harbor."

I chuckled, "It's always about the money."

"So my wife says, m'lord." We laughed.

"I will look around, carry on." They bowed.

I walked to the end of the wall. The smell of the ocean on the wind made me smile. I looked out across the cove and out to sea. If David was right, there was nothing to stop Hinterland from sailing right in and taking the town.

I sat down on the wall, studying the shape of the cove.

I imagined how we could get the most out of our cove and make this a real port. I would have to do this differently. There were too many people here about to just raise what I wanted. But then I had a thought and smiled. Earthquake!

I concentrated and held the picture of what I wanted in my mind, putting my hand on the fort wall.

Grow it. The runes on my hand glowed. The ground started shaking and craggy cliffs rose from the water, closing off most of the mouth of the cove. I left a narrow opening in front of the fort and raised a reef on the ocean side of the crags stretching out one hundred feet.

I lowered the cove bottom on this side of the crags, making a deep-water port. On the cove side of the crags I made a twenty-foot-wide shelf just above the high tide water level and extended the shelf all the way around the far side of the cove to beach. The ground continued to shake, and I raised the foot area up twenty feet above the water on solid rocks. I let the shaking slow then stop. Everyone in the area was yelling and pointing, some running.

"Baron!" I heard the guard calling.

"I'm all right," I made my way to them. When I got to them, we stared at the crag wall that enclosed the cove. "I wouldn't have believed it if I hadn't seen it."

"I see it, and I'm still not sure I believe it," the young guard said.

"This will be a tale to tell your grandkids about." I said. "It looks like the whole town is coming down to see it."

"I reckon so, ain't nothing like this ever happened, they want to see it for themselves."

"I reckon so," I said, smiling.

The provost came riding up, "My Lord above! Are you all right, Baron?"

"Yes fine, thank you. Tell me, provost, are there any stone masons in West Gate?"

"There are, m'lord."

"Good, would you be so kind as to send them to me? I think I have a job for them."

"Yes M'lord." he turned his horse and rode to complete his task.

CHAPTER 13

It didn't take long for the stonemasons to show up, since they were already on their way to the cove see what all the excitement was about. I gave them some time to take in the new sight... I must admit it's not something you see every day.

"God works in mysterious way," one said.

I smiled, "Yes He does."

They turned to me, bowing, "Baron."

"Quite a sight, isn't it?"

"It is, m'lord."

"I think we should capitalize on this event. I want to add to the fort, the pier, the quay ... well, to the harbor as a whole." I took a paper and charcoal out of my pouch and drew a sketch of what I wanted done to the fort, and emphasized that I wanted it started right away.

"I want you to survey the cove and come up with a plan to best use what has been given to us," I said. "With the looming Hinterland threat, we need to get the fort ready to protect our town. I will have cannons delivered shortly to install in the fort.

"Use heavy timbers, if you must, to get us started — but get us started! Also, we'll need a powder house for the black powder for the guns." I took a large purse of gold out of my pouch and gave it to them.

"Yes m'lord," they bowed, and I went on to other business.

"That's the best I can do for now," I thought to myself.

***

I rose early and had breakfast at the inn, then mounted Mare and rode out to meet Captain Chard and his company outside of town. We started for Black Stag Keep as soon as I joined them.

The captain followed the same well-proven procedure as Master Sargent Miller had: scouts led the way, with flankers out left and right, scouts following behind.

My mind was busy, trying to think if I had missed anything. One big question was what was I going to do about the king and queen's letters to Prince Kade? Did they mention my special powers?

Once one thing comes out, I worried, the avalanche would start.

Of course, when the prince finally saw the king in person, I was sure those details would come out, anyway. I guessed I'd better get my story ready — not the whole truth, of course, just a good story.

"Everyone loves a good story," I thought, then smiled to myself.

We could have made the trip in one day, but I saw no need to push. We arrived at the keep by mid-afternoon the following day, and Chard set up his company area outside the Keep until we could get everything sorted.

They took my horse to the stables while I joined the prince on the battlements where he was watching the new company set up.

"All is well?" he asked.

"Well enough, but there have been some developments."

"How many men in the new company?"

"Eighty-odd. I've also bought one hundred cattle, and they should be here in a week or so."

He nodded and smiled," let's go inside and have some wine. You can regale me with tales of your adventures."

Over wine I gave him the cleaned up version of being attacked and the Baronette being killed. I also told him of the "earthquake" that almost blocked off the cove.

As he poured us another cup of wine, I took out the letters and laid them before him.

He looked at them, frowning at me, but I said nothing He opened the king's first and read. I sipped my wine and waited while he reread the letter.

"This letter is only a day old."

"Roughly."

He sat it down opened the one from the queen and read, perusing it twice as well.

He lay the letter down and sat back with his cup of wine in thought. "You can get to the capital in a day?"

I nodded, "Yes."

"Do you know what is in these letters?"

"I do not. They were sealed and they did not share their content with me."

"My father says you saved his life, and he is not given to false praise."

"He looked like he would have done all right, he just needed a little help."

"My mother says it was three against one. Had you not intervened he would have surely been killed and she might have been next."

"After the king read your letter, in which I'm guessing you told him the spymaster was behind the assassination attempts, he confronted him, but didn't expected there to be plans for if they found him out. Two of his guards turned out to be the spymaster's men, and they caught your father unaware. I finished paying a debt I owed."

"He also says you cleaned out the castle of spies."

"Before the spymaster died, I convinced him to tell me who else was working with him. I also found papers naming them, so I removed them from service."

He stared at me thinking, "you're a mage!"

"I can do a few tricks that helped me in my career as a thief. I guess you could call me a mage, but an untrained, minor one, at best."

"That's why they called you Ghost."

"Yes, and no. Everyone just thought I was a good thief and I kept my talents hidden; you know how superstitious people are. You are the first person to guess the truth."

"No one ever suspected?"

"I always worked alone and was careful about what I did, and where."

"The king knows?"

"He did not say?"

"No."

"To save him, I had to appear through the wall behind his attackers and he saw me. Then the queen saw me leave through the same wall."

"That's how you were able to save me when the building collapsed on me." I nodded. "So only the three of us know of your talents."

"Yes."

"The king also said he would have to think of some reward to give you for saving his life."

"Great, he'll probably give me more land, so I have to pay more taxes!"

The prince laughed, "such is the price of service. He also says he is sending an army of three thousand men, under the command of my brother the Crown Prince. But we must hold until they get here. They will move faster than we did, but it will still take them three or four weeks."

"We are in a good position here; we'll see how many men those knights come back with, and how many make it in with Master Sargent Miller." He nodded.

"Port West Gate is a weak point. A Hinterland ship was already in port, but something happened and it burned to the waterline, or so they told me. I've got them started on improving the Fort there. That was the best I could do at the time."

"We must start sending out scouts to see how far away

the Hinterlanders are." He stopped and looked at me. "You could do that couldn't you? The way you travel to the capital?"

I nodded," I could."

"How long would it take you?"

"That depends on how far away they are."

"We need to know where they are, how many they are, and how long before they get here."

"I'll eat, then I'll go. Are you going to continue to be "Captain Drake," or are you coming out into the open?"

"It's already pretty much an open secret, so I see no reason to keep hiding my true identity."

"Very well, let's go get something to eat, and I'll head out."

***

I fast-traveled to the narrow pass that I had blocked. No one was there, and as far as I could tell, no one had been there, so I headed north. When I found the army, they were two days march from the blocked pass.

I glided along under them, counting. They had pikemen, men-at-arms, archers, and both heavy and light cavalry. There must have been fifty knights and between three and four thousand men. Following the main army were the support troops with supply wagons, some fifty in all.

The trip back around the crags, forced by the blocked shortcut, would take two or three weeks, making them use up some supplies. Then it was three to four weeks back to Black Stag Keep, again using more supplies and tiring the marchers. That meant we had maybe two months before they would get to us, and a lot could happen in two months.

I fast-traveled to where we had left the Black Stag Company wagons. The Master Sergeant had made it back to them and all was well. I noticed that there were more than just Black Stag men present: the other mercenary company was also there.

I stopped to listen.

"We'll hire you on at winter pay," said the sergeant, "and provide horses to get you into Black Stag Keep. After that you must get your own horses."

"Agreed."

"We'll get your wagon teams hitched at first light. We leave right away." The other company was mostly intact, just lacking horses. This would give us more men at the Keep and was a good deal for all of us.

I went back to the Keep and rested in the earth beneath it.

***

Prince Kade was in the mess hall for breakfast the next morning. I got a plate of food and joined him at his table, and we talked as we ate.

"What news?"

"Fifty knights, four thousand men, and a supply train of fifty wagons are two days from the Northern Pass." He nodded thinking.

"So, they'll be here in a week."

"No, six weeks to two months, if they don't go home. I left them a surprise."

He stopped eating, "what kind of surprise?"

"I put some rocks across the passes narrowing and blocking them."

"Rocks?" How big are these rocks?"

"You know the rocks that surround our valley?"

"You mean the crags?"

"Yeah, like those."

"You blocked the pass with crags? Did you make the crags somehow?"

"No, they were already there, I just asked them to come up out of the ground."

He stared at me, "you enjoy doing this to me, don't you?"

I smiled.

"Next time, start with that kind of information."

I shrugged my shoulders. "Our company will be here in a week, with what's left of the company that attacked us on the road."

He nodded, "we can man the Keep and start sending them out scouting and as a show of force."

"I'll go back to the pass in two days and see how they react to the blockage."

"What can they do?"

"Unless they have a mage, the only thing they can do is turn back." I looked around, "we need to hire some servants."

"We need to hire a whole servant staff for the whole keep."

"Tenant farmers and tradesmen too. Let's take the war-horses out for some exercise, I want to show you something."

He nodded, "they could use it."

***

We rode north to the river ford, then east along the crag wall, pulling up when we got to the exposed coal vein.

"Coal?" He asked. We dismounted.

"Yes, this whole area has exposed veins of it. It will be easy to mine."

"With this you won't have to worry about your holdings being profitable. You must hire workmen to dig it out. We can haul it to Port West Gate to be shipped out."

I said nothing about Black Stag Cove, I'd rather have all the major shipping go out of Port West Gate.

We rode the rest of the estate looking over the forest and noting a surplus of game. "Sir Edwin had a gem here. I wonder why he never lived here?"

"The king. He always said he needed him, so, he stayed in the capital."

"Well, thank you, Sir Edwin."

"Amen!" said the prince.

***

A few days later, I was waiting at the blocked Northern Pass when the Hinterland army arrived. The main body stopped short of the pass, since their scout had reported that it was now blocked.

The commanders were sitting in a pavilion and discussing their options.

"So general, what have you to report?"

"My prince, our scouts reported this pass open two weeks ago, but we have reports that there have been earthquakes in this area and Port West gate's harbor has been nearly closed off by crags raising from the sea. This must have resulted from that same event."

"So, we must go around. How? Is there another pass?"

"No, your Highness. There are no other passes. We must backtrack and goes east around the crags."

"A two-week journey?"

"Yes, your highness."

The prince stood looking down at the map. "So, it's two weeks back tracking before we clear these crags, then it's another four to six weeks before we reach Port West Gate. All the while we will be using our limited supplies, with no place between here and there to replenish them.

"Other reports say their port has been closed off because of this earthquake. Does that about cover it?"

"Yes, my prince."

"The Fates have been busy!" He studied the map. "How long to reach their northern keep, the one called Vigil?"

"The same amount of time. But the land there is much richer, and easier for us to live off."

"Send messages that we are being forced to backtrack. Have re-supply wagons meet us as we turn east. We will head to Vigil Keep instead of Port West Gate. Send the Navy to take Port West Gate. We rest here tonight and start back tomorrow. Inform the priests. General, stay behind a moment." Everyone bowed and left the pavilion.

The general waited. Once they were alone, "Vigil Keep?" the prince asked.

"It will be a challenge."

"That is why my father, the king, set me this task. This is a test to see if it will be me or my brother who rules Hinterland."

The general said nothing.

"Send messages to our spies at Vigil Keep. Have them set plans in motion for us."

"Yes, my prince." Bowing, he left the pavilion.

I followed the general to the messenger bird wagon. He gave instruction to the message man, what messages he wanted sent and where.

When the general left, I pulled the message man under. *Teach me,* and his corpse crumpled. I now knew how to raise and care for messenger birds, but more importantly, I knew the Hinterland message codes. I searched his wagon for his code book and released all the birds.

Now there would be no resupply wagons and no enemy action against Vigil Keep until this army got closer to them.

Once everyone had settled down for the night, I located their spare horse corral. After the midnight guard changed, I found three guards at a campfire on the outskirts of the main cavalry camp. I pulled all three under, saying, *Improve me* and their bodies turned to husks.

I rose from the earth, took the three horses the guards had been using and rode out among the spare herd. My hand tingled, and the three hundred horses began to follow me as I rode away from the Hinterland army.

I instructed the ground not to show signs of us passing as I walked the herd down a side canyon and opened the crag wall into the next valley. Once we were all through, I closed the wall behind us.

This was a beautiful land. If there had been no stony up-thrusts, this could have all been farmland. Now it was forest and open grazing land with plenty of water. I stopped and un-saddled the three horses and turned them loose.

Then I sank into the earth, taking the saddles with me. It seemed the more time I spent in the earth the more my powers grew. I concentrated and let my consciousness expand. I felt the crags as they expanded all around me. I closed all the gaps and walled off my lands from the outside. Now no one could get in, as there were no passes.

I sank the crags that divided my lands, opening up the plains, leaving the last rocky wall in place between this valley and the one my keep was in. I'd let my herds increase until I needed them.

I took the saddles and went back to Black Stag Keep.

CHAPTER 14

I left the saddles in the stables at the Keep, and fast-traveled to Port West Gate. I looked at the work that had done on the fort and was pleased to see that they had started the stone work, but had also emplaced a lot of heavy timbers. They had built a sturdy black powder building, so I moved all the former Hinterland Navy powder from the pier vault into it. I moved the cannons into the emplacements, along with all their equipment and closed the pier vault.

Then I fast-traveled back to my keep.

At breakfast the next morning, I told the Prince what I had learned.

"So, there were no messages sent, and therefore no resupply wagons."

"And no skullduggery at Vigil Keep, and no navy being sent to Port West Gate."

He nodded, "we need to let the king know, so he can send the Crown Prince and his army to Vigil instead of here. Then we need to improve Port West Gate's Fort and harbor defenses. We can't depend on their Navy to do anything."

"We also need to go to the slave market. We need craftsmen, farmers, and servants, some to hire and some to buy. If you will write the king the letter, I'll take it to him."

***

But when I arrived to deliver the letter the castle was in an uproar. The keep's gates were closed and guards were everywhere. Servants were running around at some task or other. I flew up through the walls to the king's office. No one was there, and the royal quarters were empty as well.

I heard shouting from another room in the royal wing and found the king and queen at the foot of a bed where a young woman lay, convulsing with her skin turning blue.

The queen was shouting at a man I guessed was a physician.

"Do something!"

"My queen, I have tried all I know how to do — this is beyond my learning."

My hand tingled sharply, pulsing. There was magic at work here. Before I thought, I stepped through the wall to her bedside. Everyone jumped and the guards shouted and drew their swords.

"Hold!" The king's command froze them in place.

The queen came to my side, "help my daughter if you can, Sir Ghost."

I nodded, leaning down, and placed my hand on her forehead. The convulsions stopped, and she quieted, breathing easier. The queen went to her knees holding the princess and crying tears of relief.

But I sensed there was something in this room that was the source of whatever was attacking the girl.

I looked around the room, and saw a maid who was cringing, shaking like a leaf. I walked around the room, looking at the items on shelves. One was a small castle, finely carved, but to my eyes it wavered like something in the hot sun. When I picked it up, the princess relaxed and went to sleep. I walked over to the maid, staring at her. No one said a word, but their eyes never left me.

The maid dropped to her knees. "You brought this to the Princess?"

She nodded, weeping. "But you didn't make it."

She shook her head.

"You know who did?"

She nodded.

I walked over to the fireplace and set the castle down.

Fire consume. The little wooden castle was soon ashes.

"Hear me well!" the king said, his voice dropping to a menacing whisper. "If anyone says one word about what they have seen here today, I will have all of you drawn and quartered. Then, what's left of your bodies will be fed to the pigs. Leave us!"

They all bowed and scurried out of the room. The maid also started to get up, but I put my hand on her and shook my head, so she dropped back to the floor. The king moved to the queen's side. I moved back to look at the princess. She looked like her brother, Kade, as well as her mother the queen. Not beautiful but fetching.

I lay my hand upon her brow and the runes on my hand glowed gold and ran all the way to my elbow, forming the outline of a gauntlet. The princess took a deep breath and her eyes fluttered open. The queen sat back on her heels putting her hand to her mouth while tears ran down her face. The princess looked at me, her deep brown eyes showing no fear, only curiosity.

"How do you feel m'lady?"

"Fine. I had a headache, but it's gone now."

"Do you know where you are?"

"Yes, in my room, I just laid down for a nap."

"That was yesterday, dear," said the queen.

I removed my hand and stepped back.

"Yesterday? Mother, why are you crying?"

"We thought you were dying, but Sir Ghost saved you. He's a friend of Kade's."

She looked at me with a twinkle of mischief in her eyes. "Did my brother name you? It sounds like something he would do."

I laughed, "It does, doesn't it? No, m'lady, my first name is Draugur, which means ghost."

"Princess Maddison," The king said, "May I present Baron, Sir Draugur de Crypta, of Black Stag Keep."

I bowed, "Your Highness."

"Well met, Sir Draugur. Did my brother send you to help me?"

"No m'lady, we knew nothing of your plight. He sent me on another matter." I took out the letter and handed it to the King.

He opened it and read.

He glanced up at me, "So the stories of an earthquake are true."

"Yes, sire."

He continued reading. He looked at me, "Eight weeks, then."

"Roughly, sire. Depending on what they do about resupplying."

He nodded. "You will conclude this other matter quickly?"

I nodded, "I will, sire."

"I will have a letter for you in the morning."

"Will you sup with us, Sir Draugur?" The princess asked.

"Yes, he will... we eat one hour after evening prayers," the queen said.

I bowed, "Yes my queen."

"Lacey," the king said.

"Yes, sire." The maid answered.

"Go with Sir Draugur."

"Yes, sire."

I led Lacey from the room and out of the castle. Once we got to the courtyard I stopped.

"Tell me who gave you the castle for the princess."

"I can't speak her name, or I'll die." I smiled.

"Then take me to her." she nodded.

Lacey led me out the castle gates and toward lower city. Just before we crossed over the river bridge, she turned off the main street.

We walked on a way, then she stopped. She was nervous. "One block on is a cross street. There is an apothecary on the west corner, that's her shop. She's the only one that runs the shop, there's no mistaking her." I nodded, looking down the street. "Are you going to kill me?"

I looked at her. "Only if you speak of this, as the king said."

She shook her head.

"Then return to the castle and go about your duties."

"Yes m'lord." She turned and hurried away.

I stepped into the alley out of sight and dropped into the earth, then traveled to the west corner of the cross street and looked up into the apothecary. An old lady was working in the back, but she didn't look right ... something was off about her. I came up through the floor behind and across the room from her, watching her for a moment. Then I saw her shoulders tense and she reached into a pouch at her side. She quickly turned and threw a handful of powder toward me; powder that sparkled as it left her hand.

My left hand waved itself before me, and the sparkling dust fell dead to the floor. That also nullified the illusion of the gray-haired old crone. Instead, a middle-aged woman with black hair stood before me.

I smiled, "nice trick."

She saw her illusion was gone, "it has its uses."

She looked at me, studying, "why have you come?"

"You sent a death token to Princess Maddison and the king is not happy."

He eyes grew wider. "It's true, they paid me to make a death token, but I did not know they meant it for the princess."

She pointed with her chin, "we are of a kind, and I see that you wear an artifact, too, although yours is more powerful. They allow us to do what we can do. A smith makes a knife but is not responsible for who it kills."

"That's not quite the same, but I understand your point,"

"Perhaps we can bargain, help each other."

"I'm listening."

"The man who paid for the token... I'll give you his name

if you forget about me."

"You could never show up looking like the old lady again."

"Easy enough."

"OK, you give me his name, and if he's the one, you have a deal, but if not..." I left the rest unsaid.

She nodded, "His name is Richter Schmid. He is a jeweler, but a special one, an arcane jeweler. He creates magic jewelry with runes inscribed on them. He made the ring that puts me in a disguise when I want it to."

"Where can I find Master Schmid?" She told me, and I left, saying, "I know the area."

The name Schmid sounded familiar, but there were Schmids, Smiths and Schmits everywhere.

I went into the alley and dropped into the earth, moving rapidly to the area where Schmid was supposed to have his shop. I found the shop and went under it to check everything, sensing a lot of rune magic. He was working alone in his shop.

I went across the street to an alley and came up, then crossed the street to Master Schmid's jewelry store and went inside.

"Good afternoon m'lord, how can I be of service?"

"Good afternoon, I'm looking for something special. We have a mutual friend and she recommended you."

"Excellent, who might that be?"

"The lady apothecary."

He studied me a moment, "I see."

"She had a ring that helped her looks. I'd be interested in one of those, and perhaps some others if you have them."

He seemed to relax, "I think I have what you are looking for." He locked the door and closed the curtains. "Now we won't be interrupted."

He took out a display pad with rings on them. "The ring the lady has is a simple guise ring. It changes your face and hair appearance, but that's all. This one," He picked up a ring, "is much more complex. It causes your total appearance, including your clothes to change. You just think of the way you want to look, and you do. It takes some practice to get it right."

"You guarantee this to work?"

"I do."

"How much?"

"I mean no offence m'lord, but I do not haggle: five hundred gold."

I nodded, "I'll take it, what else do you have?"

He showed me his other rings, including:

The Ring of Armor, which made any clothing you were wearing into armor and also multiplied the strength of any armor you were wearing. It also shielded you to some extent against magic being used against you.

The Ring of Divination recognized magic objects, magic being used, people lying and also could counter magic being used against you.

The Ring of Quick Reflexes, to no surprise gave you lightning fast reflexes.

The Ring of Levitation, which allowed you to levitate, even while carrying heavy weight.

The Ring of Strength and Stamina, which made you incredibly strong and fit.

"I have another thing that may interest you." He took out a bracelet with five chains attached to it.

"What does it do?" I said, already suspecting the answer.

"This is a bracelet of magnification. When you wear this bracelet with rings attached to it by these chains, it magnifies the power of each rings exponentially."

"Will anyone be able to see them while I'm wearing them?"

"Yes, but I can add runes that will put them under your skin, they will attach to your bones. No one can see them, and no one can steal them."

"Can you do five that way and the sixth one just be invisible?"

He nodded, "I can."

"Total cost of all the rings, bracelet, and additional rune work?"

"Fifty thousand golds."

"I'll pay fifty-five thousand, if you can have it done by tomorrow."

He nodded, "half in advance." I took a wallet out of my pouch with thirty thousand in bills in it and handed it to him.

He took it and thumbed through the bills, nodding, "which ring do you want invisible?"

"The guise."

He nodded, "good choice, the magnifier would not help it much. They will be ready for pickup by mid-morning."

I nodded, "mid-morning then." He showed me out of the shop and locked the door behind me. I went back across the street to the alley and, once out of sight, I dropped into the earth. Then I went back under the jewelry shop and watched Master Schmid as he took all the jewelry I had purchased to his workbench and started working on it.

I'd wait until the morrow, after he finishes my work, then question him about the token. If he lies, I'll gain the knowledge of how to make magic jewelry. I smiled.

Right now, I needed to get dressed for dinner, knowing I'd need nicer clothes for a private dinner with the Royals. I sped to a tailor's shop near the castle to see what clothes he had that might fit me.

"Good afternoon m'lord, how may we assist you."

"I need some nice clothes to wear to an important dinner tonight. What do you have that will fit that bill?"

"Let me take your measurements then I'll see what I have." He took my measurements, then went into the back. He and a servant returned in a few minutes." I think these will do for a short notice dinner."

The clothes fit and were of good quality. "I'll take them." They packaged them for me, and I left. I went down the closest alley, dropped into the earth, and headed for the castle.

CHAPTER 15

I moved under the Castle, created a vault and opened my backpack, dressing in my new clothes. When I was ready, I went up into the chapel.

The royal family was there at prayer, so I watched the princess, who was dressed in well-tailored clothes that showed off her figure. I decided she was a good-looking woman. I waited for them to finish their prayers, then came up on the side of the chapel out of sight and moved around to the front. There, I waited for them to come out.

I bowed, "my queen, sire."

"Ah, Sir Draugur, well timed," he said, smiling. "Will you escort Lady Maddison?"

"Of course, lady?" I offered her my arm.

"Thank you, Sir Draugur. You look nice this evening."

"I could wear rags, and no one would notice... all eyes are on you."

"Watch this one, my dear, he has a smooth tongue!" The queen said.

"Only made smoother by speaking the truth, m'lady."

The ladies chuckled, "entirely too smooth," added the queen.

The four of us went into the private royal dining room and were seated at the table, made in the shape of a "U" so we could all see each other as we talked. The menu was varied, and all of the several courses were very good.

"My brother, Prince Kade, is well?" asked Maddison.

"He is, m'lady, at Black Stag Keep awaiting the rest of our troops."

"How many will you have?"

"Roughly three hundred, but I plan on hiring more. We intend to man the Fort at Port West Gate. The earthquake changed the cove to more of a harbor, closing off most of the cove with rocky bluffs rising up from the sea. The fort now overlooks a narrow entrance to the harbor, and we have workmen improving the fort as we speak. Once that is complete, we will start improving the harbor."

"Prince Kade made you Baron of Port West Gate?" asked the king.

"He did, sire, after Sir Gordon attacked us and tried to kill him. I captured the traitor, and under questioning he pleaded guilty of working for Hinterland and attacking us. Hinterland had apparently promised to make him Duke of the Western District and his ambition overrode his common sense — he was a greedy man."

"His wife?" the queen asked.

"Killed when six thugs from the Criminal Guild attacked her home trying to kill me. They did not survive the encounter."

"The Guild?" The king asked.

I shrugged my shoulders, "those in Port West Gate won't bother us again."

"Are you a dangerous man, Sir Ghost?" The princess asked, suddenly.

I looked into her eyes, "only to those who attack me, or my friends. As I told your brother, I don't like to kill, but it is something I'm very good at."

She fell silent, contemplating my words.

Servants then brought in dessert and more wine. I picked up my wine cup, but my hand tingled.

"STOP! Don't drink the wine! It's poison!"

Two men dressed as guards rushed in with swords drawn, with two others came behind them with crossbows, quickly aiming at the royal couple.

The crossbowmen fired. Time slowed. *No!* Stones shot up from the floor in front of the king and queen, stopping the crossbow bolts. Then two stone dogs rose from the floor at my order, savagely attacking the assassins. One had headed for the princess but I threw my knife, burying it up to the hilt into his temple. The impact drove him into the wall. The other three were dead an instant later.

The three royals were all in combat crouches, holding daggers and staring at me.

Enough! The stone shields slid back into the floor, as did the stone dogs. I stepped over to look at the bodies and saw that they all wore Assassin's Guild tattoos. I felt the king step beside me, and I showed him. "These are from Hinterland." He nodded. *Take them under the castle.* The bodies and blood sank into the stone, startling the royals and several servants drawn by the shouting.

"I'll be back, sire, I think there is another one, probably the leader, trying to escape the castle."

"Alive, if possible."

"Yes, sire." I stepped through the wall and moved around the castle looking for the missing killer. I saw a slave with a shimmer around him that I recognized. He was strolling to the stables, but once he was out of sight, I pulled him down. It was the woman apothecary, in a magical disguise. *Teach me.*

Her body turned to a husk and I instantly had a headache — she was a nasty piece of work. I took her ring and a few golds, but she carried nothing else of importance. I went to the four assassins and searched them, retrieving my knife and a few golds.

I fast-traveled to her shop and searched it, recovering her code book, a compendium of poisons, and her gold and currency.

I moved back the jewelry shop, where Master Schmid was still working, but it seemed he was not part of this plot, so I went back to the Castle.

***

They royal family were resting from their ordeal in their apartments.

I came out of the wall in the Kings Office. The door was open, so I announced myself. "Sire, I have returned."

"Come in, Sir Draugur."

I stepped into the sitting room of the king's quarters. The three of them were sitting there.

I bowed, "Sire, M'ladies."

"Were you successful?"

"Partially. I caught the ringleader, but she did not survive. They were, as we thought, from the Hinterland Assassin's Guild. It seems she was also the spymaster's lover and an intermediary for Hinterland. The poisoned wine was supposed to kill you, and the assassins were there as a backup in case something went wrong. I believe we've cleaned out this group, since none of them survived."

The king nodded, wearily. "I've sent messages to the Keeps in the North and the East. The Crown Prince marches north for Vigil Keep at dawn. Once again, we find ourselves in your debt, not only for my life but for the lives of the queen and my daughter."

"Sit and have tea with us."

"Are you a mage, Sir Ghost?" Maddison asked.

"A minor one perhaps, and untrained."

"Your powers didn't look minor to me; your parents were mages?"

"I never knew my parents, so I guess it is possible."

"Does Kade know how powerful you are?" asked the king.

"He suspects, but he lets my secrets be mine. You are the first ones to see this much of my powers."

"And live?"

I nodded my head slowly, "and live."

"I'm glad we're your friends, Sir Ghost," said the princess.

I looked into her eyes and she quickly looked down, blushing.

"Yes, well," interposed the king. "What boon would you ask of us?"

I sat thinking a moment. "As I've said, I have no father or mother, so what advice would you give one of your sons, sire?"

His eyebrows climbed. He looked at the queen, then back at me. "Well, you have a title, lands, money ... you have money, don't you?"

I smiled, "yes, sire."

"A wife, then?"

"I know I will want a wife someday, but the women I've been around are only invested in wealth and what a man can give her, not in the man himself."

"That is why you must make your choice carefully," commented the queen said.

I noticed that Maddison was watching me closely. " What about a strong-minded woman? One that knows her mind and wants a partner and not a keeper? Do you prize beauty over intellect?"

"Strong-minded women do not intimidate me. And it should be a partnership, two facing what life throws at them. As for beauty, I heard an old man say one time 'I don't care how good looking you are, someone, somewhere is tired of your, umm.. stuff...'" The princess chuckled.

The queen was looking back and forth between us, a small smile on her face. "Would you give up your lands, and titles for the woman you loved?"

I thought for a moment. "If I loved her, yes. Together we would have lands anew."

"And your titles?"

"Husband would be title enough." They stared at me, saying nothing.

"I'll continue to think on how we can best reward you, Sir Draugur. I'll have the letter to Prince Kade ready tomorrow afternoon."

I took that as a dismissal. "Good night sire, my queen, princess." I left by the door, smiling and I slept in the earth under the jeweler's shop the rest of the night.

***

I was waiting at the his door the next morning when he opened. He let me in, then re-locked the door.

"I believe you will be pleased with the results," he said as he walked over to the display counter.

He put the rings and the bracelet on the counter. They looked nice, but I was more concerned with them working their magic while not melting through my hand down to the bone.

"We will put each ring on a finger then fasten the bracelet. Once it fastens, they will blend into your hand and wrist becoming part of you. Understand, you cannot take them off. There may also be some discomfort, pain even, when they bond with you."

I nodded, "proceed."

I put the rings on and gave them a moment to size themselves to my fingers. He then took the sides of the bracelet, "last chance to back out."

I shook my head. "Do it."

I prepared myself for the pain; He snapped the bracelet closed. Nothing happened for a moment. Then the stinging started, then heat, as they sank beneath my skin.

It was painful, but nothing like the other hand. Runes glowed gold through the skin of my hand. "I've never seen that before!" He looked up at me suddenly, "and I saw nothing this time either."

I nodded, paid him the rest of his money and left.

In the alley I dropped into the earth and opened a vault, sitting in it and concentrating on levitation. *Up one hand span.* I lifted, when I did both hands began to glow and runes ran up my arms to the elbow. There was an outline of gauntlets on each arm. At first, they pulsated randomly, then synced to each other. They grew brighter, then faded. I was not sure, but both hands felt more powerful.

I took my knife and tried to cut my shirt sleeve. The blade slid across the sleeve like trying to cut steel. That spell seemed to work as well. I closed the vault, traveled to an inn and had a meal and tea.

I sat for a while thinking of all the things I needed to do, and wondering what the king had in mind for me.

***

I went to the his office and waited until he arrived. "Good afternoon, sire."

"Good afternoon, Sir Draugur," he said as he put a letter on his desk.

"The ladies have asked me to escort you to the ladies' sitting room. Once there, you are on your own, my young friend," he chuckled.

Frowning in confusion, I followed him through their quarters and down a hall to a room in which the queen and the princess were waiting.

"Sir Ghost! How nice to see you again. The princess and I were wondering..." "Here it comes," the king mumbled.

"What was that, dear?"

"Nothing, please continue."

She nodded, smiling, "as I was saying, we were wondering, having seen your influence over stone, if you could change the castle."

"Some, m'lady, what did you have in mind?"

She walked over to a set of double doors that opened onto a small balcony.

"We'd like a larger balcony."

"A large covered balcony," Maddison added.

"Yes, covered... a large covered balcony."

I knew I could easily do it, but I made a show of looking at the situation. "Can you draw a sketch of how big you are thinking?"

"Yes," the princess answered, and she got paper and some charcoal and started sketching. Their backs were to the balcony, so as she sketched, I grew a balcony out of the stone wall to match her drawing. The king watched, smiling broadly. When she finished, she showed me the sketch, "something like this."

I took the sketch looking at it, "something like this, or something like that?" I said, holding it up to the new balcony. Both the ladies spun around and covered their mouths as they took in my work. The new construction was approximately 20 by 12 feet, with lattice covering the third at each end, leaving the middle open. A roof covered it entirely.

"Can you make this wall a little longer?" I moved it and they nodded. "Perfect."

"You should have said you couldn't," laughed the king. "Now, every time you come they'll have something for you to fix."

"And risk being thrown in the dungeon? Not likely," I whispered.

"I'd have pardoned you."

"And then you'd be in the cell next to me. This was easier."

"Coward."

"Where those two are concerned, absolutely." We both laughed.

"What was that, dear?"

"Nothing!" We answered in unison, and the ladies laughed.

"Thank you, Sir Ghost this is perfect. All the ladies will enjoy it."

"My pleasure, my queen." I said bowing.

CHAPTER 16

Back in his office the king handed me the letter to Prince Kade, and I read: "Continue to improve and fortify the port. If you get the chance to take a Hinterland spy or navy ship please do so, I want a navy and at the moment we only have few ships, most armed merchantmen, but what I really want are naval ships of the line."

Turning to me: "As to your reward," the queen came in and took a seat and he paused.

"As to your reward, we have increased the holdings at Black Stag Keep. They now include all the lands north of Black Stag Keep to the northern border. From the sea, inland to the crag walls. You are no longer Baron of Port West Gate, but EARL of Port West Gate, which entitles you to a 'third-penny' of all taxes collected from your lands. Also, you are a peer of the realm and therefore eligible to pay court to Princess Maddison."

My mouth dropped open; I was speechless. I looked at the queen and saw she was smiling, and I knew the princess was standing on the other side or the wall listening.

"I am deeply honored sire, by the elevation in rank, but more especially that you honor me by allowing me to pay court to your daughter, especially since I'm sure she has many suitors. Maybe I should have built her a bigger balcony!" I said smiling. We all heard a stifled laugh from the other side of the wall, and the queen hung her head and covered her smile with her hand.

"Knowing those two, I'm sure you'll get the chance. This is a greater responsibility for you and Prince Kade, since it is now your responsibility to protect the North-West Border

Pass."

I looked at the map. "If I build a fort and finance it, will you send troops to man it?"

"How long will it take you to build it?"

"How many men will it need to house?"

"Five hundred total, troops and support people, plus horses and wagons."

I calculated. "A few days, once I get started."

"A few days?" He stared at me.

I shrugged, "If you recall, I have a way with stone."

"Yes, of course. If you build and finance it, I'll send troops to man it. So, once we push the Hinterlanders back across the border, get right to it."

He gave me all at the seals, a license and signet ring for Port West Gate, all of which went in my pouch. "I will also send out notices of your appointment."

"Thank you, sire."

The queen handed me two letters, one from Maddison.

"My queen."

"Earl de Crypta," she said, smiling at my new title.

***

Before I left the Capital, I stopped at the Williamson's trading house. Taking out the lumps of coal I held them in my hands and began to squeezing them, harder and harder and applying heat. After a few moments I held several diamonds.

I went into Williamson's and announced, "Lord Draugur to see Arthur Williamson." They took me to his office.

"Lord Draugur, how good to see you!"

"And you, Arthur."

"What can I do for you?"

"Are you the master of this house?"

"No, I am second here, and I'm still building capital to open my trading house."

"What if I financed you? Would you come to Port West

Gate and open a trading house there? I need someone to help me bring in more trade, to handle cargo ships and negotiate deals with other countries. Would you be interested?"

"I would!"

I took the purse of new diamonds and put them on the desk where he could appraise them.

"Will that be enough?"

"Yes, with this and what I have already saved, more than enough. The port is still open, then?"

"It is, and it will be better than before."

"Then I shall leave within the week for Port West Gate."

I nodded, "bring a caravan with you of farm supplies and seeds." I set another purse, of gold, on his desk." Bring enough household goods to supply ten farmsteads … plates, bowls, cups, cook pots, and whatever else you can think of."

He was making notes and nodding. "The caravan shall leave within the week."

"Good, I look forward to seeing you there. Safe travels."

***

I fast-traveled to Black Stag Keep, and zipped under the surrounding grounds, ensuring all was well. I found the prince in the stable alone, working with Beast.

"He's looking better," I said.

"He is, and I think he will make a full recovery. How was your trip to the Capital?"

"Interesting, I have letters for you."

He nodded," let's go inside." I followed him to his office and handed him the letters. He opened them and began to read, then, as he usually did, he read the letters twice.

He looked up, "my family is well?"

"Yes, they are all well, but those who attacked them are not."

He nodded, "you've been busy. Thank you for saving my sister, and my parents."

"I was there, and I could do no less."

"Tell me what happened from your point of view." I told the tale, leaving out the parts that did not pertain to him or the royal family. Then I gave him the apothecary/assassin's guise ring and told him how to use it.

"Thank you, this will come in handy! But whether you realize it or not, Earl, you are in trouble."

My eyebrows lifted, "in what way?"

"My sister has set her eyes on you. I'm sure she and the queen, were the driving force behind you becoming and earl, so that you can pay court to her. Yes, my friend you are in trouble."

"What about all of her other suitors?"

He harrumphed, "she scared all of those off long ago. She is too strong-willed for them. They want someone to bring money to their coffers, bear their children and stay in the background. My sister will not do that.

"They want her because she will eventually — if they don't marry her to a foreign king — be Duchess of the Southern District. Whoever marries her will be the princess' consort, and many can't stand not having a title equal to, or higher than, hers."

I nodded, "that was why she was asking me all those questions about lands and titles."

"Probably. The other downside is the Southern District, which although it's a lot of land is about half marsh. It has no port, and over all, it is underdeveloped and makes little in the way of income. Too bad we don't know anyone who knows how to work with, and change the land!"

"Maybe we'll think of someone." I said smiling. "And speaking of land, your father gave me even more land so I could pay even more taxes."

We laughed.

"True, but as an earl, you have more income. Welcome to the peerage, Earl de Crypta. The king wants us to march to support Vigil Keep, coming in behind Hinterland's forces, cutting their supply lines and harassing their rear."

I nodded, "I thought that might be the case."

"We leave in a week."

"Then we have a lot to do."

***

By the end of the week, the cattle drovers had delivered my cattle. One asked for a job, which I gave him. The rest of the Black Stag Company arrived right behind them, with our supply wagons and men. The Elms mercenary company were with them.

Master Sergeant Miller set the other companies up outside the Keep and moved the Black stag Company inside to man the walls.

We detailed a wagon to go out to the coal vein and bring a load in so we could burn coal in addition to wood.

Our five knights arrived, with twenty men at arms each, followed quickly by Williamson's supply caravan... which was good because I had a lot of men to feed.

That evening at dinner we gave the captains and Master Sergeant Miller orders to be ready to march in one week. The Elms Company was to give us a list of their needs, which turned out to be extensive.

The next morning Prince Kade, Captain Elms, I, with five of his wagons, set out for Port West Gate. It was an uneventful trip, Prince Kade and Beast enjoying the outing after their convalescence. We made Port West Gate by early evening and stayed at my house since there was room enough for the wagons in the yard. We all ate at the inn and made it an early night as we had a lot to do on the morrow.

The next morning, I gave Captain Elms a purse of gold, so he and his wagons could go to fill their supplies and then head back to the Keep.

Kade and I went back to the inn for breakfast. "Just for the sake of conversation," I said, "suppose we hired a professional mage to raise a fort, keep, castle, or what every you would call it nearby. At great expense, I might add."

"Oh, no doubt!"

"And, as it would be the seat of the Western District, it would need to be more than just a small fort designed to guard the harbor's mouth."

"Oh, yes, of course." he said, smiling.

"Anyway, would you have a design in mind for this undertaking?"

"Well, as you say, it would be the district center, and would need to make that statement. I could spare no expense."

"Oh, of course not."

"I might sketch something out that I've been working on."

"Good, let's go to the port and have a look."

We walked down to the water. "That earthquake changed the cove into a harbor, and the fort is now in a better position to defend it." We walked up to the cannon emplacements and looked out over the harbor. The masons were already hard at work.

"Master Mason, may I present Prince Kade, Duke of the Western District."

He bowed, "Your Highness, an honor."

"You are making good headway, Master Mason."

"Thank you, sire."

"You know of the menace of the Hinterland's army and navy?"

"We do, sire."

"We have, at great expense, hired a mage to speed some construction along. Fear not, he will not put you out of a job. We have many plans, and we will need you to complete them."

"Of course, sire."

"Do you have a paper and charcoal that I might use to make a sketch?"

We walked over to the mason's worktable and the prince began to sketch the castle he wanted... high walls and towers with no moat. Covered firing platforms for the cannons, a courtyard with a curtain wall separating it from the Castle proper. Stables, barracks, a smithy and plenty of storage. He added a large chain that stretched across the harbor mouth to prevent water-borne attacks. It was all very detailed, so he must have been planning this for a long time.

The Master Mason looked at it and joked, "I'm glad you hired the mage, that is if you want it finished in my lifetime!"

The prince chuckled. "He assures me it will be completed soon."

I added, "Whatever he does not finish, Master Mason, you will continue the work."

"Yes, sire."

I placed a large purse of gold on his table.

"Thank you, m'lords."

As we walked away, "nice castle, and with just a quick sketch, too."

"Another royal gift ... we can all do it."

"Now THAT I believe, since I've seen your sister do it," I said laughing. I told him about the balcony, and what the king had said.

"I wish I could have been there for that! Let's go to the slave pens and see what they have."

It surprised me how many slaves were being held. Apparently Port West Gate was a major market for slaves coming in from foreign lands.

"Slave Master!" I called, and a man approached.

"Yes m'lord?"

"May I present Prince Kade, Duke of the Western District."

He bowed deeply. "sire, an honor to meet you."

"We have needs, slave master," said the prince, "and I only want to see the best. I'm not looking for any concubines, just good quality servants for whom I will pay a good price. Don't push any leftovers off on me!

"We are looking for tradesmen, blacksmiths, cooks and household servants. We also need farmers, and we'll take whole families if you have them... in fact, I would prefer them."

He bowed again. "Of course, sire, I understand. If you will come this way, I will have them brought to you to inspect."

The slave master started bringing the slaves up and did as the prince had asked bringing the best. There were a lot from Hinterland, most of whom were made slaves because of a debt or some infraction with the law. They brought in a large group of fifteen —an older man and woman and four younger couples with older children.

"Speak." the slave master said,

The older man bowed, "Lord, we were the household servants of a knight and had managed and cared for his keep for years. But he was killed and his keep taken. They ransomed his wife, but we were left for slavery." They spoke truly, according to my ring said.

"How many were in his household?"

"Ten, Lord, but we cared for others that worked in the Keep."

"We'll take these, slave master, continue." They brought in the next group and by the time we were through we had bought fifty slaves. We did not find all we wanted, but it was a good start, and they would be delivered to my Keep on the morrow.

We then went to the stables and bought horses. Finding that the liveryman had eighty good horses, we bought them all.

We ate our midday meal at a different inn and found the food a little better. "Are you ready for the mage to make his appearance?" I asked.

"How do you plan to do it?"

"I have a guise ring, so I will appear as an aloof mage. I'll raise the castle, and you make corrections or additions as we go."

"OK, sounds like fun."

"You go down to the fort, and your new mage will make his entrance." We finished our meal and he left for the fort. I gave him a while to get there before I started.

I slipped under to the other side at the harbor and took on the appearance of a classical old mage with white hair and a long white beard, dark blue robes and a staff. I levitated, using my new ring, and flew around practicing. It would not do to fall on my face making my grand entrance!

CHAPTER 17

When I felt ready, I rose and flew across the harbor and around the fort site, making my grand entrance. I landed near the prince where a crowd had grown watching me fly around.

"Which one of you Is Prince Kade?" I said, gruffly.

"That would be me, Sir Mage."

"Ah, yes, so you want a castle, do you? Well, you paid, so I guess I shall give you what you want. You want it here, I suppose?"

"Yes, I do, right here."

"Your father will not give me any grief about this will he? It costs just as much to take one down as it does to put it up, though I will admit taking them down is easier."

"No, my father the king knows and approves of this."

"What was that? Speak up!" I put my hand to my ear, pretending to be hard of hearing.

"I said, my father knows and approves."

"Good, good. Met him once, you know, loved to fish, told me himself. Always talked too much for a child" And I turned away, mumbling.

I decided to put on a bit of a show. I raised my staff, and the wind began to blow, stabbed it into the ground and there was an answering thunderclap. Then the ground started to tremble and stones began to rise. I pointed and gestured, and walls rose and took shape high and wide. I kept the sketch that the prince had drawn in my mind, but continued making meaningless gestures as the castle took shape.

I rose up for a better view of what I was doing. I drifted over the walls, and around the towers, out over the cannon platforms and up to the top terraces, down around the royal gardens. I grew doors, and windows already filled with glass.

I built a set of massive gates and a portcullis.

Acting the part of crazy old mage I raised piers, quays and docks along the crag wall back to the shore, and made the harbor deep all the way in..

Inshore, I raised warehouses lining the harbor and created a stone road joining everything between the main street and the new castle gate.

Once I was satisfied, I landed back near the prince and the crowd, which had swelled.

"Something like that?" I asked.

"Where are the wells?"

"The what?"

"Wells, water wells!"

"Yes, Yes, Yes, wells... not deaf you know." I pointed, and artesian wells sprang from the ground, with pure water flowing from them.

"Did you make a dungeon and underground storage?"

"Of course, there's a dungeon, you can't have a proper castle without a dungeon!" People with the prince were chuckling, amused at our little bit of theater.

"As a gift to you, Prince Kade." At that, two stone lions the size of horses rose from the ground, walked up the steps to the castle proper, turned to face us and roared. Then they sat down on guard and froze.

Everyone applauded, and I bowed.

"Sir Mage, let's go look at your good work. Provost, would you set guards at the gate, please?"

"Yes, sire."

We took a walk through of the Castle. "Adequate Sir Mage, adequate."

"One tries sire, in my youth I could have done better."

"I suppose that's true of all of us, right, provost?" They laughed, and I held my face straight... with difficulty.

Once we had seen the lower area and the cannon emplacement, we dismissed the provost and inspected the upper areas and the castle proper.

"It's better than I could have hoped for... well done, my friend."

"It's your castle, sire, the Seat of the Western District."

"Thank you, it is beautiful."

"I added a few things while I was at it, including apartments for the king and queen when they come, as well as plenty of room for visiting royals, so you won't have to give up your rooms. And, although Princess Maddison will be upset, your balcony is bigger than hers." We laughed.

We went up to the Royal Garden and looked out over the harbor and ocean where torches burned at the harbor entrance showing the chain stretched across the opening. "At dawn the chain will lower and at dusk it will rise."

"Brother, is Hinterland going to be surprised!" .

"Wondrous. I hope my sister marries you, since we can't afford to pay you." He said laughing. "Speaking of pay." He tossed me a gold and I caught it. "Paid," he said.

I laughed, walked over to the fireplace and pushed the gold coin into the mantle face.
"Paid," I repeated.

***

We rose early and went to the inn for breakfast. The talk there was mostly about the castle and the crazy old mage, and how their prince made him put things in proper order. We just smiled.
The provost came in and the prince asked him to join us. As we ate, we talked.

"Provost, I have a task for you," I said.

"Yes, sire?"

"I want you to hire the walking wounded from the mercenary companies to guard our castle, especially those with experience with cannons. You may quarter them in the castle barracks."

"Yes sire, I shall see to it."

I sat a large purse of gold on the table, "Pay them the going rate plus food and shelter."

"Yes, sire."

"Also, keep a close watch on ships coming in, as we expect Hinterlanders to make more incursions."

"We will, sire, and if I need more troops?"

"Hire them, I leave that to your discretion. Take what funds you need from the city; I will replace them. Also increase the city watch, as I expect the city to grow up around our new protected port. Do not scrimp on equipment, as I believe it is better to lose a little money than lose a life."

"That is a subject I needed to talk to you and the prince about... there is no City Fund, sire."

"I see my predecessor was remiss." I took out a wallet and passed it to the provost.
"Thank you for bringing this to our attention. I'm sure you have someone who keeps accurate accounts?" I asked.

"We do m'lord."

"Also, if there are inquiries about renting the warehouses, you may rent them, except the large one on the far end. That is for the Williamson's trading house who will arrive within the month. Put the monies in the city fund. You now have the additional duty of City Treasurer. With your promotion you may move into the former baron's house and use it as your own." I said.

"Thank you m'lord!"

"Any other business?"

"No sire, it will be as you say."

***

We rode past the slave master's wagons, crammed with new workers. Further on, we passed our new horses, on the way to be delivered.

"Do we have enough horses for all of our support wagons

and for everyone to be mounted?" the prince asked.

"With the eighty we bought I think we have enough. We'll do a head count tomorrow when we do a full inspection." He nodded.

I hesitated. "Tell me about the Princess, what's she like?"

"Oh, nasty temper on that one... you saw the hunched back, yes?"

I laughed, "Oh, here we go!"

He laughed, "In truth, she's probably the smartest of us. Mother made her train as hard as any of the boys, and then some. She has a mind for business and is already running the Royal Houses' affairs under mother's scrutiny."

"She has a sweet, kind soul, unless you cross her. If you do that, you will see her temper. She has a mind of her own and it's a sharp one. She is not one who will be set on a shelf and ignored. If you win her hand, you will gain a prize, that few can equal. I hope to find one such as her someday."

I shook my head, "I'm not sure I can overlook that hunched back, though." We laughed and enjoyed the ride into Black Stag Keep.

***

When the slaves arrived, we took them into the mess hall and fed them. Once they had eaten, I spoke to them. "I am Earl de Crypta and this is Black Stag Keep. You will not be chained or caged here, because there is nowhere for you to run. The gate you came through at the pass is the only way in or out. My whole valley is enclosed by craggy cliffs. Serve me well, and you will be treated well.

"If you are more trouble than you are worth, I will send you back to the pens to be resold. Tonight, those serving in the Keep will go into their quarters. We will take the farmers to their farms on the morrow, and also show tradesmen where they will set up their shops."

"You will eat after the soldiers eat, but you will not eat

scraps — we all eat the same food here. I pointed to the major-domo, "move your people into the hall. Everyone else will be in the stable loft tonight. Go!" Everyone started toward their places and I went to the Keep's Great Hall.

When the major-domo and his people were all gathered, "on the morrow you will not prepare your own food, but will eat in the mess hall like everyone else. After that you will start putting the Keep to right. You will find supplies through there." I pointed. "Anything we don't have, we'll get. Your rooms are down the same hall as the supplies. That is all for tonight, get some sleep."

They all bowed, "yes m'lord." I left the hall, to find their rooms.

I had a lot still to do before I slept. I dropped into the earth and moved out into the valley. I imagined my valley like a chessboard with each square being some forty acres in area. I removed all large stones from the fields and used them to raise a stone fence about four feet high around each field.

Each got a stone three-room house with a loft, plus a four-stall barn with a hayloft and a stone corral. I bored a water well between the house and the barn, and repeated this pattern ten times.

As an afterthought, I closed the wall between the cove and my Keep. We were leaving soon, and I didn't want any surprises. Then I went to sleep, cradled in the arms of the earth, recovering my strength.

***

Everyone seemed to be up before dawn. The mercenary companies were getting ready for their pre-march inspection. Realizing I would just be in the way, I let Master Sergeant Miller take care of the details.

"Miller?"

"Sire?"

"Will there be someone staying behind who can serve as

quartermaster?"

"Yes sir, Sergeant Pickens. I'll send him to you."

Once Pickens had found me, I gave instructions on the supplies I wanted bought for the farmers, including livestock, and gave him a purse to cover expenses.

I let the five knights look to their own. It was their responsibility to do so, and if they didn't understand that, I wanted to know about it now.

After everyone had eaten, we loaded the farmers into wagons and took them out to their farms. When we stopped at the first one everyone just stared.

A child asked, "Truly m'lord?" His mother shushed him.

"Truly what, lad?" I asked.

"This is the farm we are to work and the house we get to live in?"

I smiled, "yes, this is the farm, or one like it, that you and your family will work and live on." They could not believe this warm, cozy area was where theirs in which to live and work.

"Everyone, let's look, it will save time," so they all un-loaded. "All the farms, houses, and barns are the same. Tools, seed and livestock will be provided. But you will have to work hard. Everyone will get a milk cow, chickens, maybe sheep, goat or pigs. You will feed your family and my fam-ily and the soldiers. There is no need to hide food to feed your families. If you are not healthy, you don't work and pro-duce. It is in all our interests that you are fed and healthy.

"Now go walk through the house and barn. Then we'll get everyone onto a farm." It didn't take long as everyone was excited to get to their farms.

By noon, we had all the farmers installed on their farm-s. I told them more things would be delivered so they could start work. We gave families supplies to live on until they could start raising their own. I figured it would take most of a year before they could support themselves.

I rode back to the Keep and checked in with Master Sergeant Miller. "How do we look?"

"Not bad sir, few things need fixin' but we're working them out."

"Do we have enough horses?"

"Barely sir, I'd feel better if we had spares."

"How many do we need?"

"Forty, but fifty would be better."

"I'll bring you fifty. If we need, we can make a last supply run to Port West Gate."

"No sir, the horses are what we need."

I rode back to the stables and put Mare away, then grabbed got a saddle and tack and dropped into the earth. I flew under to my "found" horses, safely grazing in their little valley. They came to me; I separated fifty geldings and sent the rest back to grazing.

I saddled one and headed back to the Keep, trailing the others, opening and closing passes as needed. I was back to the Keep by mid-afternoon. When I delivered them to the spare horse holding area, the sergeant was shaking his head.

"You know sir, they hang horse thieves."

"I've heard that, awful narrow-minded of them! But it's not stealing if you purloin them from the enemy. I happened to have found these poor beasts lost in the wilderness."

"You sound like my first recruiter. Promised me the world, he did."

"I just hate to see you doing without, Master Sergeant."

"That is the same thing he said." He shook his head walking away yelling orders. The man loved his job.

They had checked and double checked, loaded and re-loaded. Finally, everyone was satisfied, and they stood down for a day's rest. We would leave day after tomorrow.

Tomorrow everyone would rest, but also do last-minute repairs on their personal equipment

CHAPTER 18

Our major-domo was getting the house in order. Beds were being made, clothes washed, windows opened, floors swept. I never noticed that sort of thing until someone cleaned, then appreciated it.

Over dinner with the prince, I asked, "Beast has heavy armor, right?"

"He does."

"I'd like to see it. I have an idea that I can strengthen it and make it lighter."

"That would be a godsend."

We finished eating, went to the stables and laid out all of Beast's heavy, armor. "No wonder the horses tire so quickly — all this weighs a ton."

"Plus my weight in my armor."

"Is all of this necessary?"

"Some is ornamental, but all of it helps protect him, yes."

"Ok, let's lay all of it on the floor."

Once I had it all — human and animal — in a pile, I knelt on it. "I'll be back." With that I sank into the earth, moving the armor to a place in the earth that held a lot of metals and minerals. I first concentrated on the princes' armor, changed it, then on to my armor, all the while holding the thought in my mind of how strong, and lightweight it should be. The runes on my hands and arms began to glow and the armor ring on my finger became warm. My strength and stamina ring become warm, as well as my quick reflexes ring.

My hand began to pulsate and draw metals and minerals from the surrounding earth as I held onto the image of what I wanted. Minutes passed until the pulsating stopped, and under my hand lay a set of heavy horse armor that matched the prince's. I moved under back to the stable, to the prince.

I emerged from the ground with Beast's new armor. As we picked it up and began to examine it, we realized it now weighed half of what it used to. It was marked by runes were on its underside and it had the same dragon scale design as ours.

"Lord above!" said the prince.

We put it on Beast — it was all black and the head and neck pieces were shaped to look like a dragon's head, face, and neck. Beast seemed to like it and stood taller.

"Magnificent. You need to make a set for your warhorse."

"And a light set for Mare."

We gathered The Queen of Battle's heavy armor, mare's light armor and piled all of it in the floor. I took the heavy armor first and the process worked just as it had the first time, including the dragon motif.

We dressed Queen in her new armor and she liked it, especially since it weighed half as much as her old set. She looked fearsome. The heavy shield that hung on her saddle now featured dragon scales and a rampant black stag. We removed their and put it away for the night, planning to dress them again on the morrow and let them become accustomed to it.

I took Mare's light armor and went back to the metal and mineral spot and went through the same process, but this time my guise ring became warm, so I knew this set would be different.

And Mare's armor WAS different. It had the same black dragon scale motif, but this one was a deep shimmering non-reflective blue-black. And, instead of the dragon head and neck, hers had the imprints of stag's horns. Her vital areas were fully covered, but the whole outfit weighed no more than leather armor would have.

We dressed her in her new armor. She shook her head and stomped her feet, then settled down. At the rider's left knee hung a quiver and bow scabbard, but the quiver looked odd; I'd have to check it later. The small shield that hung on her saddle had the same rampant black stag as the shield.

When I mounted, everything looked and felt good.

"What did you do?" The Prince asked.

"Nothing, why? What happened?"

"As you mounted, she changed to look like a black stag... actually, two black stags, one with you riding and one with no rider."

I concentrated on the idea of a black stag by itself. "What do you see?"

"A black stag, with no rider!"

I thought of me riding a black stag. "And now?"

"You are riding a black stag."

I laughed, "That will come in handy."

"When you were sitting there on her, unmoving, you almost faded onto the background shadows and darkness."

"With this new armor, she'll make a better scout." We got her undressed and put her armor away, figuring that she, too, would get more practice the next day.

***

We were all up early, getting started on the day, when I heard the knights grumbling about not being fed better food than the commoners, when they are the high table. However, since the prince was eating the same fare, they kept their complaints to themselves.

After I had eaten, I walked through the company area as everyone was working on their personal equipment. My hand tingled as I passed one trooper, so I stopped and looked. .

"Let me see your sword, trooper."

"Yes captain," he said handing it to me as the Master Sergeant came over to see if he had missed anything.

"There is a fault in the steel." I hit it against the wagon and it broke. Both men's mouths hung open. "That would have been bad."

"It would, sir."

"Let's get another one."

"Yes, sir."

They got another one from the supply wagon and brought it to me. I looked at it. The steel was OK for what it was. I took it, nodding my head, and ran my hand down It. A rune on my hand glowed and the sword morphed into a finely crafted sword, razor sharp, that weighed half as much as the old one.

Everyone stared at me and the sword, and I mumbled, "Sorry for breaking yours, trooper."

"Yes sir, Thank you, sir!"

The trooper next to him said, "can you break mine too, captain?" Everyone laughed and I smiled, taking his sword and improving it with a quick pass. That started a line forming.

By noon I had touched and changed over two thousand swords, knives, daggers, lances, spears, bows and arrows. The list included the five knights and their men-at-arms.

I had not planned on doing anything like this, but the cat was out of the bag now. They knew I was a mage.

"I guess I kind of am," I told them, "but not a naturally born one. If it saves the life of one of my people, it will be worth it."

"Master Sergeant?"

"Sir?"

"Form up the company with shields."

"Yes, sir. Fall in, company formation, with shields!" The troopers lined up. "Open ranks, march!" The company opened so I could walk down the line.

As I walked, I touched each shield, and they became lighter and stronger, also turning black with a raised rampant black stag on the face.

I was finishing the last rank of my men, when I noticed that the other two companies had formed up. On the other side of them, the five knights and their men-at-arms were also formed.

I moved to the next company and came to their captain. "What sigil would you have on your shields?" He looked left and right, knowing everyone was listening.

"The Black Stag, m'lord."

"Ah-ooh! Ah-ooh! Ah-ooh!" came the shout from his company behind him. I touched the captain's shield, and it changed to match the others. I could have changed them all at once, but sometimes pomp and circumstance are needed, so I walked down each line, moving to deal with the next company as well.

When I approached the knights, I remembered the prince's charge that they regain their honor — lost when backing a traitor — on the battlefield. Each knight stood beside his warhorse, in full armor, with their men-at-arms behind them.

"Sir Knights, The Prince has charged you to regain your honor on the field of battle, and I know you will do just that. So that all may see your honor, you will wear your house sigil on your shields and armor as you go into battle."

I walked forward, touching each knight, his warhorse, and his shield. All were changed, and their revised house sigil appeared. Their armor was much improved, but wasn't as good as mine and the Princes'. I walked the ranks of their men-at-arms, touching and changing their shields.

When I finished, the 'Close ranks' command was given, and I returned to the front of the formation. As I neared the front, I looked out across the field and there stood a large twelve-point black stag.

I stopped, startled and awed. He looked over the formation as no one made a sound. He looked at me and bowed his head. I bowed in return. He then turned and moved majestically back toward the forest. It was quite a surreal moment.

Master Sergeant Miller, in his parade ground voice, shouted, "Black Stag!"
"Ah-ooh! Ah-ooh! Ah-ooh!" Was shouted in return by everyone on parade, and it echoed across the valley.

"Master Sergeant Miller, Post!" He came to the front of

the formation and faced me. "As of this moment you are pro-moted to Sergeant Major!" I shouted. "Take charge of the for-mation, Sergeant Major!"

"Yes, sir!" He saluted and I walked away.

"Well done, my friend." The Prince said.

I smiled, "everyone loves a show."

He chuckled, "send a runner around, tell the com-manders that there will be a meeting tonight at six in the Great Hall. It's best if they eat before they come."

"Yes, Sire."

***

I raised a table in the middle of the floor in the Great Hall and created a relief map of the North-West from Port West Gate north to the Northern Border, then over to Vigil Keep. My map also showed the route the Crown Prince was taking to Vigil Keep. But I left my lands vague and covered in crags.

The Prince looked at the relief map. "Is the pass still blocked?" I showed it open on the map.

"It is at the moment, I'll open it before we get there, so we can follow behind them if we want to."

"No, leave it closed. We'll take the outside route and come in behind them after they've passed. I closed the pass on the map."

"Can you make watering holes for us at the end of every day's travel?"

"I can," and I indicated some at intervals along our route. He nodded.

"Thoughts?"

I was looking at the map. "I've read that when the Romans, at the end of a day's march, made quick forts. A circled moat of spikes and a timber palisade before they slept. That way they slept securely inside walls."

"Yes, I've read that, too."

"What if I took a small scouting force ahead of the main

army and did the same? I could make us forts of stone so we could be secure behind walls every night, with water for us and the horses." I raised little forts up on the map along own planned route.

He smiled, "now that, I like."

The knights, captains, and Sergeant Major Miller came in.

"Gentlemen, this will be quick. Prince Kade is in overall command of our forces." I stepped back.

The prince stepped forward and everyone bowed. "We have been tasked by the King to follow the invading Hinterland army to Vigil Keep. We are to cut their supply lines and harass them as opportunities present themselves. We will bleed them all the way to Vigil Keep but will not directly engage them. The Crown Prince is approaching Vigil Keep from the south and we will join his forces for the main battle.

"You can see our planned route here on the map. We have, or will have, overnight forts and water for us after our day's march so we will be secure inside walls almost every night. Our enemy will not."

Everyone was studying the map. He gave them a moment.

"Questions?" There were none. "We leave at dawn. We'll eat on the move, and march until we reach the first overnight fort."

"I suggest we all get some sleep since we won't rest for some time after tonight." They all bowed and departed.

"I think I'll go check on the Hinterland Army and make sure they are still moving where we think they are."

"Good idea."

"Good night, Sire."

"Good night, Ghost," he said smiling.

I fast-traveled to the north pass then flew on until I found the army. They were still on track heading north, which was the only way they could go.

On a whim, I fast-traveled to the capital and up into the castle. I went up into Princess Maddison's room wall. She was asleep. I went to one of the windows and made it a double door, and grew a covered balcony outside the new doors that It matched the sitting room balcony, only a little smaller.

I added sliding panels of clear glass with stained glass depicting climbing rose vines in full bloom. They could be closed during bad weather or winter so she could still enjoy the balcony. I added a small brazier and lit it to give warmth and light.

When I was finished, I opened the double doors. After a few minutes the breeze and the light coming through woke her. She sat up looking around, then she looked at the open door where a window used to be.

She got up, wrapping a sheet around her and walked to the doors, looking. "Oh, Ghost, it's beautiful!" she said to the room She smiled and lightly touched the stained-glass slides. "Truly beautiful." She giggled. "My father will have you hanged if he catches you in his daughter's bedchambers. But I suppose he'd have to catch you first." She sat on one of the stone couches looking out over the city.

She held her hand out, reaching toward the door. I knew she could not know that I was still there, but hoping... I stepped out of the wall onto the balcony, taking her hand bowing over it.

"Thank you, my Ghost."

"You are welcome, my Princess."

She held onto my hand. "My brother is well?"

"He is, Princess, we march north at dawn."

She stood, drawing close to me. "Stay safe, my Ghost." She kissed me, our hands lingering together, as she went back into her room.

I watched her walk away. *"No hunched back."* I smiled. "Yes, my Princess." I stepped back into the wall and fast-traveled back to Black Stag Keep and slept in the earth to restore my strength.

CHAPTER 19

I rose early and ate, then dressed in my light armor and adorned Mare with her new armor. I put my bow in its saddle scabbard and arrows in the quiver. It was then I found out why the quiver didn't look right. It was a "blessed" quiver, allowing me to put two hundred arrows in it without filling it.

Thatcher helped the prince get ready, and he would carry the banner when we rode out. Another trooper would carry the Company's Black Stag banner. We marched at dawn, with a scout squad, and I moving out early.

As we rode, flankers were out scouting, although there was little need since I could feel everything around me for hundreds of yards. But they were following established orders. We walked our horses at a steady pace throughout the day, with regular breaks for water. When we reached our first camp site, one that our companies could reach well before dark, we stopped. The scouts set out to survey the surrounding area.

I looked around and pictured in my mind what I wanted in our overnight fort. Concentrating, I raised an eight-foot stone wall with a watch step on the inside so the guard could see over the wall and the archers could fire over it. The fort was a square that took in enough land for everyone to be inside, with all our horses and wagons.

I pushed the woods and brush back two hundred yards so we'd have open ground approaching the walls, then raised fifteen-foot-tall covered wooden watchtowers in each corner, and then added one in the middle of each wall, giving us eight.

I raised a gated four-foot wooden fence inside and across the back for the horses and dug a watering hole in that area. I created a well for the men and raised a covered kitchen with worktables and ovens in the cook's areas. I made the ovens and cook grills hot and kept them that way... we would not have to gather wood.

The moat that surrounded us was full of spikes, there was a bridge over it and a large gate to close us in. The scouts acted as if they saw this sort of thing every day. The only thing said was, "wish you had been with us before, Captain."

When the companies arrived, the spare horses moved in first to the walled off watering hole. Then the mounted companies, then the wagons. Once everyone was inside, we closed the gates. Camp was set up, guard duties assigned. The cooks went right to work, as I had already done the hard work for them.

The prince stopped where I was standing inside the gate. "Well done, Captain, Well done."

I bowed, "Thank you, Sire. We'll see how this design works and make improvements as needed."

He nodded, "see you at dinner, then."

When I saw the Sergeant Major, I motioned him over.

"Yes, sir?"

"Look over the camp layout and design and tell me where I can improve it."

He looked around nodding, "Yes, sir." He walked away shouting orders.

It wasn't long before they served dinner. I walked through the camp as I ate. looking over everything. I made my way back to our Command Wagon where the prince was. T-hatcher and the wagon driver were taking care of the setup.

"Good idea, this fort." The Prince said.

"Yes, I think it will work out well."

"Have you thought about leaving them up when we leave? We could use them as caravan stops and it would help with the trade route."

"That's an option, and if it helps trade, it will improve all of our lives."

***

As we left the next morning no improvements to the fort had been requested, so I left it standing as a new caravan stop. The scouts and I left out early as we had done the day before, and once again walked our horses, eating on the move. Just short of our planned time to stop we came to a small river with a ford. The land around was all fields so it was a good place for another overnight fort.

I raised one like the one the night before, but made it a little bigger. I had in mind to come back at some point and raise an inn at this important crossing. I raised the land to make a low hill on this side of the ford, just in case the river every flooded, so the fort would be safe and dry. As an afterthought I raised a wide low stone bridge, making the ford unnecessary.

All was ready when the main body arrived. The Prince looked everything over, seeing the bridge, He smiled. "Show off!" and moved into the fort.

As we moved toward the future battle, this became our pattern: scouts out, move all day, fort up at night. At the end of the sixth day, we had reached the end of the crag divide. The Hinterland army had passed this point the day before, or so it appeared. We forted up for the night and sent scouts out to see how close the enemy was. I could have done it, but they needed to stay in practice. Plus, I didn't want anyone else knowing all I could do. They had already seen too much as it was.

The scouts reported back late that night that the Hinterlanders were a half-day march ahead of us. We decided that in the morning, the wagons and support people would stay here in the overnight fort while our cavalry moved forward to harass the enemy. Then we could withdraw back here for the night.

We ate and checked our personal weapons and gear,

thinking that, more than likely, we would fight tomorrow. We did not dress our horses in heavy armor, since we planned hit and run harassment.

We moved out before dawn the next morning and I sent two scouts ahead to find the enemy while I led the other scouts and the archers. The prince and the five knights led the vanguard of our main body.

Three hours later our scouts reported they had found their rear guard, noting that there was a bend in the road in two miles. I sent them back to keep watch while I reported to the prince.

"Sounds like a good place for our first combat. Set your archers in the woods at the bend, push the scouts forward to harass, and when their rear guard gives chase fall back around this side of the bend. We'll be waiting for them here. Archers are to engage as soon as the enemy is in sight. That will thin their ranks."

I took the archers and placed them in the woods. All the scouts were also archers, so had our bows ready as we moved forward. We caught up with the rear guard quicker than I expected.

They must have been sleeping, and we were almost upon them before they realized it. We loosed arrows into them as we galloped past, doing the same to the last three wagons. The wagon's horse teams panicked and ran down the road, causing the wagons to roll over spilling supplies.

The rear guard finally reacted and gave chase. We headed back toward our main body to spring the ambush, with them fast on our heels. As soon as the prince saw us rounding the bend he and the knights charged, lances down. They flowed around us and drove a gap in the middle of their line. The fifty rear guardsmen never had a chance: the prince's charge decimated them, and our archers finished them, taking no prisoners.

Our archers remounted and set up a blocking force on the road as we picked up our dead and wounded and fell back toward the overnight fort. Most of their now riderless horses followed right along after us.

I made sure that the Prince was unhurt, then I set scouts behind to wait for at least six hours to see if we would be followed. We made the fort by mid-afternoon, and once everyone was inside the gates were closed.

At nightfall our scouts reported in, saying the enemy had followed us with a force numbering one hundred light and heavy cavalry, but had turned back after two hours because their heavy cavalry could not keep up the pace.

We had lost six troopers and fifteen wounded. Surprisingly, most of the dead and wounded were from the knight's men-at-arms, who apparently weren't professional soldiers, and so were unused to real, life and death fighting.

The Hinterlanders had lost fifty troopers and forty horses, most of which were in our hands. We tended our wounded and buried our dead, then rested the next day with scouts out.

Our whole force pulled out the following day at dawn, following the enemy. They had recovered their supplies lost when their wagons rolled over, and the wagons as well. We forted-up again before sundown, sending scouts out to make sure we did not come upon the enemy unprepared ... or that they did not sneak up on us.

As we ate that night we talked, "How far to Vigil Keep?" I asked.

"I'd say ten days march from here."

"What are they thinking?"

"What do you mean?"

"Well, they know, or should know, that there is no re-supply caravan coming or that it's late. So why did the commander push on? Why not wait? He's got to be getting low on supplies."

The prince nodded thinking, "He might think had can live off the locals, or resupply by taking Vigil Keep."

"That is not a sound strategy, and if I can see it, certainly their prince has a general that can see it."

"Perhaps he overruled his general... it happens."

I shook my head, "I suppose, but it bothers me when things make little sense, makes me nervous. I think I'll go check on our friends."

I went to our wagon, out of sight, and dropped into the earth. I moved rapidly underground until I reached their rear guard, which now numbered more than a hundred. I moved forward up the supply wagon line and started getting an uneasy feeling. There were more wagons than there were before. Did they get a message through somehow?

I found the Hinterland Prince's pavilion. He was in his cups, pacing, venting at his general.

"Relegated to guarding the supply wagons! He could not stand to let me fight my way! No, I might be victorious and steal his glory!"

"Sire, the King did not come to take your place, he was marching on Vigil Keep as a separate front and did not know about the earthquake and the blocked pass."

"Yet still he blames me for the delays, saying I should have used the outside route around the crags." The general said nothing.

"That's not good, a second army led by the King of Hinterland himself," I thought as I moved up the line of march to find the king's camp. When I found it, it held a twenty-thousand-man army and one hundred knights. *"Not good! Not good at all! I don't think he intends to stop with just taking Vigil Keep. He intends to resupply, then push south into the heart of our kingdom."*

I went back to the supply wagons thinking I needed to slow them down. I went to the rear wheel of a wagon and hollowed out three spokes on one side of the hub. As long as the wagon sat in place nothing would happen. But when the wagon moved forward, putting those spokes on the bottom or top, they would collapse. I did the same thing to the same wheel on every wagon.

"That should hold you for a bit," I muttered to myself.

I fast-traveled back to our overnight fort, came up at our Command Wagon and went to see the prince. He was inside looking at maps.

"We've got a problem."

"Only one?" He chuckled.

"Well, it's a big one."

"How big?"

"Twenty thousand big,"

He lost his smile, "Tell me." I told him what I had heard and found. I told him what I had done to the wagons to slow them down, but warned it would not hold them long.

"That means a total force of almost twenty-five thousand men, mused the prince. "You are right, they will gain a foothold at Vigil Keep and then push south."

"And the Crown Prince is heading straight into them, thinking it's only four thousand men. Hopefully, he makes Vigil before they do."

"It hardly makes a difference. I doubt Vigil can hold long against twenty-five thousand men. Did you see any siege engines?"

"I did not."

He nodded. "You must go to the King with this news. He will decide what they should do. He will probably have you take orders to the Crown Prince. Return as soon as you can, we'll hold here for orders."

"Yes, Sire."

I dropped into the earth and fast-traveled to the Capital and up into the kings office wall. He was not in his office as he, the queen, and the princess were in their quarters in discussion. I stepped from the wall and knocked on the door to their quarters, then stepped back in plain sight. The King opened the door, dagger at the ready.

He looked at me intently, "what's wrong?"

"Hinterland has invaded with a second army of twenty thousand men. They are eight days march from Vigil Keep and I don't think they plan to stop there."

He came into his office followed by the Queen and the Princess.

I bowed, "My Queen, Princess."

"Sir Ghost", the queen answered, the princess smiled. The three of them sat down.

"Take a seat and tell me all."

I reported events from the time we started following the Hinterland prince's army, then what I found when I scouted forward.

"And you think their king intends Vigil Keep as a base to push south from?"

"I do, Sire. I don't think he would have sent his son to Port West Gate, then brought twenty thousand more men to stop at Vigil Keep. This was intended as a two-pronged attack from the start, and his goal is this capital."

He nodded, "I agree, he is a greedy man, never satisfied with what he has."

He sat back thinking, looking at the wall map. I waited.

"Prince Kade and his army's task is the same as it was: harass the enemy and cut his supply lines, but not engage in a major battle. If they run for home, let them, and dog them all the way to the border."

"You will take an order to the Crown Prince to pull back to Mid-Brook and will hold there for further orders, or until I meet them there with our army."

He looked at me, "I know you can build balconies," The Princess looked at the floor, smiling. "Can you improve Vigil Keep's defenses?"

"I can, Sire." He nodded.

"You will take the message to Prince Mathew at Vigil Keep and while there improve his defenses. Tell him he is to hold the Keep if possible, or if not, to sell it at as high a price as possible. "As for you, don't make the Keep look so formidable that they pass it by. I need time to gather our army and move to meet them either at Vigil Keep or on their way here, so the Keep's forces need to hold their attention for as long as they can."

"I understand, Sire."

He sat thinking as I waited. "Neither the Crown Prince nor Prince Mathew will believe you. They don't know you, and they will doubt who you are and the messages you carry-. My seal may carry some weight, but they will still want confirmation. We will send messenger birds, but we need to be sure the messages get through."

He looked at me, holding my gaze. "Can you take someone with you the way you travel?"

"I've never tried it over long distances, but I think I can get you there."

He shook his head, "not me, I have to raise our army." Princess Maddison stood up. "The Princess?" He nodded.

I looked at her. She raised her chin, looking directly into my eyes.

I nodded, "do you have armor, Princess?"

"Yes, but it's only ceremonial."

"It won't be when I get through with it. Take me to it, please". She and the queen took me to her bedchambers as the king started writing out orders.

Her armor was on a stand in the corner. It was a standard set of heavy armor, with the back of the legs open for riding horses, protected only by chain mail. That was fine as long as you were riding. The rest had been made of thin poorly tempered metal that looked good but wouldn't stop an angry bee. Her sword and daggers hung on the armor, and were also purely ceremonial. I walked over to the armor, putting my hand on it.

I looked at them, "I'll be right back," and sank into the floor, taking her armor with me.

CHAPTER 20

I took her armor down deep in the earth to find a metal and mineral deposit. Once there, I concentrated on her armor and, as the runes on my hands began to glow, my rings began to warm. I held my concentration until I felt the work was complete, then went back up to the princess' bedchambers.

I backed away from the standing armor, which had turned out to be a combination of mine and hers, covered with white and yellow gold, featuring a winged helm with the lower wings covering her cheeks and leaving the rest of the face was open. It had a dragon scale design with bigger scales in some areas, and with power runes on the inside.

I picked it up, noting how much lighter it was than mine. As I was touching it, I suddenly thought, *black,* and it turned all black with a non-reflective surface.

"Can I do that?" The princess asked.

"Yes, when you are wearing it, just think 'black', or if you are in the woods and need to hide, think 'woods'" and it will camouflage you. Her sword, like mine, had become incredibly sharp.

"If you will excuse us, Sir Ghost, I'll get her suited up," said the queen.

I returned to the king to find that he was still writing orders and other messages. While I waited, I looked at the map on the wall, changing Port West Gate to reflect my recent changes. I looked at the area around Vigil Keep, which seemed to be mostly rolling hills and farmlands. Mid-brook appeared to be a three-day march from the Vigil Keep.

I looked at the South Lands, but saw there was not much there. It was walled off by rocky ridges from the rest of the kingdom, and seemed to be roughly a third of the size of the rest of the king's domain. Since it was marshy and isolated, it remained largely unimproved and unpopulated, with no ports to encourage development.

I heard the queen and the princess approaching the office and saw that the princess looked splendid — and I hoped, safer — in her new armor.

The king got up and examined her. "Excellent," he said nodding, then drew her sword and dropped the blade on the corner of his desk. The blade sliced through the wood, never slowing down. "That will do," he said, and handed the princess the letters.

Then he looked me in the eyes and said, "protect my daughter!"

"With my life, sire."

"What happens if she slips from your grasp while you are traveling, or whatever it is you do?" the queen asked.

"Well, let's just say it would not be good, so I'll hold her tight!"

She nodded and looked at us, then said "wait!" She left the room and returned shortly, with a short royal blue length of rope. .

"Hold hands," She ordered, and we obeyed while she wrapped the rope around our wrists and hands. As she tightened it, the princess sucked in a breath, wincing. "I know dear, but this is the strongest knot I know. It will never come undone, unless YOU untie it."

When finished, she stepped back and the king stepped forward. "This is the old way, not practiced in many years. You see, this is a betrothal knot." Now I felt like wincing! "Do you accept this man, daughter, to be your husband and consort?"

The princess looked at me, her eyes big. "I do, father."

Then he looked at me with a piercing glance. "Do you accept this woman to be your wife, renouncing claim to all titles in becoming the princess' Consort?"

I stood straighter, "I do, sire."

"Then, as her father and king of the realm I pronounce you married. You may kiss the bride."

I leaned down and kissed my princess. Our clasped gauntlets locked together, the runes glowing. She smiled up at me.

The queen hugged me and the king shook my hand.

"I know this is not the way you wanted it to happen," her mother said to my new bride, "but needs must."

"Go," said the king, and we bowed as they left.

I looked at my princess, now my wife, and muttered, just loud enough for her to hear, "just breath normally!"

She nodded and we stepped through the wall, fast-traveling to the Castle at Port West Gate. We came out of a wall in the Royal Gardens overlooking the city, port, and ocean, and despite the unusual experience, she kept her composure... she was an aristocrat.

She looked around, "Is this your castle?"

"No, this is Prince Kade's, the seat of the Western District in Port West Gate."

"Kade has a castle? Did you build it?"

"Yes, and yes," I chuckled, "but he paid for it."

"It must have cost him a fortune."

"I gave him a good deal on it."

"Yes, but wait, how good of a deal did you give him?"

"He paid in gold."

"How much gold?"

I was smiling. "One."

"You built this castle for one gold?"

"No."

"I should hope not!"

"I built, the castle, harbor, and warehouses for one gold,"

She shook her head, "You two need keepers!" and she laughed and hugged me.

We spent our wedding night in our apartment in Castle West Gate and no longer needed the knot to bind us... and I started calling her by her private family name, "Maddie."

***

We arrived at Crown Prince Luke's pavilion at sunrise to find him alone and dressing. We rose through the earth while his back was turned.

Maddison spoke, "brother?"

He whirled around, dagger in hand. "Maddie?" We removed our helms and I bowed.

Prince Luke, put his dagger away, stepping to her but keeping his eyes warily on me. They hugged.

"Crown Prince Luke, may I present Earl Draugur de Crypto, my husband, and consort."

He stared at her, then at me. "Well met, Sir Draugur."

I bowed again," sire."

"When did you wed?"

"Last night. Father handled the ceremony."

"And then sent you?"

"It was the only way to be sure you trusted the message."

She handed him the letter, which he took, broke the seal and read. He read it twice.

Nodding his head, he looked back at me. "My father says he trusts you with his life. He says you are a mage and will help Prince Matthew at Vigil Keep... and that Prince Kade will join me at Mid-Brook."

"That is the essence of our tasks, yes sire."

He nodded again, "then be about your mission, and take good care of my sister. She's a brat, but she's the only sister I have!"

He kissed Maddie on the cheek, and we put our helmets on, clasped hands and dropped into the earth.

We fast-traveled to the overnight fort where Prince Kade was waiting, coming up between the wagons where no one could see us, then walking around to the front of the Command Wagon.

I stuck my head in, "we have a guest!"

Prince Kade looked up and saw Maddie, frowned, then looked at me quizzically and started laughing.

"You are wed?"

I nodded.

"Decided you could live with the hunched back after all?"

"You told him I had a hunched back? He was always telling everyone I had a hunched back!" The prince laughed even harder and then grabbed us both in a hug.

"I'm so glad for both of you. Now we are truly brothers."

She handed him one of the king's letters, "no rest for the wicked!."

He read it, and nodded his approval of the plan. "You go to Vigil Keep."

"Yes, I'll fortify that position and try to keep the Hinterlander's attention."

"Very well. Now sink this fort so they can't use it as they retreat."

I nodded, and thought instructions to the fort, and the earth began to reclaim its walls.

"All right be on your way, then." He kissed the princess on the check. We clasped hands again and sank into the earth, fast-traveling to Vigil Keep and coming up in the stables. We removed our helms and as walked out no one gave us a second glance.

As we walked into the Great Hall, children started shouting, "Aunt Maddie!" and ran to meet her. She knelt and hugged them.

"Maddie?" A woman, who I assume was the duchess, called. "When did you arrive?"

"Emily!" They hugged, "just now."

"Duchess, may I present Earl Draugur de Crypta, my new husband?"

I bowed," Duchess."

She squealed and grabbed both of us in a hug.

A hearty laugh came from the hall, "so father finally found someone to take you off his hands!"

As the duke approached us I bowed, "m'lord."

"Sir Draugur." He hugged Maddie and clasped my wrist.

"Where's my message? I can't imagine any other reason you would show up here." She handed him the letter, he broke the seal and read it. He looked up at me, then reread the letter.. the habit seemed to run in the family.

He folded the letter, thinking. "A mage. Father says you can fortify my keep."

"I can, m'lord."

"Have you done this kind of thing before?"

Maddie chuckled, "he built Kade a whole new castle at Port West Gate, and then rebuilt the port and added warehouses!"

The Duke looked at me, his eyebrows raised. "I was bored, and he paid me for it." Maddie laughed.

"I hear a story in there somewhere." The duchess said, well, perhaps later.

***

We toured the keep and found it was crowded, since he had gathered all the farmers and merchants from the area around for protection. There were over a thousand men and twenty knights as defenders plus all his people who served him.

After we finished the tour, we all went to his office. I raised up a stone platform from the floor, then added a model of the keep and its surrounding town and fields.

"If we are going to do this, we may as well do it right. If you could change anything, what would it be? More walls, expanded storage areas, more space whatever. What would those things be?"

"Anything?" the Duke asked and I nodded.

"Move the walls out make the courtyard bigger."

I reached over and pushed the model's walls further out. "Like that?"

He nodded, then reached and moved a wall himself.

"Can you take the roof off so we can see inside?" the duchess asked. She looked inside and started moving walls making their living areas larger, the kitchen larger, the hall larger. I smiled. "I've always wanted more room," she said.

The Duke made the stables larger and added another well. We moved all the walls out, doubling the size of the keep. At the same time, I thickened the walls and made them taller, bringing up bedrock to support the extra weight.

We made the moat wider and deeper and lined it with stone. I made the watch towers bigger, the gate thicker, and added a portcullis. For raw material, I would call all the large stones from the surrounding fields, helping the farmers.

Maddie was studying the model, "what are you thinking, Maddie?"

"Can you raise another wall all the way around the village, so they don't have to rush into the keep for safety?"

I raised a wall around the village but left room for a perimeter road wide enough for two wagons to pass between the houses and the wall. I added a wide stone road leaving the Keep — now really a castle — heading south.

"Like that?"

"Yes." she smiled.

"Can I add another thing?" the duchess asked sheepishly.

"Of course!"

"A grist mill. We could really use one."

We looked for a likely place to put it by the river and decided on a spot next to the castle but inside the village wall. A quick stone dam would provide motive power for the mill. Then I added the wall around the village. That made the castle wall a secondary barrier, separating the fortifications from the village while leaving a large open space for festivals.

"OK, let's leave this alone for a while and see if we think of anything else to add."

"One problem I see is that the new walls may look too formidable for the Hinterlanders. Don't forget the king wants us to delay them for at least ten days, if at all possible."

I nodded, "I have some ideas to slow them getting here. Then we'll see." We ate dinner as a family, which was enjoyable, especially hearing stories about Maddie as a child, fighting with her brothers and throwing tantrums. She was not as amused as the rest of us.

***

After dinner we looked at the model again and everyone had more things to add, from more servant's quarters to bigger barracks for more soldiers. I pushed the walls over to the riverbank and added a quay on a road by the wall. I also decided to extend the moat around the village wall and join the river. I added a large bridge over the river, crossing into the village right at the castle wall, so the bridge was protected by a large gate, portcullis and the Keep itself. We added more wells in the protected part of the village and, while we were at it, better drainage everywhere.

I stood for a while, concentrating on the model. Maddie finally asked, "What's wrong?"

"This will be expensive."

She smiled, "how expensive?" The duke and duchess were listening intently.

"I'm sorry to say, at least two."

"Two what?" The Duke asked

"Two golds," Maddie said. "Kade only paid him one."

"This will be twice as big... I would guess."

The Duke put two golds on the table. "Done!"

I picked up the golds, and announced, "kids, who wants to see a magic trick?"

"I do, I do!" they shouted. Everyone followed me to the Great Hall. I stepped up to the grand hearth, held the two golds to the mantel, and concentrated. The mantel changed as the golds became part of it, while above the fireplace mantel their house shield was displayed, but with no sigil on it.

The children, as well as most of the adults, were staring wide-eyed.

I gathered them around me, "now watch!" I pointed to an open place in the middle of the room.

I couldn't resist: "Uh oh, something must be wrong! Who can whistle?"

"I can," said one small boy, proudly.

"OK, you whistle, just like calling a dog, right?" He nodded and started whistling.

Slowly a large stone lion rose from the floor, all black with red markings, and everyone stared at it.

"Now, where do you think he belongs?" The children pointed to the shield over the mantel.

A little girl, all eyes, was beside me, holding on to my pant leg. "Would you like to help me?" I asked her and she nodded shyly. "Can you say, "up?" she bobbed her head. I picked her up and stepped closer to the hearth. "OK, point to the shield and say 'up'!"

She pointed and said, "Up, lion!" The lion rose, flowing up onto the shield and becoming a Rampant Black Lion with red outlines. The children cheered and everyone clapped. I put the little girl down and she ran to the duchess.

"Mommy, did you see the lion? I made him jump!" Everyone laughed.

I took firm hold of the mantel and sent the orders for all the changes to be made through the wall, floors, and earth. We soon heard a commotion from outside. "I guess we should see what's going on."

We walked out onto the new balcony and looked out over all the changes. People were running up the walls to see what was going on.

The captain of the guard came running up, sword in hand. "No need to worry, captain," the duke assured him. "We hired a mage to make some improvements."

"Well, sire, I don't know what you paid, but it looks like you got your money's worth!"

"I think so." The duke answered smiling.

"We will all be busy in the morning." I said, to nods all around.

Then Maddie led me to our new bedchambers.

CHAPTER 21

I rose from our bed, put on clothes and sank into the earth, moving rapidly Vigil Castle and the village. All was well, and everyone had settled down for the night.

Then I flew to the Hinterland army's encampment and found the King's pavilion. He was sleeping soundly, so I stole his armor and his weapons, silently pulling them into the ground. I left them solidly encased in the earth under his pavilion.

I then found his warhorse — a beautiful animal that had its own tent. First I moved its heavy armor into the ground, then rose slowly. As the horse looked at me a rune on my hand glowed, apparently quieting the animal. I covered its eyes and pulled both of us into the ground. He never flinched as I moved both us to the new stables at the castle.

I went back and retrieved both sets of armor, as well as the king's war chest, stuffed with gold. I saw there were knights' pavilions encircling the king's. Working my way methodically along the line of tents, I stole ten of the richest knight's armor, weapons and gold. Then I did the same with their warhorses and armor.

Once back home, I stood their suits of armor, swords and shields along the wall in the new Great Hall. The loot would come in handy ... after all, it costs a lot to defend a castle!

Then I slept in the earth for a short time, restoring my strength. I rose back up into our bed before dawn. Before settling down, I placed my ten new chests of gold along the bedroom wall.

"You've been gone a long time, is everything ok?" asked Maddie sleepily.

"Yes, I caused some trouble with the invading army, but it took longer than I expected." I went back to sleep.

Sometime after dawn Maddie snuggled up to me. "Ghost?"

"Hmmm?"

"What's in the ten chests along the wall?"

"I don't know, I haven't looked. Did you look?"

"They are all locked,"

I smiled.

"Ghost?"

"Hmm?"

"Where are the keys?"

"Probably with the owners back at the Hinterland army camp, nosy."

She bit my ear, "Ow!" she jumped up to run. But I caught her before she could get away.

"You wench."

"You can open the chests, can't you?"

"I can."

"Open them, I want to see."

We got up, and I touched each one, unlocking them. Each was full of gold. She looked at me. "Spoils of war, and the beginning of the Southern District's Treasury," I said.

She jumped into my arms, and, well, we were late to breakfast!

Before we left the room, I pushed the chests into the stone wall as Maddie watched and nodded her approval.

***

We walked through the Great Hall on the way to breakfast and found the Duke and Duchess were there looking at the armor. We walked over to see them too.

"Ah, Sir Draugur, Good morning. I don't suppose you'd know anything about this armor?"

"Yes, Your Grace, they go with the Castle."

"I see, but where did they come from?"

"Well, that's a long story ... the short version is that I stole them. That one over there belonged to the King of Hinterland. The chest in front of his armor is a tax I collected, in your name, for trespassing on your lands." I walked over and opened a chest. It was full of gold.

The Duke started laughing, "he will lose his mind, and people will lose their heads." Maddie was laughing as well.

"There are also eleven warhorses and heavy armor in your stables, including the king's. Did you know his horse had his own tent, so he's quite spoiled I'd expect." We all laughed.

"We'll go see the horses after we eat." The Duke said. "I doubt their army will move today, since their king will be in a rage."

"That was my thinking."

***

The castle was a beehive of activity, with soldiers and people racing everywhere. The people of the village had gone back home, feeling safer since they now lived inside a sturdy wall.

We went to the stables to see the war horses, and the duke loved the King's magnificent animal. "What will you do with them?"

"They are yours; I only need two, and not that one, which is yours. I want two mares."

He was all smiles. "If you are still here when your mares come in season, we'll let him cover them, and that will start the Southern District's herd." We picked out what we thought were the two best mares, Maddie and I saddled them and rode around the village wall inside and out.

"Ghost?"

"Yes?"

"You said the gold was for the Southern District's treasury, but what do you intend to do with it?"

"I've already done it; I gave it to you. You are the brains of this team, and I'm the muscle."

"Do you mean that, or are you just saying nice things to your new bride?"

I stopped, "I mean it. You will handle the district's finances. I have some investments of my own, but you take care of that money.

"At some point, I have to talk to Prince Kade about the other lands and incomes."

"You get to keep those; you just can't claim any of my lands. The Southern District lands that will pass on to our children, if we have any."

I nodded, "then we'll make them the best lands we can to pass down to them."

***

I slept for a while, then visited the Hinterland Army again, systematically looting . I opened a vault and laid out my backpack. I opened my chests, there was room in them to put in more gold. I went to every money chest I could find and drawing the gold out through their bottoms while replacing the contents with sand. This trip would be expensive for their country.

When I had finished taking all their gold I closed, the backpack, and it put away. I filled the vault back in. I flew under their camp looking for opportunities to cause trouble. It looked like half the camp was on guard duty, so I smiled ... one goal accomplished.

I raised twenty stone dogs and ordered them to *scatter all their horses. Chase the horses for a mile then go back to the earth. Go!* The dogs rose from the ground and started barking and snarling, running through the camp scattering horses, causing chaos. As each dog reached a mile from the camp, it crumbled into dirt. A second goal reached ... they wouldn't be moving for at least another day.

I returned to Vigil Castle and slept in the earth for a while, then returning to our bed well before sunrise. Maddie snuggled into my arms and we slept.

In the morning, we went down to the family breakfast to meet the children, who had adopted me as their "Uncle Ghost." They were convinced that having a mage for an uncle was the best!

We sat down and tucked into the food. "So, you own Black Stag Keep?" asked the duke.

"I do, Your Grace, but it is nothing as grand a Vigil Castle."

"I should think not; I spent a small fortune having it built." We all chuckled. "And, while we are with family, please call me Mathew."

"And me, Emily," the duchess chimed in.

"Thanks to both of you, you are most kind."

"I would say Black Stag is a medium-sized keep, with some two thousand acres in an enclosed valley that is completely surrounded by stony outcroppings. Only a small pass allows entry to the valley, and I built a gate fort to guard it, which makes it very secure."

"Farmland?"

"Probably half is cleared, and with good water. My problem right now is tenants. I just established ten 40-acre farms, each with a house and a barn and installed farmers and their families in them. I also bought one hundred cows to start a herd, and left instructions for ten milk cows and chickens to be bought for the farms."

"Stone houses and barns, I'll bet."

Then he paused. "My problem is that all my farmers live in the village and go out every day to work the farms, which means there are no farms farther than a few miles from town."

"I'd bet that if you built houses and barns surrounded by walls for protection," I suggested, "you'd get tenants to move out there. Why not offer a better percentage of the harvest for those who go? Give them, say, five percent more of the harvest. If you add livestock, you have more to tax."

He nodded. "After breakfast we'll ride out and look at the land. You can show me what you've done."

"Any excuse to go riding," Emily said, smiling.

***

Mathew, Maddie, myself and a squad of cavalry rode out the east road, stopping where the last field was being worked, which was a couple of miles out from the castle.

"Here, Your Grace?" I asked.

"Yes, about here."

I got down and took a handful of soil. It was good soil, not too rocky. I stood and looked around, then concentrated, building in my mind the same style of farm I had raised at Black Stag, but adding a wall rather than a fence. Stone began rising out at the ground. In a short time, we had a farmstead with a twelve-foot wall around it and a twelve-foot tower at the front corner by a reinforced gate. We went inside and looked around.

"Better than the farm I grew up on," one cavalryman commented.

The duke winked at me and asked Maddie, "Princess, what would it cost to build a farmstead like this using wood?"

"Three golds." she answered right away. "seven, if you mixed wood and stone. Twelve if you only used stone."

He laughed, "she always does that ... she's sharp!"

I nodded, "so I'm learning."

"Build me another like this right across the road, so they'll have neighbors." It was finished by the time we walked out the front gate, and the duke laughed, "let's go do some planning."

We rode back to the castle at an easy pace, entering the village at what was now known as the "bridge gate." We rode slowly through the village and everyone seemed at peace, feeling safe behind their new walls, and with no feeling of impending doom despite an invading army closing in.

The grooms took our horses and we went up to the Duke's office to look at the map of the Northern District on the wall. "Show us a model of the castle and village area, please," asked the duke.

I raised a platform from the floor with scale models of the castle, the village, roads, and the surrounding ten miles.

The duke looked at it. "How far out is that?"

"About ten miles." Then I added models of the farmsteads I had created a few hours before.

He nodded, "those you built today."

"Yes."

Horns sounded from the gate. "Company is coming," the duke said. "We'll continue this later, Ghost, thank you."

I let the tabletop platform drop and become the floor again.

A messenger met the duke in the Great Hall. "The Crown Prince approaches with his army, your Grace."

"Impatient, arrogant...!" Maddie fulminated. "He was to wait at Mid-Brook for father, but just can't wait to show what a great war leader he is!"

"Maddie, watch what you say, he will be king one day" Mathew cautioned.

"More's the pity!" We went down to the courtyard to greet the him as his party rode in.

"You've been busy improving things, I see." He looked at me, but I said nothing.

"We have, brother," said the duke.

"How far away are the Hinterlanders?"

"Five days march," replied Matthew.

"I thought they'd be closer by now."

"Sir Draugur attacks them every night, slowing their progress."

"He has taken spoils?"

"He has."

The Crown Prince looked at me and I saw his jaw muscles bunching. "You will turn over half of those spoils to me, this is

MY campaign!"

The duke's eyes grew larger and Maddie became stone-faced.

I bowed, "Of course, Your Highness, where would you like your five and a half sets of armor sent?"

The duke closed his eyes and winced.

"What was that?"

"You wanted half of the spoils I took. I took 11 sets of armor, so your half is five and a half sets. Oh, and five and half war horses."

"You took armor, not gold or hostages?" His voice was rising.

"And warhorses, Your Highness."

I could see that he felt I was beneath him in status, but did not fear him, and he could not stand it.

"You were told to improve the defenses and hold the invaders here by making them reduce the Keep."

"Actually, I was told to improve the defenses and delay the enemy as long as I could, which I have done with no loss of life on our side."

"Well, as you have accomplished your task, you may leave. Take what you came with and go! Be glad you married the princess, or I'd have you in the dungeon."

I bowed, "Yes, Your Highness."

As he left, over his shoulder he said, "enjoy the swamps of the Southern District," And he laughed.

I just smiled.

I bowed to the duke. "Thank you, Your Grace, for your hospitality. I apologize for any trouble I may have caused you."

He nodded, "go before he does something stupid, and please take care of my sister."

"With my life," I said, then turned to Maddie.

"You could have handled that better," she said reproachfully.

"I'm sure, but I can't stand bullies."

"I can't either, but this one happens to be my brother. We'll let father handle him."

"For as long as he lives, anyway. Once he's king, it will be a whole new mess."

"We'll worry about that when it happens."

I took her hand and dropped through the floor and into the earth, opening a comfortable vault.

"I don't trust the crown prince, I'll be right back with our belongings."

"You are wise not to trust him."

I rose up and got our clothes, armor and other things, threw them all on the bed and took it down to Maddie. She laughed when I showed up with the bed. Then I went back and got our 10 chests of gold and brought them down.

"Before we change and go, let's go see something." She nodded and took my hand. We fast-traveled out to the East Road farmstead. We stepped off the acreage the duke wanted and raised two more farmsteads, then I changed the dirt road to a wide stone one extending ten miles to the east.

We went to the North Road area and did the same thing, creating four farmsteads and improved the road as well.

I figured it wouldn't be long before the duke heard about the new farmsteads and found tenants for them.

"Let's go get changed and go find Prince Kade."

Maddie clasped my hand, and we quickly traveled back to our vault, changed into our armor and returned the bed to the bedchamber.

"The chests of gold?"

I shrugged, "I'll come back for them later."

We clasped hands and left Vigil Castle.

CHAPTER 22

We found Prince Kade just arriving at Mid-Brook and I raised an overnight fort just short of the town for the companies to set up camp. Prince Kade rode forward, "is there trouble?"

"Not at the moment."

He saw Maddie and looked around, "the Crown Prince?"

"At Vigil Castle."

His face lost expression, "the King?"

"Has not yet arrived."

He shook his head looking at Maddie, "still the same Luke."

She nodded, "worse!"

"Well, it's good to see you two. We'll talk later." He rode to the center of the camp and watched as the companies arrived and moved into the fort in good order. You could tell they had done this maneuver plenty of times before.

I discreetly took Maddie's hand and dropped into the earth, creating a vault for us to change clothes in. This time I made chairs to sit on and a table to put clothes on. Once we had changed into our traveling clothes, I shrank my light armor to fit Maddie and put her in it. I really didn't need it with my armor ring.

When the camp settled, we went to the Command Wagon. We went inside and sat down. "So, he could not wait for father as instructed, he had to show he was in charge of an army."

"It's worse than that," Maddie said. "He ordered Ghost to leave and take what he came with. "He was angry that he could not attack the Hinterland Army right away."

He looked at me, "tell me all that has happened." I nodded and told him most of what we had done since we had seen him last. He listened, asking a few questions. When I finished, he just shook his head.

"Perhaps some time in the army would have done him good, as it did with me. Father will not be happy... how far away is he?"

"I don't know, we've only just arrived ourselves."

"If you would, Ghost, go see how far away he is. You don't have to speak to him, I would just like to know how long we must wait."

I nodded and looked at Maddie, "I'll be back." She nodded and kissed me.

I dropped into the earth and found the king and his army some three day's march away. But it was not as large as I had expected. His 10,000 men were only half the number that we were facing.

I went back and found the siblings laughing, so I eavesdropped. "Then he asked him where he wanted his five and a half sets of armor delivered!"

"He didn't!"

"He did!"

"Then he told him he also had five and a half warhorses" and Kade laughed all the harder.

"Our brother was NOT amused."

"And that's when he threw him out?"

"About then, yes. He could have handled that better, but it was worth it to see the expression on Luke's face. He was infuriated because Ghost is so obviously not afraid of him."

"My dear sister, from what I've seen, our Ghost isn't afraid of much of anything."

"He said he didn't like to kill, but he was good at it."

The Prince nodded, "the night they came to kill me, he took revenge on the Assassins' Guild. He probably killed fifty assassins, in their Guild house, in one night. He doesn't talk about it. I would say he is very good at it indeed."

I gave them a moment, then stuck my head into the wagon. "Three days march, ten thousand men or thereabouts."

The Prince frowned. "That gives us roughly 15,000 against 24,000. Not the best odds. We need to catch them at Vigil Castle, if the Crown Prince can hold his water."

***

"Sergeant Major Miller, have the quartermaster buy all he can of supplies here. I don't know when we'll get another chance and even if they have supplies, they will get expensive." I gave him a large purse.

"Yes sir, I'll send them straight away with escorts."

I traveled underground to the Hinterland's cattle herd, reached up through the ground and touched two cattle until they calmed. I pulled them under and they didn't struggle or make a sound. I delivered them to the cooks.

"How many to feed everyone fresh beef?" He looked at the cattle.

"One more will do, two would be better." I brought him two more.

I took advantage of the situation to expand my herd. I took two young bulls and thirty cows to the fields where my horses were grazing. I'd let them build a herd there and perhaps add more cows later.

The Sergeant Major found me later, "you were right, sir. Supplies are short and prices are high."

"Give me a list of things we are short on." He smiled and handed me a list.

I chuckled, taking the list. "I'll see what I can do." His list included the standard list of needs: beans, flour, salt, pork, beef, etc. I went back to the enemy's supply wagons, slipped up through their bottoms and found what we needed. By late afternoon I had filled his list.

The three of us ate together. "I see by our meal of beef you're up to your old tricks," the prince said.

"Those poor cows were lost and needed a home. The one you need to question is the cook. Those cows were fine when I left them!" We smiled as we enjoyed our meal.

"So, we rest and fatten up for three days, with scouts out?" I asked.

"That's the way I see it. We'll let my troublesome brother explain his own actions."

I introduce Maddie to Mare and unsurprisingly they took to each other right away. So, Maddie rode Mare and I rode Queen, traveling around each day to pass the time. I kept the companies in Hinterland beef and added another hundred to my herd.

Their army was on the move and would probably reach Vigil Castle a day before the King could, even if he marched straight through.

I traveled under to the enemy camp, but as I approached; it became harder for me to move through the earth. Surprised, I found that if I went deeper I could move freely but close to the surface was harder.

I realized they had brought in another mage to counter my moves against them. I could have forced my way through, but there was no need. I'd let him think he had shut me out, and maybe he had, they seemed to have found a powerful mage. But there was no need to challenge him directly now. I'd bide my time.

***

We sat down with Prince Kade at breakfast. "I was checking on our friends last night, but they have brought in a mage of their own to counter me."

He stopped eating and looked at me. "More powerful than you?"

"At least as powerful, but I don't know, I didn't push it. I let him think he had stopped me. I'll go back and challenge him later."

"That will make things more interesting." I nodded my head and continued eating.

He thought a moment. "Can you build a stone road from here to the king to speed his arrival?"

"I can, but it won't get done fast."

"Do it, once you get to him, start heading toward Vigil Castle with it."

I nodded, "I'd better get started." I dropped into the earth and flew under to Mid-brook, fixed in my mind what I wanted and started creating a road. I moved along, making the road as I went, traveling at about the speed that a fast man could run.

I stopped a half mile short of the king and his army, then fast-traveled back to Mid-Brook and started the road toward Vigil Castle. When I made it to Vigil Castle, I went back to the overnight fort. Then I had to sleep in the earth for a while to restore my strength.

I came up at dinnertime and ate. "You look tired." Maddie said.

"A little, that was a lot of road, and it's complete."

"Eat, them go rest."

I nodded, "After I've rested, I'm going back to see how strong the enemy mage is."

"Is that wise?"

"We need to know." She nodded and I sank down deep into the earth and went into a sound deep sleep.

***

When I awoke, I was rested and felt great, but was very hungry. I headed up to get something to eat, maybe Maddie or Kade would be ready to eat. I headed for the Command Wagon and found the King was there with Kade and Maddie. This was not good! When I went to sleep, the King was two days march from Mid-Brook.

I must have slept for two days! I didn't want to burst from the ground in front of them, so I started around back.

"You were supposed to control him!" said the king angrily.

That stopped me, and I started to listen.

"I had him under control until Luke showed up playing god." Maddie answered.

"I'll take care of Luke later. What I need to know is where Ghost is now. I need him to fight this war. I only brought 10,000 men, because Ghost was going to do all the fighting for us."

"I don't know, we haven't seen him for two days, when he said the Hinterlanders had a powerful mage now and he needed to see how powerful he was. Nothing since then."

The king looked at Kade, "Did he say anything to you?"

Kade was staring at them. "What have you done? Did you marry Ghost to control him? You weren't in love with him? This was all about you, wasn't it, Maddie?"

"We did what we had to do," the king answered for her. "There hasn't been a mage in our kingdom for generations. We needed to tie him to us... think of all the things he can do for us."

"Yes, it was about me!" she burst out. "All I had waiting for me was swampland or some fat old man for a husband. G-host was an opportunity to change that. With him I could make the Southern District into a Garden of Eden. Marriage for us is not about love, it's about power, wealth or alliances. You have to make the best deal you can. Well, I did! He'll do what we want him to father, I promise, or I'll make his life a living hell."

When she said that I remembered the "Grandmother" that had betrayed me for a small purse of money. She had said I was too trusting, and I guess she was right.

"He was doing all that we asked out of friendship and mutual benefit. Why go through all this manipulation and betrayal?" asked the prince.

"We could not risk losing him to someone else, or some other kingdom. We had to secure him with a marriage." The

King answered.

"You don't know what you've done. You are not dealing with some weak-minded courtier."

"I will bring him to heel," Maddie said confidently.

"When he finds out you've betrayed his trust, you'll be lucky if he doesn't kill the bunch of you."

"He would never dare such a thing!" Maddie said.

Kade laughed. "You really do not understand who you are dealing with. Let me enlighten you to some facts about Ghost.

"Ghost, which is his real name by the way, was a thief in the Criminal Guild. They wanted him to kill me to get out of some trouble he was in with them over a theft or share of a theft. But before he killed me, he found out they betrayed him, double crossed him, and were going to kill both of us.

"Do you know what he did? He killed them. Not just the ones who masterminded the betrayal, he killed them all, everyone in that Guild House."

"When they later sent assassins, he saved me and slaughtered all eight trained killers.

" Sir Edwin offered him friendship and a new life away from the guilds, and Ghost accepted his offer. When they destroyed Sir Edwin's house, killing that gallant old man, he killed them, all of them.

"Then moved on to kill everyone in the Assassins' Guild house, every assassin in there. I told you he had killed fifty of them, and I was telling you the truth. There is no more Assassins' Guild in the capital, because he wiped them out."

"When he found out who had betrayed him, which was the Top-man in the local Criminal Guild House, he killed all of them. Everyone in the Guild House. All of them. Are you seeing a pattern here? He told you he did not like to kill, but he is good at it. Well, sister mine, I can guarantee that if he feels you have betrayed him, and he decides to kill you for it, you are DEAD. With his powers there is nothing anyone can do to stop him."

"I'll tell you Ghost is not a fighter, though he is good at

it. He is not a warrior. He is a killer. What's the difference, you may wonder? A warrior or fighter will fight you straight on, kind of even odds. A killer just kills, efficiently, quickly, anyway he can, and moves on. That is what your conniving ways have bought you. You'll be lucky if you live to be married to a fat old man."

Neither one spoke, stunned to silence as the prince shook his head in sorrow and shock.

"Surely, he will listen to reason." Maddie said.

"Reason is what you should have used before you went ahead with this farce of a marriage."

"He will lose his lands, his titles, his wealth," the king said.

"Father, he's a mage, he can make his own lands, and he does not care about titles, which he proved when he gave them up to be the Princess' Consort. As for wealth, do you know where he keeps his wealth? In my vaults, for me to use as my own. He doesn't care about those things. He's a thief and he can always get more."

"If Ghost is dead, I mourn the loss of a true friend, and you should rejoice that you outlived him. But then you have to worry about fighting a 25,000-man army with just 15,000 men. But if he's not dead, and he finds out that you've betrayed him... You won't have to worry about fighting that army. That problem will fall to someone else."

Kade stood up and bowed, "Sire," and stepped out the door.

"Where are you going?"

He stopped and looked back. "To my company... we have a war to prepare for. If I lead them well enough, some of us may survive." He turned and walked away.

The king and the princess sat in shock. "What are we going to do?" she asked

"If Ghost comes back, act normal, we need him to win this war. After that, we'll try to reason with him to make him see we did it for the betterment of the kingdom."

"And if that doesn't work?"

"Kill him before he kills us."

"What if he is already dead?"

"Then my daughter, you'd better practice your Hinterlandish for your new husband."

The King walked out of the Command Wagon and Maddie slammed the door, screaming.

CHAPTER 23

I lay there in the earth for a while thinking, or rather trying not to think. I decided I would not kill them, but I would not help them further. I went over to Maddie's armor and weapons and removed the runes from them, returning them to their weaker state.

I found Mare and took her down into a vault with some hay, grateful that she stayed perfectly calm despite her unusual surroundings. I left Queen for now, since taking her would be a giveaway I was still alive.

I flew under to Vigil Castle and retrieved my ten chests of gold, bringing them back to the vault, then putting them into my backpack, which I closed, folded and put back in my pouch.

If the king's army left now, I figured, it would take them two days to reach Vigil Castle, which gave me that much time to plan and take care of things before any fighting would start.

As far as I was concerned, the king, Maddie, and the crown prince were on their own. They made this pot of soup, let them eat it!

On the other hand, I cared deeply about Prince Kade, Duke Mathew and his family, and my Black Stag Company.

My big problem at the moment was their mage. I didn't know how strong he was and where his king might send him to attack. If he were to attack the castle — and if I was their king that is what I'd have him do — he would have to go. If that gave him a chance to kill me, he would, another reason I would have to deal with him.

If he was a normal person, I'd just pull him under, but I didn't think that would work. So, I would have to distract him in order to kill him before he killed me. Perhaps, use stone dogs to distract, some steel through his throat, then under? Or just figure out a way to take his head, and that would be the end of that.

I wondered if he would talk, maybe make a deal... but I couldn't. So that was that, he's definitely got to go.

***

I checked my armor, weapons and face guard locked in place. There could be no mistakes — one false move could very well mean my death. I'd like to avoid that event for as long as possible.

I moved underground to the rear of the enemy army and started moving toward the mage. As soon as I began sensing resistance, I stopped, backed away and found an empty tent in which to rise.

Then I took on the guise of one of their common soldiers, left the tent and started walking toward the mage's area. I didn't feel any resistance or other feeling of power, but I wasn't taking anything for granted.

Then I sat down and leaned against a wagon wheel like many other soldiers were doing and concentrated. I readied 20 large stone dogs ... 10 to cause chaos in the area and 10 to attack the mage directly, distracting him or her. I rose and walked toward the tent that I sensed held the mage, and when I was halfway there, I raised the dogs and turned them loose.

When the dogs started barking and attacking people, I ran, shouting like everyone else. I had made it to the mage's tent when he came out and the dogs attacked. He was holding his own, using lightning bolts to strike the stone dogs and keep them away. Disregarding me as just another soldier, he stepped past, chanting and casting lightnings.

Time slowed for me, and as I drew my sword, my runes glowed. He must have sensed something and started to look back, but it was too late and my sword took his head off smoothly at his shoulders.

Quickly I pulled his head and body under the earth as several residual lightning bolts hit me. But my rings held them off, for the most part and I was able to remain conscious.

Then I concentrated on the dying mage, *teach me.* He knew he was dying, and he fought me to keep me from taking his knowledge. We struggled, but he finally succumbed. The power of his mind and the depth of his knowledge jolted me. It was overwhelming and I almost blacked out.

I ordered the dogs to run away, keep causing trouble then go back to the earth. When my mind began to clear, I searched his body and took every artifact he had, leaving his naked husk of a body there. I needed healing from the lightning bolts; even with my ring, since they had burned me severely. I pulled down a few bodies the dogs had wounded and took their life force, using it to heal myself.

When I was healed, I assumed the mage's likeness and rose just outside his pavilion. Frightened, none of the soldiers would even look at me. I stepped inside the pavilion. The inside of the tent was much larger than the outside — my new knowledge of magic called it a "dimensional pocket." It was much, in fact, like my backpack and pouch. I closed the flaps on the pavilion and once closed it was like locking a door. The only way in was to use the door, you could not come through the sides, even though they seemed to be simple canvas. No one would bother me, since everyone had feared the mage, but I raised two large stone dogs to guard me, just in case.

I walked around examining my new home. It felt odd; I knew what everything was, even though this was my first time seeing it. The pavilion had four rooms... a main room where the mage would meet people was also the dining room with a table and chairs. Then there was an office, with a desk, chair, and all his working papers and account books.

There was a bedchamber with a big bed, clothes cabinets, and dressers. The fourth room was a storage room. To my surprise, what at first appeared to be a short hall or closet was actually a double stairway, with one set of steps going up, another down into a basement!

Downstairs was more storage, a dungeon and stables, with a doorway leading outside. Upstairs was a library with maps and works of art on the walls. Sir Edwin would have loved this! The mage must have spent a lot of time on the road. I "remembered" that he was a traveling magician, moving from job to job.

I went back downstairs and opened the stable, fast-traveling to Mare I brought her to the stable. I put her into a stall and watched as hay, oats, and water magically filled the troughs. I had to go back and get her armor. When I returned, I closed and sealed the curtain wall.

I looked around for a treasure vault, and found it in the bed chamber, along with a privy and a bath with hot running water. Well, I thought, if you had to be on the road, you might as well be comfortable!

I went to the dining room table and sat at its head as food appeared on the table — hot, freshly cooked food. I had not realized how hungry I was until I saw it.

I knew the Hinterland camp would move in the morning and I needed to be gone by then. How to do it was the question.

I went to the office and found the dead mage's Staff of Power behind the desk in a stand. It was a richly colored wooden staff with a silvered blue stone within a twisted wood knot at the top. It was at the same time plain, yet beautiful. I held it and concentrated on sinking the whole pavilion into the earth.

Once safely within the earth, I placed the Staff of Power back in its stand and went to the bedchambers. One of the stone dogs followed me for guard duty so I took a hot bath and went to bed, where I fell into a deep restful sleep.

***

When I awoke, I realized I had slept eighteen hours. And,

since the pavilion had been in the earth, my strength was re-stored and I was totally healed. I seemed to have completed the mage's information assimilation.

It was dinnertime and I had to get going... I had things to do. I reached for my clothes and stopped. They had been washed and folded. I shrugged my shoulders, "more mage magic."

I got dressed, ate, and went to find if the enemy army had moved. I went out through the front door of the pavilion and sealed it behind me, leaving the dogs inside on guard.

I moved under the Hinterland king's pavilion and eaves-dropped as they discussed battle plans.

"The mage, when he returns," the king was saying, "will open the castle's gate and freeze it open. When that happens, our center force will rush their defensive line in front of the gate. Everyone else will follow as they break through and cap-ture the castle. Our remaining forces will turn left and right and roll-up the defensive lines."

Good luck with that!" I thought, then moved to where King John and his army were on the move. Maddie was riding with him on Queen, who looked tired. For that matter, Maddie didn't look very good either, that caused me to smile. I then found Kade and the mercenary companies following as rear guards, which on reflection was probably the safest place for them.

Taking a quick detour, I fast-traveled back to the army's last overnight fort and sank it back into the earth, leaving not a trace. Perhaps my mistake was in giving things away too quickly, at least that was what the mage's memories, coupled with my own experiences, were telling me.

I fast-traveled back to my new pavilion and dressed in my armor. I started to put on my helmet and face mask but then decided on a change. I ran my hand over it and added an upper portion that covered my whole face. The upper part was now black dragon glass that was unbreakable. I donned it and went downstairs to get Mare.

Before I put her armor on, I changed it to look like dragon armor. We rose to the surface and I quickly to the office and got the Staff of Power. I raised my pavilion, stepped outside, and touched it with the staff, *close!*

The pavilion folded down, then began to swirl like sheets of paper driven by a magical wind. When it stopped, a book lay on the ground. I picked it up and slipped it into my pouch along with the powerful staff.

"Mare, let's go watch the show, and of course, we have to take care of Kade and the companies." Mare snorted. I smiled, "you're going to have to do better holding up your side of the conversation!" I had never tried to travel underground while mounted, but I might need to someday, so I slowly eased us under. She stayed calm, so I moved us forward slowly with no problems.

We fast-traveled to the overnight fort I had sunk, to find an enemy force of some 500 mounted lancers heading toward Kade and the companies. I slipped along until I found our rear scouts and came up just out of sight, put a guise of my old armor on and approached a scout.

"Good to see you back, captain!"

"Well, tell no one I'm back, I have other work to do. Get back to the company and tell them there is a mounted lancer force of 500 headed their way. They need to prepare for the attack."

"Yes, captain!" He turned his mount and galloped toward the army.

I trotted along on Mare, knowing she needed her exercise. We sank into the ground just before arriving at Kade's ambush point, set up just around a curve in the road. To help, I made the brush thicker along the sides of the approach road.

He had dismounted one company and would use them as pike men, to stop the cavalry. Their pikes were longer than the Hinterland lances. His archers were behind them on the left and right flanks. He had his cavalry in the middle rear. There were no lights showing among our men so the enemy would run headlong into our pike men.

I came up in back of the companies and no one noticed me as they were all watching the road. I pulled my staff out of my pouch, its crystal quiet and dark. I eased Mare up beside Kade.

"Did you miss me?" I asked.

He looked at me and smiled, "why, did you go somewhere?" We both chuckled. He looked at my new staff, "I see you've been up to your old tricks again."

"What? this old thing? It was just lying there, I mean come on, that hardly counts."

"I don't suppose the previous owner needed it anymore."

"He did not."

He laughed, "it's good to have you back, brother." I smiled.

I raised a four-foot stone wall bristling with sharp points in front of our men.   Men with lances raised them and waited for any enemies who made it over the wall.

"When you are ready," I told Kade, "give the word and I'll drop the pike wall and light the road in front of us."

He nodded, "when they run into the barrier, give us light."

It wasn't long before we heard horses coming, not at a gallop but at a good trot. Silently we waited, and then their first ranks hit the pike wall without breaking stride. The first several rows piled up on top of each other before man or horse could react.

I raised my staff, sending a fireball above the road and lighting the whole area.   No orders had to be given to these professional soldiers. The archers started loosing their armor-piercing arrows as soon as I gave them light, slaughtering those within range. The lancers speared all who got over the wall.

I raised and released 10 stone lions on each side of the rear of their force. Panicked horses and men started screaming and dying as they tried to escape through the brush at the sides of the road, That drove the rear forces harder into the front ranks, who found themselves packed so tightly that they could not fight.

Our ambush had completely blunted their attack and they were finished.

"Lower the wall," Kade ordered. I dropped it into the earth and our companies surged into the decimated enemy.

I pulled my lions back and used them as containment, and before long the army had surrendered. We had taken eight knights and 162 prisoners, while our losses were light: just 16 killed and 30 wounded. Their task completed, my lions went back to earth.

I slipped my staff back with my pouch, let the guise of my old armor fall away and my dragon armor now appeared. No one questioned me as I sat beside the Prince.

Eight knights surrendered to Prince Kade to be ransomed, giving their parole and they were allowed to keep their swords. Two of our companies stayed on guard. The others stripped our fallen, laying them out beside the road.

At sunrise, before we left, I rode Mare to the ranks of the dead. "Honored dead," I amplified my voice. "You fought well, go to your rest in peace." Stone crypts formed over each body and took them into the earth.

Behind me the three companies shouted, "Aa-ooh! Aa-ooh! Aa-ooh!"

I turned and rode forward and took my place beside the Prince, glancing down at Hound. "I see you still have that dog."

"Not me, that's Beast's dog. We just feed him." We laughed.

We had just started back when we saw riders... a handful of knights and some 50 lancers, approaching. We reined-up and waited for them.

"Why have you fallen behind?" barked their leader. "I think you'll find..." that was as far as I got.

Then he saw the knights that had surrendered to Kade. "You will turn those prisoners over to me!" He shouted. Faster than he could react, I drew my sword and in one motion smoothly slashed the crest from his helm.

"If you interrupt me again, your head will be on the ground beside that useless crest." He looked at the ground, feeling the top of his helm and no one moved.

"As I was saying," I continued, "allow me to introduce the Duke of the Western District, Prince Kade, who is also commander of the Black Stag mercenary company."

He looked at the prince. "My apologies, your highness," he said as he bowed his head, "I did not know."

"Not to worry, Sir Knight, there are many upon the field this day. You must forgive Captain Drake," he cut his eyes at me, "his blood is still up from the battle. They attacked our rear guard with 500 cavalry. We are catching up now."

"Yes, Your Highness, I will take the word." He looked at me, "Elias Drake?"

I shook my head, "No, that would be my brother." Kade smiled. "I'm Captain Elijah Drake." He looked me up and down, marking me. He nodded.

He bowed to Prince Kade, "Your Highness."

"Sir Knight." He turned his horse and led his force back the way he came and we moved out, following the army.

"You can't kill everyone." Kade said.

"What? Is that a new rule?" He smiled. "I won't have to, only half. After that, the other half will leave me alone."

His face lost expression. "The king and my sister?"

"Last I saw them, they were fine. As far as they are concerned, Sir Draugur died fighting the enemy mage. Since I'm dead, I don't have to take revenge. I think Sir Edwin would have liked my remedy to the problem. On the bright side, I don't have to pay taxes anymore since I have no titles or lands. I'm just a poor mercenary Captain." I laughed, and after a pause to digest the idea, he joined me.

"I'll catch up with you later — there is something I have to do." I turned out of the formation and headed back down the road, sliding underground, once I was out of sight we fast-traveled to the valley where my herds were and came up overlooking the valley pasture. I dismounted and stripped off Mare's armor.

"Today is your lucky day. You are being retired. Go make me some great warhorses." She looked at me, then toward the grazing herd. I could almost see her shrug her shoulders as she trotted away toward the herd.

I took my staff and my pavilion book out of my pouch. I laid the book on the ground and touched my staff to it. *Open! * The book opened, and pages began flying around in a whirlwind, and my pavilion formed itself.

I took Mare's armor down to the stable and put it away, thinking I might need it again someday. My stone dogs were still on guard duty. As I put the armor in the storage room, I saw there was a set of heavy horse armor stored in there already.

I began to think. If I were a mage with a magic pavilion that included a stable and heavy horse armor, wouldn't I have a war horse? Or another sort of magic beast? I searched the mage's memories but found only a vague memory of an animal that wasn't his, but had belonged to an earlier mage.

I took my staff out and concentrated on the stables to see if anything happened. After a moment I remembered a book up in the library, I went up the stairs and found it.

It was a reference book of enchanted beasts, many of which I had never heard of — or could even imagine. I lay the book on the table and sat down, and was startled when it started flipping pages on its own. It stopped at horses and riding beasts.

I addressed the book: "I need a horse or something like it to ride on a battlefield. It needs to have instincts and intelligence, not like a drone. It needs to be strong, quick and have endurance, like a warhorse only better."

Pages began to turn, then stopped at the title, "Talon Footed Dragon Horse." A drawing showed an animal with the shape and head of a horse but with horns. It was heavily scaled, and had a mouth full of teeth like a dragon.

It had talons on its front feet and hoofs in the rear. It was thickly scaled on the chest, shoulders and rear. It was also scaled and bony on the backsides of its legs protecting its tendons. Its tail was like a dragon's, ending with what looked like short feathers but were actually long slim sharp scales.

The book said it ate both vegetables and meat, what it called an "omnivore."

The description continued: "Although heavily muscled, they are extremely fast and capable of quick movements and strikes with their mouths, talons, and tail. Their endurance is exceptional, having no equal in the equine species. They are extremely intelligent and intuitive. Their relationship is more of a partnership rather than subservient.

"I think that is what I'm looking for!" I suddenly felt the need to touch the staff to the page, did so, and watched the blue stone in the staff glow briefly. I waited a moment, but nothing else happened, so I shrugged and put the book back on the shelf.

I was getting hungry so I went down to the main floor and sat at the table, waited until food appeared and ate. When I had finished, I said to myself, "just out of curiosity, let's go look." As I started downstairs to the stable, I heard noises and as I reached the bottom of the stairs I saw there, in the stall, my new black and red Talon Footed Dragon Horse.

CHAPTER 24

The beast raised her head from the feed trough as I approached and her nostrils flared as she tasted my scent. The runes in my hand glowed for a moment and she quieted. She was a big as any warhorse I had ever seen, muscular, but streamlined, and she looked fast standing still.

She came and stuck her head over the fence, putting her head against my chest. I scratched behind her ears and she gave a contented rumble, just like a cat, if the cat weighed 2,000 pounds! She looked like the drawing in the book, and her talons were huge, powerful enough to take a man down with one swipe or tear a horse to shreds.

I went to the storage room to get her heavy armor, thinking I'd probably have to change it to make it fit. But what I found was a completely different set of armor, only medium weight, but I figured that, since she was naturally armored, this was all she needed.

It was good armor but had no power runes inscribed on it, so I gathered it all together and took it through the floor deep into the earth. Using the metals and minerals I needed, as the runes in my hands began to glow and my rings became warm. I held my concentration until the runes stopped glowing and the rings cooled.

I took the armor back up to the pavilion stable and saw that it matched her coloring and scales. "Excellent!" I thought, when I saw that the inside of the armor was covered in runes. Harbinger came, sniffed it, and seemed to approve.

The name "Harbinger" had come to my mind unbidden and seemed for some reason to fit her. More importantly, I liked it. She stood still as I put on and adjusted her armor fitting her head and face guards perfectly around her horns.

Once I finished, she checked my work, shaking and stretching. She stood on her hind legs and stretched out her front legs, striking with her talons. She stood back down on all fours, then kicked out with her hind hooves. When she finished, she stood still, apparently approving the fit.

I opened the wall curtain and walked her out into the earth, led her around a minute on the surface and then mounted her. We rode around a bit, allowing her to become accustomed to me. We moved to a trot, then I gave her a small tap with my heels and she took off at a full gallop. Reading the words "fast and quick" in the a book was nothing compared to riding her when it happened!

I rode her around for a while, then lowered us into the earth and went back into the pavilion. I took off her armor, brushed her hair and scrubbed her scales and she enjoyed the attention.

I decided I needed to change my whole appearance with a new heavy set of dragon armor to match hers. "I need a set of heavy armor to match Harbinger's." I said out loud to the pavilion. Nothing seemed to happened, but thought I'd look around when I finished with Harbinger.

I made sure she had food and water, and I went upstairs to eat. There was always plenty of food on the table. When I finished, I went to my bedchamber and I found a set of dragon armor standing in the corner that matched Harbinger's. It was not heavy, more of a medium, which weighed no more than my light armor.

The helm was a horned dragon face made of black dragon glass that actually looked a lot like Harbinger's face. I could see through the dragon glass, so I lost no visibility with the helmet design.

I changed into it, and found it fit perfectly with no binding, and it didn't slow any of my movements. My sigil, displayed on my shield and banner, was a rampant dragon. This was the new look of Captain Sir Elijah Drake.

***

After I dressed Harbinger in her armor, we moved up and I closed the pavilion and put the book in my pouch. Then we dropped into the earth and fast-traveled to the place where I had last seen Prince Kade. We soon caught up with him and the companies and found they had caught up with the army and were once again set as their rear guard.

Since Sir Draugur was "dead", I needed a new guise, so I made my hair darker and added a close-trimmed beard. Feeling a bit theatrical, I added a scar that ran from my forehead over my right eye and down past my mouth. I made my right eye white but could still see out of it. I modeled this new face on that of my old friend Dane, the guard from the guild. The girls always said he was handsome. The hair close to my scar, I made white, then put light burn scars on my left hand and finally made my voice deeper.

As I was checking everything, I realized this was not a normal illusion, but real, so there was no need to worry about how close people got or some errant spell seeing through my disguise.

The companies had stopped for the day and set up their rearguard position on the road. Once it got darker, we rose between the Command Wagon and my old wagon. As I took off my helm and started taking off Harbinger's armor, Prince Kade appeared and walked up to us.

"I like the look, 'Captain Drake.' "

"How did you know?"

"Who else would be out here unsaddling a warhorse?" I had to laugh.

"Have you eaten?"

"Not yet."

"Let's go get something, so the companies get to see their captain, Sir Elijah Drake, with me."

I nodded, "good idea."

We got our food and returned to the Command Wagon and talked strategy over dinner. "We move up tomorrow, and the leading element has reached Vigil Castle." Kade said. "We'll be acting as right flank rear guard and reserve."

"I would have thought they would have placed you in a more honorable position."

He shook his head. "My brother, the Crown Prince, is jealous. Don't forget that I have actually served in the army and in combat. He doesn't want me near the front, and I think he's afraid I may steal his glory."

"I wonder if he'll feel the same when the killing starts."

"Who knows? He has his own idea of how things should be, and reality has no bearing on them."

There was a commotion on our perimeter and one of our men came running up, shouting "the King approaches."

We stood and waited, and when he arrived, the crown prince, and Maddie were with him, surrounded by their personal guards.

"Sire."

"Have you seen him?" the king was agitated.

"I have not." Prince Kade answered.

"You believe he is dead, then?"

"I do, if he was coming back, he would have by now."

I was watching Maddie out of the corner of my eye, noticing that she was looking intently at me and I could tell she was suspicious.

She stepped forward, "Brother, introduce us to your knight."

"This is Captain Sir Elijah Drake. Captain, my sister, Princess Maddison."

I bowed, "Your Highness."

"May I touch your face, Captain Drake? The scar, does it hurt?"

Oh, she was suspicious all right! "No longer, Your Highness." She touched my scar, ensuring it was real and not an illusion.

"Do you know Sir Draugur, Captain?"

"I did. He gave me my sight back and I see things much more clearly now."

She drew back, looking at me strangely.

I pointed to the white eye, "this eye was dead and he used magic to make it see again."

She nodded and turned away.

"Drake?" The crown prince said, laughing, "are you the one who cut the crest off Sir Stallings helm?"

Prince Kade jumped in before I could say anything. "He is," he said, "Sir Stallings was being rude. Captain Drake has little patience for rudeness. Sir Stallings didn't recognize me and was being disrespectful."

"And what if he comes looking for satisfaction, Captain Drake?" The crown prince asked.

"Then I shall pay someone to bury his body, Your Highness." His jaws tightened.

"We will all have more than enough killing by this time tomorrow," the King said.

He turned and walked away, his party following him. We sat back down, finishing our food in silence.

***

We were up early the next morning, eating an early breakfast and moving out within the hour. As we assumed the right flank rear guard position, I added fifty yards of thick brush and briers behind us. We were on a bit of a rise and could see a lot of the battlefield. We dismounted, knowing nothing would happen for a while, and agreeing to rest the horses, knowing we would need them later.

The sergeant major joined us. "So now we wait. Hopefully, the kings will bluster a bit and then come to an arrangement and then we can all go home."

"How often does that actually happen? I asked.

"About half the time, providing neither loses their temper. If that happens, of course, we'll fight. How hard and long depends on how mad they get... and how big an army they have."

He moved on down the line checking the troops.

"In that case I hope my brother doesn't go out to meet with the King's group. He has the unique gift of making anyone hate him almost instantly."

I chuckled.

"You have an illusion on your horse, don't you?"

"How can you tell?"

"Her foot prints. The front ones are not hooves."

"Ah! Yes, you're right."

"What is she?"

"She is a Talon Footed Dragon Horse."

He looked at me, "is that a real thing or did you just pull that out of your behind?" .

"Of course, it's a real thing, I'm not smart enough to make that up."

"OK you got me there, you AREN'T that smart."

We chuckled and Harbinger nodded her head in seeming agreement.

"You had better keep her, whatever she is, she's way smarter than you." We laughed.

"Movement up front!" someone yelled.

We looked out over the field to where two parties approached each other under white flags and then talked for a while.

The king had set our main force up with one end anchored on the castle's main gate. The Hinterland army stretched from the river to the forest, and their ranks were deeper than ours. The castle was our biggest advantage.

After a time, the two parties separated and returned to their respective lines and we remounted in case we had to move. There was more activity at the front, and a cheer went up.

Someone rode from our army onto the open field between the two armies, his lance held high. I could not make out the banner, but he was apparently issuing a challenge to single combat to the other side. There was chanting coming from both armies.

"That arrogant fool!" Kade said, as I realized that it was the crown prince who was issuing the challenge.

"Sergeant Major, you have command until we return."

"Yes, sir."

Prince Kade looked at me, "let's go join the fool's party." We headed out and arrived just as the crown princes' challenge was answered by a Hinterland champion.

I watched as their champion rode to the far end of the field, and my powers showed me that both the knight and his steed were wearing armor festooned with power runes.

When they were both ready, they spurred their horses, who leaped into action. They were both at a full gallop when their lances struck shields. Both lances shattered from the impact, which ripped the crown prince from his saddle. Landing hard, he did not move.

Their champion went back to his side and raised his visor, signaling his downed opponent could be helped. The medicos and pages rushed out and clustered around his still body.

The king sat stone faced as they took the prince off the field, indicating that he was not dead... yet.

When the field was clear, the Hinterland champion lowered his visor and rode along their lines to their cheers. Then he turned toward ours and rode down our line, reined up in front of the king, and barked, "challenge!"

He knew the king would not accept; the challenge was intended as an additional insult.

I saw Prince Kade tense, but before he could answer, I yelled, "answered!" as I walked Harbinger out onto the field. Their champion nodded and rode back to his end of the field.

"Lance!" I called.

Kade brought me one. "What are you doing?"

"His and his horse's armor are runed and he is using magic to enhance his skill. I'm the only one that has a chance of defeating him."

Kade looked across the field at their champion, knotting his jaw in anger. "Then kill him and let's get on with this."

"That is exactly what I intend to do!"

He handed me the lance, "luck, brother."

I nodded and rode to the other end of the field.

As I rode, my runes glowed, locking me into my saddle. I strengthened and hardened my jousting lance. I got the distinct feeling that Harbinger had done this before. As we trotted out, she nodded, and I smiled behind my visor.

I reached my starting place and turned toward their champion. He lowered his lance as his mount leaped toward me.

Harbinger and I waited calmly as they thundered towards us. We were forcing his steed to use more of his endurance and strength to run further, and then, when he reached the halfway point, I felt Harbinger gathering herself. She didn't rear, just dug her talons into the earth and accelerated, reaching a full gallop in three strides.

Time slowed for me. The distance between us was closing fast and I leaned into my lance aiming for his chest. Then I saw him change his aiming point to Harbinger's chest, but at the last second Harbinger used a taloned foot to deflect his lance over and up missing us both.

My lance held true as it struck his chest, breaking through his rune's magic and plunging into his chest and out his back. Skewered, he hit the ground and did not move.

I could tell he was dead.

I had started to turn when an arrow hit me in the back but did not penetrate my armor. Harbinger whirled, and I caught a second arrow on my shield, deflecting it.

Both armies shouted at this treachery. The two archers were standing at the Hinterland king's pavilion and were notching their next arrows when two stone dogs rose from the ground, attacking and eating them alive as the army gasped.

No one moved to stop the dogs or me as I rode to the enemy pavilion. The Hinterland king stepped forward, scowling. "The dogs can stop now — I think you've made your point."

"I wasn't making a point, that was the punishment for shooting me in the back. But they were under your orders..." That was as far as the king let me get.

"You bore me, boy! Go back to your king so your betters can conclude our business."

Harbinger's guise dropped and she roared as I ordered 1,000 snarling war dogs to rise from the ground. A giant dragon rose from the river, screaming its challenge, as I sank Hinterland's king to his waist into the ground.

Neither army moved... both were stunned. "You interrupt me again and I'll be dealing with your heir, the next king." He had turned white with fear.

"Do something!" he shouted, "help your king!" I waited, but no one came to his defense and he sagged in defeat.

I dismounted Harbinger, "as I was saying, those men were under your orders, so the dishonor is on you. You have one hour to reach a settlement with King John. If, after one hour, no settlement is reached I'll kill you and deal with your son."

"You!" I pointed to a nearby soldier, "ride over to the other side and ask King John to come over." He nodded and rode out, waving a white flag.

The two blood-covered dogs that had eaten the archers moved over and sat staring at the half-buried king.

I took out my staff and changed to a mage guise — you know, standard stuff: an old man with long gray hair, in dark blue and red robes, with crazy blue eyes.

King John arrived and walked into the pavilion, and before he could speak, I sank him down to his waist into the ground next to the Hinterland ruler.

"Now you both have a motive to reach a settlement and end this. You have one hour to settle, or I'll kill the two of you and deal with your sons."

"If they can't settle, I'll make myself King of Hinterland, then take my army home.

"Your time starts now."

"Can't you do anything with him? He's your mage." King Manfred sputtered.

"He's not MY mage!"

"I'm no one's mage. I'm my own. No one owns me ... and you're wasting time." I walked out.

After thirty minutes of yelling and cursing, resulting in no meaningful negotiations, I sank them to their armpits and made the ground warmer. That got them started talking seriously. With fifteen minutes left, I dropped them down to their necks. But with two minutes left, there still was no agreement.

I looked at the two dogs, saying "dig them up, then eat them!" The dogs jumped up and started digging, throwing dirt everywhere.

The kings were screaming and shouting.

"Wait! Wait!"

I let the dogs stop, "you have something to say before I serve lunch?"

"We agree!"

"What is the agreement?"

"Hinterland will give King John ten new ships, five warships and five cargo ships." I nodded and looked at King John.

"Princess Maddison will marry their Prince."

"When will the wedding take place?"

"When the ten ships are delivered."

"Not good enough, they will marry today."

"Impossible! You can't expect a princess to marry in one day," King John blustered.

I knelt down and looked at him. My eyes turned red, the war dogs started growling and barking and the dragon screamed even louder and moved toward the pavilion. "Isn't that exactly what you did to the boy named Ghost, oh great and honorable King John?"

He looked at the ground. "Very well, they will marry today."

"King Manfred, you shall remain here at Vigil Castle until your navy delivers the ten new ships to Port West Gate."

He nodded, "agreed."

I turned to one of the pages standing nearby, nervously eyeing the dogs. "Send word and have your prince brought here. You," I pointed to another, "send word to have Princess Madison come as well."

The two nodded and left.

CHAPTER 25

Prince Manfred II of Hinterland returned within minutes. Not surprisingly, Princess Maddison took longer. When she walked into the pavilion escorted by Prince Kade she was in a rage. But seeing her father buried up to his neck in the ground quickly snapped her out of it.

Before she could say anything, he announced, "You are to marry Prince Manfred as part of our settlement."

She blinked her eyes several times. "I cannot, I am already married!"

"Your husband is dead, Princess," I said.

"How can you be so sure?"

"Because I killed him, along with the other mage. You had killed his heart and I killed his body."

She abruptly sat down on the ground, tears running down her face. "We have no priest." she whimpered.

"Your father, as king of the realm, will tie the knot."

She hung her head. I raised the kings up from the ground and gave King John the royal blue rope. As the prince and the princess stepped forward, facing the king, Kade moved closer to me, observing the ceremony.

King John tied the special knot. "As your father, and King of the Realm I pronounce you man and wife. You may kiss the bride." As he did, her eyes said she was elsewhere.

"At least he's not old and fat," Kade muttered for my ears, and I secretly smiled. News quickly spread through the armies of the settlement, and cheers went up as celebrations started.

While everyone's attention was on the newly married couple, I quickly sank the stone dogs, the dragon, Harbinger and myself into the ground.

***

There was a celebration in Vigil Castle that night, but of course I was not invited. I assumed the newlyweds consummated their vows, that is, unless she killed him, which I doubted. It was late the following day when Prince Kade returned to the company and joined me in the Command Wagon for dinner.

"How was the celebration?"

"Not much happiness. The only good thing to come out of this," he stopped and looked at me. "Well, one of the good things to come out of this was there is no war. You saved a lot of lives by intervening. I am truly sorry about what happened between you and Maddie."

I shrugged my shoulders, "better to find out early, rather than later, after we had children." We left it at that.

"King Manfred became a guest of Vigil Castle until they deliver the promised ships."

"Unless his son decides now is a good opportunity to make himself king and keeps his ships and his new queen."

Prince Kade laughed, "what an irony that would be!" He became somber. "My brother's injuries were, as you know, too great for the medicos to save him. That makes Mathew Crown Prince. I suppose, in the grand scheme of things, that's better for the kingdom. He will remain at Vigil Castle until his succession to the throne."

"My father and half of the army leaves on the morrow, taking Luke home for burial. I have been ordered to return with him, and it seems I have fallen from favor. He apparently blames me for not helping keep Ghost under control. I predict he is about to strip lands from me to pay his army for coming to fight for him, as he has no ready gold. He had hoped to take King Manfred's gold."

"Half of Hinterland's army left for home this morning, and I'm told Prince Manfred and Maddison will follow with the other half of their army by week's end. Once they have departed, the rest of our army will go back to the capital."

"Then back to Port West Gate?"

"Who can say? The succession has not changed for me and I may be sent back to the army." We moved outside and cared for our horses. Harbinger loved the attention. Then we looked to our equipment's repair and care. Those chores done, we sat outside by our fire and I brought out a bottle of wine.

"What took you so long?"

"You always get into trouble when you drink."

"Not always, I didn't last night."

"Why, did the king threaten you?"

"Of course, not... The duchess did." We laughed and I poured the wine.

"Oh, I forgot!" said Kade. "The king is looking for the 'Crazy Mage'. I think he wants to hire him." I chuckled.

"What are your plans, brother?"

I shrugged my shoulders, "I guess that's up to you, I'm still sworn to you."

He shook his head, thinking, "no longer, I release you from your bond. But I hope our friendship remains."

"Our friendship was never in danger and remains strong. Truth be told, you are my only friend. What of Black Stag Keep?"

"We must wait and see what the king decides about my lands. What of the Black Stag Mercenary Company?"

"My suggestion would be to use Black Stag Keep as a training area for the company, keeping it as your army and guards at your castle at Port West Gate. I supposed that also depends on the king. If the companies want to stay in that role, that is. Ask the sergeant major, when I first met him, he was about to retire. This may work for him."

"Thatcher!"

"Yes, captain," came an answering call.

"Find the sergeant major and ask him to join me at my fire, please."

We waited for the sergeant major to join us.

"Good evening, sergeant major, please sit with us."

"I have a proposition for you after your winter contract is up." He nodded, not saying anything. "I intend to make Black Stag Keep the training area for my army. I'd like you to run it and the training, as well as oversee that guard at Black Stag and Port West Gate."

He looked at me, then back to Prince Kade. "What of Captain de Crypta?"

"Dead, I'm afraid."

The sergeant major looked at me. "Sorry to hear that. If I could have had him for ten more years, he would have made a good captain. I will say this, he was the best supply officer I ever had, but they would have caught him eventually and hanged him for a cattle or horse theft.

"Good man he was, not that I'd say it in front of him, since it might swell his head, him being a mage and all."

"Yes, I know what you mean, he thought he knew everything. Like those overnight forts I had him build, he said he thought of it first."

"Ah, the bloody Romans thought of them, now didn't they?"

"That's what I said," The prince said.

A small stone dog came out of the ground, walked over, peed on the sergeant major's boot. then went back into the ground.

"See what happens when you speak ill of the dead!" I could not hold a straight face any longer and we all burst out laughing.

Still chuckling, we poured the sergeant major a cup of wine.

"What think you, sergeant major? Is that something that would interest you and the men? No more going off to war unless one comes to us."

He took a swallow of wine. "I think we would, sir. I was ready to retire from that life anyway and training your army would be right easy life compared to our past."

"Good, you take the company and return to Black Stag. I'll return from the capital as quickly as I can. We'll discuss the finer points then. As you leave, trail the last of the Hinterland Army to our border. Once you've seen them off, take the route home using the overnight forts."

"Yes sir, thank you for the wine, sir. Good night, gentlemen."

"Good night sergeant major."

"I would ask a favor."

I nodded, "You want me to close off the pass at the border?" He nodded. "Done."

"Where will you go next, my friend?"

"Well, after I'm done at the border, I'm going to Black Stag, where I will build barracks for 500 men and a training area. After that, I'm not sure. I may go see what the Southlands looks like. I hear there is plenty of land to be had there."

"What if the king takes over Black Stag?"

"I can always sink everything back into the earth and let the next guy pay to have it rebuilt."

He laughed, "I'd bet good gold that we have an earthquake in that area sometime soon."

"We might, you can never tell."

***

The Prince left early the next morning becoming part of the army returning to the capital.

The companies were to stay in this position for another week. I found the Sergeant Major, "Tell me, what would the ideal training area look like? I was thinking of barracks for 500 men." We sat and talked, drawing pictures in the dirt of what he would like to have if he could have his wish.

Once I had a clear idea of what they needed, I decided to leave for Black Stag, and build the training area and barracks while the companies waited for the Hinterland Army to leave.

I rode out on Harbinger heading west. Once out of sight, we went under and fast-traveled to my horse herd valley. I set up my pavilion, took off Harbinger's armor and released her to run free for a while. I went inside and took a hot bath. While I bathed, the pavilion cleaned my clothes. I ate a good hot meal and slept for several hours.

It was dark when I fast-traveled to Black Stag Keep. I sped under the Keep and the Pass Fort to insure all was as it should be, and all was well.

I moved away from the Keep and got an idea of how much room I needed for the training area we wanted. First, I raised the training headquarters buildings and barracks where the trainers would live. Then I raised barracks surrounding a large parade ground. Each barracks had its own well, privy and bathing rooms. Each barracks housed 50 men. A mess hall and kitchen joined each two barracks building.

I raised warehouses to hold supplies for the army, stables for 300 horses, then another 40 farms, giving us 50 to help support Black Stag.

I left written instructions, and a large purse of gold, for the quartermaster to buy livestock for the new farms. He was also to prepare for supplies to arrive to fill the new warehouses. I told him that the companies would return to Black Stag in six to eight weeks.

Before I left, I paved all the roads with stone and I raised a wide stone bridge over the river. I kept the other side of the river for our horses and cattle grazing land. The grass was thick and lush over there. I checked inside the Keep and found it had been well taken care of.

I fast-traveled back to my pavilion and slept the rest of the night in the earth to restore my strength. I rose early the next morning and ate, then went and found Harbinger in her stall. I didn't put armor on her, and I only wore my light armor. We went outside, and I closed the pavilion and put the book in my pouch.

We fast-traveled to Port West Gate's castle and came up in the stables, where I left Harbinger. As I worked, I heard a booming sound — cannons firing. I moved up through the walls to the royal garden and looked out to sea.

There were ten Hinterland ships outside our harbor, four warships, one with a large pennant flying, four armed merchantmen, and the last two either troop ships or slavers. One warship was firing at the great chain that blocked the mouth of the harbor.

The castle was not returning fire, because of the distance and angle of the ship from the cannon emplacements. I'd have to fix that. I put on the guise of the calm, middle-aged mage, and flew down to the cannon emplacements. The provost and a mercenary officer were there.

The provost greeted me, and I addressed him: "Prince Kade sent me to check on the wellbeing of Port West Gate, but it appears we have visitors. How long have they been here?"

"They arrived a week after the prince left. I fear to think of what would have happened if he had not had the castle built to protect the harbor! So far, they have concentrated on the great chain, sending men in a longboat to lower it. Our cannons put an end to that."

"This is what they have been doing lately. They will move off at dusk and anchor for the night. Then in a few days one of the other ships will move in and fire at us for the day. I believe they are waiting for something."

"They are waiting for their army to arrive and attack from the east," I replied, "then they can attack with more vigor from the seaside. What they don't know is that their army is not coming. They were defeated at Vigil Castle and the routed Hinterland army is on the march home."

"Thank God!"

"I'll go discuss their options with them tonight. This should all be over by morning."

"The Prince is well?"

"Last I saw him, he was, yes. However, Prince Luke

was killed in combat and Prince Mathew is the new crown prince. Kade should be back in a few months."

"Any news of Earl de Crypta?"

"Not that I've heard. If you will excuse me provost, I must go prepare for my night's work."

"Of course, Sir Mage."

I levitated back up into the Royal gardens and looked out over the enemy fleet. I guessed that their king had sent them while he invaded from the Northwest.

"I guess this little tidbit escaped his memory," I mused. "Well, his loss, my gain. I always wanted trading ships and Prince Kade could have the warships. I wonder what, or who, is on the slave ships."

I looked around the inside of the harbor. It appeared that the merchant Arthur Williamson had arrived and had set up shop, and I needed to talk to him. But I needed to change my appearance first. Draugur was dead, so I needed another look, something new. I couldn't use Captain Drake at the moment, so I figured my present middle-aged mage guise would do

I opened my pavilion on the royal terrace and went inside to rest and gather my thoughts. As I ate, I roamed through the extensive library, looking at one book, then another.

Just as the provost had said, at dusk the Hinterland ship that had been firing on the harbor went farther out to sea and anchored for the night. I donned my armor, then, once it was fully dark, I levitated and flew out toward the ship with the largest pennant assuming it would be the fleet commander's.

When I got there, I entered through the side of the ship at the captain's cabin but stayed inside the wall, eavesdropping on three officers who sat at the table eating and discussing logistics. I moved down through the ship, noticing something was different. On this ship, the crew ate separately from several tables of guards, who definitely had been served better food.

I realized this was a ship of conscripts... who seemed to be just one step above a slave. The officers and guards were regular navy and the rest were these ragged serfs.

I moved on to the hold and found roughly 100 regular army soldiers, along with supplies. These were not Hinterland's best troops — they looked to be second rate at best. There were also some prisoners, one apparently an officer, in the brig. They had all been whipped.

I traveled underwater to the other ships and found they were all basically the same. The armed merchantmen held the fleet's supplies, and were also crewed by conscripts. One slave ship held replacement conscripts for the other ships and the other carried two mercenary companies that were locked up.

I'd wait until the crews were asleep before I made my move.

CHAPTER 26

I had time before I struck at the ships, so I looked in their holds and tallied their supplies. I saw that the mercenary's equipment was on the ship with them, and all the vessels carried a small chest of gold and currencies. The admirals ship, however, carried several chests of gold, gems, coins and paper money.

I waited for the Admiral's guests to leave and for him to go to bed once he was in bed and nearly asleep, I struck.

The water under the keel was twenty feet deep, but I took him straight down into the earth and released him. As he shrugged, dying, I ordered, *teach me!* and I received all of his knowledge. I now understood the nautical world of ships and how mariners handled their vessels, navigation and ocean charts. I also learned, with disgust, that he had been a really-nasty fellow: vindictive and sadistic.

I now knew the fleet's warships were fourth-rate ships-of-the-line — two decked, with sixty guns. The merchant-men were converted fourth-rate warships, each with fifty guns. The slavers were unarmed troopships. Each ship had a crew of 300 to 400, which was more people than I had expected.

The deceased admiral had handpicked the two officers that were with him at dinner and they were just as bad as he was. One was his First Mate and handled supplies. The other was what their navy called a "Service Control Officer". Basically, he was in charge of punishment... and he liked his job.

I took them down to their deaths, then sought out the guards and took them down one by one. I locked and battened down the holds where the soldiers were kept, leaving them until later. All ships were at anchor, so the only watch was a two-man fire and anchor watch, who were easily handled.

I moved through the rest of the fleet doing the same to each ship.

Pausing, I thought that now the heads were taken off, I'd work on the body. Maybe I wouldn't have to kill everybody. I had posted a black stone knight at the ship's wheel as a guard as I took control of each ship, as a precaution.

I went to the slave ship that held the mercenaries. I created two more black stone knights to escort me down into the hold, not that I expected any trouble. The stone knights were just to keep them focused.

I opened the door to the steps down into the hold and let my escorts lead the way as I followed with a lantern.

I stepped onto the deck and said loudly, "who is your captain?"

"That would be me, Captain Black," came the answer.

"You, your men and this entire fleet have been captured. You are now my prisoners."

The men muttered among themselves, but were a well-disciplined group and let their captain handle matters.

"You were under contract with the Hinterlanders?"

"We are... that is, were."

"As your contract with them is no longer in effect, can you buy yourselves free?"

"If the price can be negotiated, yes."

"Would you be open to another possibility?"

"Such as?"

"You need a contract, I need men, and since we have just captured this fleet, I need help in moving the regular army soldiers from the other ships to this one. Then you would be responsible for keeping these ships secured. Once we are in port, there would be a mix of guard duties."

"And if we would rather just buy our freedom?"

"You could do that, certainly, but you are a long way from home. Finding passage without sufficient funds might be difficult."

He nodded, "terms?"

"Half the standard pay for garrison duty, twelve-month contract, and you keep all your equipment. At the end of the twelve months we renegotiate."

He nodded, making a quick decision. "Done! Your name?"

"I am Mage Orcus."

"We accept your offer, Orcus."

I concentrated on the lock of the barred section of the hold and it unlocked and the door swung open. "Gather your equipment and get ready, I'll call you when I'm ready for you. Until then, stay below decks."

"Yes sir. We'll be ready."

My stone escorts and I went to the forecastle, where the crew swung in their hammocks. I took out my staff, my escorts opened the door and stepped in. I followed and the stone in my staff glowed, lighting the area.

"My name is Orcus," I said in a loud voice. "I have captured this fleet, and you now serve me or you are my prisoners. The choice is yours. I will tell you this, I pay those who serve me loyally, but I'm harsh on disloyalty. I don't have conscripts. If you with to serve me go to your stations and stand by for orders. If you are prisoners, remain here until you are sent for." I turned and walked out, and they silently went to their stations.

I went under and returned to the admiral's ship, keeping my escorts. Once there, I went below decks to the brig. As before, my staff's stone lit the room, dazzling its occupants, shocked from their sleep. "My name is Orcus. I have captured this fleet and you are now my prisoners... but I am curious as to why you, an officer, are beaten and in the brig?"

"I refused to beat men for no reason, so they beat me in their stead."

"Your rank?"

"Third Officer, name of Hicks."

"You are now First Officer Hicks, and I'd like you to see to your fellows here. Then take them above decks." He said nothing, but nodded.

I went to the crew berthing space and gave them the same ultimatum. To my satisfaction, they all decided they wanted to work for me. I repeated the same offer on all the ships, with the same results.

But the regular army soldiers in the holds were a different matter. I didn't like the look of them, as they seemed to be second-rate troops at best.

I decided to leave them in their holds and move the mercenaries to each ship as guards over them. Later, I would make the soldiers a different offer. They could join our army and be trained by Sergeant Major Miller, or go to the slave pens. Troublemakers would soon be spotted and removed. With those extra bodies, I guessed we would shortly have a Black Stag Army.

Going back to the mercenaries' ship I found their captain. "I need a detachment of guards to go to the ship with the pennant. There, I will make the soldiers an offer of employment. If they take it, I will have them moved over here, but if they don't, they'll remain under guard.

"Prepare a few detachments to be ready to move to other ships."

"Yes, Sir Mage, they'll be on boats heading that way shortly."

I flew back under to the pennant ship and waited for the mercenaries to arrive, I talked to First Officer Hicks. "What were your orders?"

"The admiral didn't tell his subordinates much. All I heard was we were to harass Port West Gate harbor, awaiting the army arriving overland. Then we would link up with them and hold the port."

"Is it common practice in the Hinterland Navy to use conscripts?"

"Yes, half of the navy's sailors are conscripts. They keep them in line with brutality, and the smallest infractions are met with the whip, sometimes to death. That is why a slaver follows the fleet, for replacements. It's no wonder the conscripts hate the regular navy."

"And the army?"

"Much the same, unless you are in the first-line army companies, roughly about a third of the force. Everyone else is a conscript."

"If I made them the same offer?"

"They would probably take it. They hate the regular army like these men hate the regular navy."

"Do they have officers among them?"

"No, at the most they have a top-sergeant for one hundred men. We call that a "century.""

I nodded, "good to know. As of now you are the captain. See to your men and your ship, Captain Hicks."

"Yes, Sir Mage," he said with satisfaction.

Soon Captain Black arrived in several boats with the detachment. I told him what I wanted, and he deployed his men. When we were ready, I opened the hatch holding the soldiers. Striving for effect, I levitated down into the hold, my staff stone shining.

"My name is Orcus and I have captured the fleet. You are all now my prisoners."

A big man stepped forward, "What if we don't want to be your prisoners, what will you do then?"

A spike of timber shot up from the floor impaling him, killing him instantly.

"Any other questions?"

"He wasn't very smart." remarked someone in the shadows.

"Who is your Top-Sergeant?" Everyone pointed to the dead man.

I shrugged and pointed to the man who had spoken from the shadows. "What's your name?"

"Cooper, Sir Mage."

"Rank, Cooper?"

"Sergeant, Sir Mage."

"Are you the next ranking man?"

"One of four sergeants, Sir Mage."

"Congratulations! You are now acting Top-Sergeant Cooper."

"Yes, Sir Mage!"

"As I was saying, you are my prisoners. I don't keep conscripts. You are either working for me as soldiers or you are prisoners, destined for the slave pens. I pay my soldiers. But as you have witnessed, I can and will punish harshly. If you are going to be one my soldiers fall into formation behind Top-Sergeant Cooper. If you'd rather go to the slave pens, take a seat in the rear."

They only hesitated a second, "fall-in, you lot!" Top-Sergeant Cooper shouted and they all jumped to get into formation leaving no one behind.

"Top-Sergeant Cooper, when was the last time the men were let out for fresh air and sunshine?"

"Two weeks ago, Sir Mage."

I shook my head, "Captain Black!"

"The Century will come on deck under Top-Sergeant Cooper's Command."

"Yes, Sir Mage."

"Top-Sergeant, take the men up top."

I went on deck and let the new Top-Sergeant handle his soldiers.

Captain Black, his detachment and I made the rounds to the other three war ships. I made those soldiers the same offer and they all accepted my terms, and I didn't have to kill anyone else.

On all the ships, I changed the pennants and the mainsails from Hinterland to my sigil of a Rampant Black Dragon on a blue background.

"Captain Hicks, signal the fleet to prepare for getting underway. We'll be moving into the harbor."

"Yes, Sir Mage."

"I'll return in a while, so stand by, once docked inside, for further orders."

"Yes, Sir Mage." He turned and started carrying out my orders.

I levitated and to the Harbor Fort and met the provost there. "Good afternoon, Sir Mage. It seems you have solved our problem."

"I have, I have taken their ships, and they'll be moving into the harbor shortly. I want to make sure everyone is clear that these were now my ships. You may lower the Great Chain. I will have them dock against the Harbor Crags, and set a guard to maintain discipline. You may continue to set your city watch as you deem fit."

He was nodding his head. "As long as we have guards to maintain order, there should be no problems."

"They will be too tired to cause problems, and I'll hang the first one who does. They will rearrange supplies between ships. That will keep them busy."

The Provost lowered the Great Chain and I flew back out to the flagship. "Captain Hicks, signal the fleet to follow us into the Harbor."

"Aye, aye Sir."

We moved the fleet into the harbor and docked the ships along the seaward crag wall.

"Captain Black, set your guards at the end of the crag wall to keep the curious away. Mind you, the provost will probably come to visit, and you may let him pass. When he comes, please coordinate your guards with the city watch. We don't want to ruffle any feathers."

"Yes, Sir Mage."

Once we docked, the first thing I did was go into the earth, open a vault and then my pavilion. I moved all the gold chests from all the ships to my pavilion storage room. I'd sort through them later.

Going back to the ship, "Captain Hicks, I need you to see who, if anyone, may be able to fill captains or other officer's in the fleet. When you've found them bring them to me."

"Captain Black have your men move all of your equipment off the troopships, and for now, divide your company between the four warships. Once you have moved off the troopship, we'll start moving the soldiers."

"Yes, Sir Mage."

I found Top-Sergeant Cooper, "Top-Sergeant, go to the other Top-Sergeants and gather them here for further orders."

"Yes, Sir Mage."

Once they were present, I said, "Gentlemen, you will gather all of your equipment and move it out onto the docks. We will do some rearranging. All the Centuries and their equipment will move to the troopships." I saw their bodies tense. "We will not lock you in. As a matter of fact, we will take all those barred doors out. The troopships will move up the coast to Black Stag Keep, our military's training grounds, where you will be posted for the time being. We will also need enough supplies for two weeks on the troopships. As soon as the mercenaries are off the troopships, start your move. Questions?"

"Rum, sir?"

"Rum?"

"Yes sir, the men have not been getting their rum ration."

"For how long?"

"Two weeks, sir."

"Is that because there is no rum, or because those officers were stupid?"

"I really can't speak to the supply problems, sir!" We all chuckled.

"I'll see what I can find out. At the least I'm sure we can find some ale to make do for now."

"Yes sir, thank you, sir."

"Anything else?" They shook their heads.

"Right, let's get to it then."

Captain Hicks showed up a while later with 40 or so men. "What have you found, Captain Hicks?"

"Sir Mage, these men are, or were, captains, first officers, and other officers on their own ships, before they were forced into the navy."

"Are you telling me those fools took trained, experienced officers and made them ordinary seaman?" They all nodded. "That is the stupidest thing I think I have ever heard of! Why would they do such a thing?"

"They want you indoctrinated, brainwashed into thinking their way, and only their way. Not inclined to question any order... to obey, period."

"Then they are doomed to failure. That may work in the short term, but it will eventually collapse in on itself."

"OK, let's keep this simple, captains raise your hands." Eight hands went up. "Captains move over there. First officers raise your hands." Eight hands went up. "Don't tell me you've worked together, too!" They nodded. I shook my head, "Idiots! OK, move over with your captains. If any of the rest of you have worked under one of these captains move over to them." The rest moved over and, just like that, we had eight ship's officer's cadres.

"Gentlemen, I need one officer group to serve under Captain Hicks here. I want you to give me the most experienced you have, to fill those positions. And remember, you're going to be working, and probably fighting, alongside them. Call me when you've figured it out." I walked away and left them to it. In the end, to my surprise, Hicks demoted himself to first officer and gave the captaincy to a more experienced man.

"Mr. Hicks, I'll not forget this, well done!" He nodded. "Now, let's see the cadres with experience on warships, so they can move to our fighting vessels. Those with merchantman experience will go to the merchantman. The troop transports will be converted to armed merchantmen. So, raise your hand if you've had warship experience." Three raised their hands.

"Go to your ships." Those three captains and their officers left us. "merchantman?" the rest raised their hands. "Anyone with experience on the type of ships those transports are? "Two raised their hands. "You two will be the transport ship captains for now and will oversee their conversion to armed merchantmen as soon as possible. All right gentlemen, see to your ships. Troop transports will leave in two days, so be ready. More orders will follow. Let's get to it." They all went to work.

Mr. Hicks remained behind. "Sir Mage, may I have a word?"

"Of course, Mr. Hicks, what can I do for you?"

"Well, sir, as you have all the captains you need, I was wondering if you would consider moving me to be your quartermaster?"

"Really?"

"Yes sir, I'm the son of a merchant and I'm very good at, in fact, I love it. Where many try to avoid that duty, I relish it."

"You don't want to be a ship Captain?"

"Well, when I joined the Navy it was to gain experience to become a merchant ship's captain, but it hasn't worked out as I'd planned. The way the Hinterland Navy uses people makes no sense to me."

"Me, either. What do you want to do?"

"You seem to be starting your country's navy, and your own trading fleet." I smiled; this guy was sharp. "I would like to be your trading fleet's Quartermaster, and I can double, at least at the start, as your navy's Quartermaster as well."

I nodded, thinking. "Mr. Hicks you've got yourself a job, well, two, actually Your first task is to find a replacement first officer for your captain, so he's not left hanging. Then come find me, as there is someone I want you to meet."

"Yes, Sir Mage, I'll return as soon as I can. And thank you."

"Thank you, Mr. Hicks."

CHAPTER 27

Hicks returned within the hour. "I have found my replacement, sir, and he is now on his ship with the captain. Everyone is satisfied."

"Very well then, let's go to the Williamson's trading house, get accounts set up and start getting supplies." We walked over to the warehouse on the harbor front and walked in.

"Good afternoon, how may we be of service?"

"I would like to see Arthur Williamson on behalf of Earl de Crypta."

The clerk left to get Arthur, who quickly appeared and introduced himself.

"Wait here, Mr. Hicks, I'll call you in a bit."

Once we were in Arthur's office, I said, "Arthur, Earl de Crypto is a mage."

"I see, what does he need?"

I changed my image back to that of de Crypta, explaining, "I just didn't want to shock you too badly, Arthur. We've come a long way since the dungeon."

He recovered quickly. "We have, indeed, how can I serve?"

"I'm now using the name of 'the Mage Orcus.' You're going to hear that de Crypta was killed, but the reality is that the king and I had a serious falling-out and this was the easiest answer for all concerned."

"I understand. Dealing with royals is always tricky."

I laughed, "so I have learned. Anyway, all OUR deals remain the same. I may have to change guises from time to time, but that shouldn't alter our understandings."

He nodded and I continued, "I have a man outside, a Mr. Hicks, and he is my new quartermaster, and I authorize him to use my accounts.

"We also now have four armed merchantmen, so I will need to arrange for cargos for them to take out trading. Hicks is from Hinterland, from a merchant family there. See what you two can come up with to make us money."

"I will sir... four ships hauling cargo could make us a nice profit."

"One thing I need right now is 15 barrels of ale delivered to my ships on the docks, as well as any rum you may have available."

"Yes sir, I'll get that there as soon as I can."

"On another subject. I built these warehouses, but I put no secure vaults in them to keep money or important papers on site. Would you like me to put a vault in for you? Say, under your office, with a door here for you to access it?"

"That would be wonderful and take a load off my mind."

I concentrated and grew a stone vault under the office with stairs up to a false wall which I turned into a door. I got up and walked over to the hidden door, gesturing for Arthur to follow. "This is your new vault." I opened the door, and we went down the stairs to the vault. "I'll be making a deposit in there tonight, so you'll find it here when you open in the morning."

"This is wonderful!" He looked around. "I hate to presume upon you, but can you put one in my house too?"

I laughed, "yes I can do that." We left the vault, closing it behind us and I changed back into my Orcus guise. We went out, and I introduced Mr. Hicks to Arthur, then left them to get acquainted.

***

Late that afternoon, fifteen barrels of ale and ten barrels of rum were delivered to the docks and distributed, which seemed to relax some nerves and put the men at ease. They all stayed in our dock area, so any fighting or disruptions — to be expected when mixing sailors, soldiers and rum — were handled there.

I took four small chests of gold from my pavilion and put them in my pouch. I transferred the chests in Arthur's new vault to buy cargo for my cargo ships, then found Arthur's house and added a vault under it like the one in his office, with a door that opens into his home office.

I moved to the troopships and looked over the iron cells in their holds. I turned them into iron bars and moved them to the hold. I had plans to make cannons from the iron, but needed more materials. The men seemed pleased to see the cells go.

I returned to the castle terrace and set up to the pavilion, bringing Harbinger up to the stable where I could take care of her. I ate, took a bath, and sat outside looking out over the ocean. I briefly thought of Maddie, then dismissed her from my mind.

I sipped wine, wondering what I should do next, now that I didn't have to worry about money, food, or shelter. I could go look at the Southern District, but I'd have to stay at least long enough to see what the king had in mind for Prince Kade and his lands. At that thought, I smiled to myself: we might both be going to the South District! I finished my wine and went to bed.

But I awoke in the middle of the night, thinking, "why do I need warships?" I'm not going to war with anyone, and if I do, I don't need ships! I'll could just convert them all into armed merchantmen, evenly distributing the cannons between all at the ships.

If I did that, I realized, that would give each ship 44 cannons, enough to defend against pirates. I went back to sleep but was up early.

I ate, then levitated down to the ships, going aboard one of the armed merchantmen and finding her captain on the dock watching the work crew.

"Good morning, Captain."

"Good morning, Sir Mage."

"There has been a change of plans. I think we should convert all the ships to armed merchantmen, giving them all 44 guns, at least to start with."

"Do you have carpenters and workmen?"

I smiled, "one of the good things about being a mage is you don't need them. Show me around your ship. We need to pull six of her guns so she will have 22 guns per side, and I'm guessing 11 per deck?"

"Right this way, sir."

We looked over everything. "I'm thinking six guns on the upper deck, five guns on the lower deck. Take out every other gun to give the gun crews room to work their guns. We'll leave the unused gun ports in place to let air in when we want it. And to add guns back if we need them."

He nodded. "That would work fine, for a merchantman, and could fool an enemy into thinking we were more powerful an opponent. It would give us more room for cargo too."

I nodded, laid my hand on a cannon, and took it through the wall of the ship and out onto the dock. That caused quite a stir. Word spread quickly about what I was doing. A crowd gathered as the men laid to, working hard to keep up with what I was doing. We had the cannons out of the ships before lunch. I had Mr. Hicks order four cooked sides of beef brought in for the evening meal. I also told him there would be no navy, so he would be the quartermaster for just my shipping company.

Putting the cannons into the troop ships took longer than taking them out of the others, since I had to make hatches and add extra deck bracing for the guns. Once we got the positioning worked out, converting the second troop ship went faster. We were finished by late evening, and we had a celebration of beef and ale that night. I now owned a fleet of ten armed merchantmen. I ordered the captains to take each ship out for a test run, to see how they handled and determine if I could improve their performance.

Exhausted, I slept in the earth that night to restore my strength.

The first ship we took out that morning taught me a lot. I went below and laid my hand on the hull, and the runes in my hand glowed. The ship began to show me where her shape was adding drag and how to improve speed and handling. I made the bow narrower and the bottom a little wider, then narrowed the stern a little. I made her bottom slicker, cleaning off barnacles and weed, and tightened her caulking. I added runes to keep her bottom slick and her caulking tight. I added some bracing where I made her bottom wider to strengthen her and to improved her capacity for ballast for handling his rough weather. The captain was all smiles.

I repeated this with each ship, and it became a competition among the crews to take advantage of their new hulls by improving sail plan and handling. By the end of the day we probably had the best and the fastest ships on the water. You could tell the crews were proud of their ships!

I slept in the earth again that night, restoring my strength.

***

We cross-loaded supplies from the fleet to the old troop transports, planning to take a two week supply with us to Black Stag for the four Centuries. We had ordered another six months' supply from Williamson's to be shipped as soon as they could load it onto one of our other ships.

That fort was less than a half-day trip up the coast, but we would wait until morning to go since I had some things to do before the troop ships arrived.

I went down into the earth and fast-traveled to Black Stag Cove, changing en route from my Orcus guise to that of Draugur.

I found a quartermaster who was also the rear detachment commander and greeted him.

"Good evening, Captain."

"I imagine you have seen the new training grounds and buildings."

"I have, and have received your instructions about the supplies and livestock."

"Good, tomorrow we'll be arriving with two ships and four hundred soldiers who will quarter in those barracks. We will be here about midday. Come with me, I'll show you our new cove."

We walked to the crag wall where I had put the opening and he watched in awe as I made the wall into a gate and portcullis. Then adding a stone road down to the quay and docks.

"Add this to your guard list, keep it closed until we arrive."

"Yes, Captain."

"When we arrive, make sure the wagons are brought down for them to carry the new troops' equipment and supplies. Their gear will go into the barracks with them, the supplies into one of the warehouses. Oh, and I will be in another guise when I arrive, going by the name of 'Orcus the Mage'. Please don't tell anyone else that de Crypta and Orcus are the same person."

He nodded, "yes, Sir Mage, all will be ready for your arrival."

I nodded, "do you need anything for here?"

"Not at the moment sir, unless you want to order the livestock for the farms."

"I'll take care of it; we'll see you midday tomorrow."

"Yes, Sir Mage."

I levitated and flew out of sight, then went back down into the earth, and fast-traveled back to my pavilion, once again.

***

When I arrived at the docks, the next morning all the soldiers were ready, and the two ships were loaded and ready.

I boarded the lead ship and gave its captain his orders. "You may leave when ready and head north along the coast."

"Yes, Sir Mage."

The soldiers stayed below and out of the way of the ship's crew, and my changes proved themselves as we made good time and arrived at Black Stag Cove as predicted.

The ships docked, the soldiers disembarked and moved into the training area.

I introduced Top-Sergeant Cooper to the quartermaster, then we went up to the training grounds and barracks.

"The quartermaster is our rear detachment commander," I told Cooper. "Work together and he will get you started on how the Black Stag Company operates. Work in on the guard duties and prepare for training, which will start when Sergeant Major Miller and the rest of the company gets back."

"Yes, Sir Mage."

I flew back down to the ships. "Captain, when you have off-loaded everything, return to Port West Gate."

"Yes, Sir Mage."

I flew up and over the crags, then down into the earth, back to Port West Gate.

I found Mr. Hicks and gave him a list of supplies and livestock we needed for the farms. "Buy them and send them on the supply ship to Black Stag Cove."

I needed more farmers now, so I went to the slave master. "My name is Orcus, I'm here on behalf of Prince Kade. He wishes to buy more farmers; do you have any available?"

"We do, Sir Mage. Come, I'll show you what we have." I bought ten families of farmers, paid the slave master and had them delivered to the docks to ride to Black Stag on the supply ships.

I stopped by to see Arthur Williamson to show him where the door to his house vault was.

"You now have ten armed merchantmen... you have been busy, Sir Mage."

"We shall put them to work straight away. On another subject, would you be interested in another business opportunity?"

"I'm always willing to listen, what do you have in mind?"

"Money changing and moneylending."

"Go on."

"There are merchants from other lands who will need to change their money to ours, and we would make the change for a small percentage. On the lending side we would loan money to people and businesses for a percentage fee. If they can't repay the loan, of course, we could take over the business, property, or merchandise."

"You would run this business from your warehouse?"

"To start with, yes. Depending on the profitability we may move the loan side to another building further into the town proper."

"How much of an investment would this business require?"

"A similar amount to that which you left in my vault should be plenty."

"I like the idea, it would help the local people do better in business, well if they are wise, so I'll deposit the money into your vault. You may start when you are ready."

"Yes, Sir Mage, we'll start right away."

I was becoming quite the businessman!

***

The two ships were back from Black Stag by mid-morning the following day. We departed taking the next load to Black Stag shortly after their return. I went with them to watch this captain find the cove, following the updated charts

I had given him. He found it with no problems.

Once we docked the ship, we started unloading supplies and the troops moved them up to their warehouse. The quartermaster took charge of our new farmers to get them to their farms, with their livestock and supplies. Once I was satisfied, I went under and flew back to my pavilion.

I got one of the large chests of gold and put it in Arthur's vault for our money changer's business.

Then I assigned Mr. Hicks a warehouse to work in, adding an office in the front with a vault and a living area in the back. I gave him a small purse for living expenses. He and Arthur were already working together filling our ships.

I gave each of the ship's captains a small chest of gold for operating expenses before we sent them out on a trade run.

Five of our ships had already departed when the Bonnie M came into port. I let Mr. Hicks deal with Captain Wester as he unloaded his cargo and reloaded for another voyage to foreign ports.

It was time to go back and check in with Sergeant Major Miller. I saddled Harbinger and took her down to the castle stables, pulling her with me as we fast-traveled to the area where we had left the company. I put on the guise of Elijah Drake, and we came up.

The Hinterland army had moved, and therefore so had the company. They were staying a few hours behind them, but keeping them well scouted.

"Good afternoon Sergeant Major, all is well?"
"Yes, sir. We've been eating well, since the mess sergeant said if we found any stray cattle he would put them to good use." He said smiling.

I laughed, "I hear they hang cattle thieves around here."
"So, they do, sir. If they catch them!"
"I'll keep an eye out. Any changes with the Hinterlanders?"
"Not really, though they are moving faster going home."
"Don't we all!"

"Aye, that we do."

I found a couple of cattle every few nights for the mess. I would just leave them standing by the mess wagons. No one ever mentioned them. I don't think my Captain Drake guise was fooling anyone in the company. But it was company business, and no one discussed company business outside the company.

We finally reached the border, and they kept marching, so we turned south, heading home. I made sure our mess supplies were full before we turned south. They were still the enemy, after all.

I stayed at the border until both parties were out of sight, then concentrated on the bedrock, raised rocky cliffs to close off the pass between our countries, at least for the immediate future. Then Harbinger and I rode south to catch up with the company.

I rode up beside the Sergeant Major, "you should be clear all the way to Black Stag. All the overnight forts are still there. I'm going to check on Prince Kade, and we'll meet you at the Keep."

"Yes sir, we'll make good time going back."

Harbinger and I peeled off heading east. Once out of sight we went under, and fast-traveled to the capital.

CHAPTER 28

I went under the castle, settled Harbinger in her stable and took a bath and put on clean clothes.

Then I went to find Prince Kade in the stable brushing Beast. I put on the guise of a groomsman and surfaced around the corner. As I approached, Beast's hound met me wagging his tail.

"You here with all of your friends?"

The Prince glanced at me and smiled. "I am now, what took you so long?"

"I had to see your in-laws off and close the door so they couldn't come back... through that door at least."

He nodded, "good, hopefully that is the end of that problem."

"I'm sure they'll be others."

"Always."

"What news, do we still have a home, or do I need to build another?"

"I am no longer Duke of the Western District. I am out of favor with the Crown. My father and I have not spoken since leaving Vigil Castle, not even at Luke's funeral. Mother is quite wroth with both of us."

"He made me Duke of the Southern District, but I turned it down, so I am being sent away with no support from the throne. Either I make it on my own or not at all."

"I see an earthquake in the future. If it wouldn't hurt the people of West Gate, I'd drop it in the sea."

"And if it didn't, I'd let you. What news from the west?"

"The company is on its way back to Black Stag, where there are 10 more farms being worked. There are 400 new men waiting there to be trained… oh, and we now own 10 armed merchantmen that are running cargo as we speak."

He nodded, "so, nothing out of the ordinary."

"Not really." We laughed.

"When do we leave?"

"I'm allowed to leave in the morning when the gates open, with just my armor and my horse. I'm sure the King will be on the wall to make sure I go."

"Do you want to go now?"

"That's tempting, but no. Let him have his temper tantrum. Then we'll go."

"Have you eaten?"

"No, I've been taking my meals in my room. While we are not speaking, I do not wish to be ignored, or eyed with disdain while eating."

"Let's go eat," I took his arm, "close your eyes."

"Why?"

"So you don't get dizzy and throw up." He closed his eyes, and we eased down to the pavilion I'd created deep in the earth.

"OK, you can open them now."

"Where are we?"

"In my pavilion under the castle. Sit down, the food and wine are excellent." We sat and ate.

"This is good. Wait, how long have you had this?" I shrugged my shoulders. "You mean we could have been traveling using this all the time?"

"What? No… well, not all the time. But hey, I was sharing your misery all the way… mostly…"

"I always heard you could not trust a mage."

"Now that part's true."

We laughed; it was a good sound. Once again, I thought of Maddie for a second, then dismissed her memory.

***

At sunrise the Prince mounted on Beast, both in full armor, and waited. He had asked me to take the royal sigil off his shield. He and Beast moved out of the stables into the courtyard and waited for the gates to open.

The King came out on to the gate wall and stared down at him, tossing a small purse down to the ground. Prince Kade left it where it landed, put on his helm and closed the visor. He pulled his shield around from his back to his front and waited. Beast, feeling his master's agitation, began to shuffle and dance. The King left the wall and the gate opened.

Beast with Kade trotted through the gate, out of the castle and down the road. Harbinger and I, in full battle armor, joined him outside the capital and we rode west for a while not speaking.

After an hour he slowed us to a walk. Raising his visor, he said, "can you take us to the castle in West Gate?"

"We can be there in a few moments, no one will see us enter, and I'll seal the castle proper."

He nodded and reined up, "take us, please."

I moved Harbinger close to Beast, so we were knee to knee and we linked arms. "Do not let go."

I lowered us into the ground and we fast-traveled to the castle, emerging in the stables. He sat for a moment, then nodded. We dismounted and unsaddled Beast and Harbinger.

Then we walked up to the Royal Gardens and I re-opened my pavilion. "Let's have breakfast while we discuss what we shall do next." We went inside to hot tea and hot food and didn't talk much while we ate, both of us deep in thought. After we had finished, we moved outside and sat looking out to sea.

"I suppose it was grief that pushed him to lash out like he did." I said nothing, just listening. "Luke and I were never close. He was always a bully to me. He was the firstborn, I guess that made him and father closer. Mother told him he would lose two sons but he didn't seem to hear her. Through his foolishness, he's lost two sons and a daughter." He said no more.

I left him looking out over the ocean. I stepped over to the other wall to look over the harbor where I had three ships sitting at the docks. I donned my Orcus guise and went to see the captains and Mr. Hicks.

I ordered the captains to wait in the harbor for a new task and Hicks to hold off on doing anything with the three ships until I had made further arrangements.

When I arrived back at the Royal Gardens, Kade was in the pool. "You should have made this with hot water," He complained.

"I didn't make that one with hot water because that one is for fish. The hot water bathing pools are inside."

He looked down at the water, then at me. "Not a word!" He got up and we went inside to the hot baths, soaked and sat relaxing in the hot water.

"What do you think we should do?" he asked.

"Honestly, I think we should go south. I'll separate the southern District from the rest of the kingdom by raising rocky cliffs, and that will solve most of our problems. I'll leave the crags in place on this side and shift the southern lands off the coast a mile or more.

"We have ships. We have people. I can build anything we need. From what I've been told, the whole of the Southern District is surrounded by crags, so I can easily enclose it until we are ready..

"I'll make a deep-water harbor with a castle, lots of farms and a town to start with, and we can grow from there. We'll get more people by freeing them from the slave pens.

"And we trade with other nations as equals. You will no longer be Prince Kade, but King Kade! If others leave us in peace, we'll leave them in peace. If they don't..." I shrugged my shoulders.

He was thinking. "It does sound easy, but new things always do. Let's sleep on it, think about it, and talk again." I nodded. "When does the company get back to Black Stag?"

"At least a month."

He nodded, "that's what I thought," and said no more.

*****

"Let's do it," he said over breakfast.

"Which part?"

"All of it. Shift the southern district off the coast, making it a new nation — The Nation of Southland. Wall it in solid, add a deep-water harbor, make a castle, town, farms, everything. We'll bring people in. I don't see Father changing his ways. He just wants to use people to his advantage and claim it's for the good of the Kingdom."

"I've noticed that about him."

"When we leave, sink this castle back into the earth. Leave the walls for the cannon emplacements but sink everything else."

"That will cost as much to take down as it did to put up. You heard that crazy old mage."

"You can have the gold in the mantle."

"That's already mine."

"I'll owe it to you."

"Uh-huh. OK, I'll go look at what we have to work with before we make a final decision."

"Good idea, we may end up stealing the Western District instead."

"It could happen, I have been known to steal a few things, but never by the acre."

*****

I flew along the craggy wall that divided the southern lands from the rest of the kingdom. Overall, it was fairly thick, close to breaking through only in a few places. I raised huge stones to fill in those areas. I saw there were two major underground rivers that fed the southern rivers south of the crags. I would have to make sure those passages stayed open when I moved everything.

I surveyed the area's low-lying lands, estimating that more than half the country was marshland. I would have to raise some of those areas and make ditches to drain the rest. The rest was a land with a good mix of thick forest and flat open fields. There was plenty of water and the soil was rich and fertile. I flew around the coast and found one break in the cliffs. There had once been a small fishing village there, but it had been completely abandoned. I raised adjacent cliffs to close that opening.

As I ranged across the area, I found coal, gold, silver, gemstones, and even oil. The rocky outcroppings were from 50 to 80 feet tall but were only 30 feet thick in some areas. I traveled back and forth under the whole region, which took me all day. I'm not sure anyone realized how big the Southern District was. It was easily a third of the size of the rest of the kingdom, maybe more.

I zipped back to my pavilion to find the Prince sitting in the garden. "Have you eaten?" I asked.

"Not yet." We went inside and sat as I told him what I had found and described the few changes I had made.

"And you found no people?"

"I only saw the one abandoned fishing village. I guess it was so remote that getting supplies was too difficult." We took our wine out onto the garden terrace and I raised a table from the floor that showed a relief map of the Southern District.

He looked the model over, "and these areas are marsh?"

"Yes, but I can raise most of that up to the same level as the surrounding areas and drain the rest. In these areas here, I think we should lower the terrain even more, creating a lake so all the water will have somewhere to go."

He nodded. "Where are you thinking of putting the harbor?"

"Well, I thought it should be away from the lake. That

still leaves us a lot of options. If we put it on the north side, that would quickly lead to a confrontation with the Northern Kingdom. Which is also why we just can't leave it where it is and put a gate in the wall. They would be beating on the gate in no time.

"I'm leaning toward the southern parts of the island that it will become."

"Will ocean currents to cause trouble at a harbor in that location?"

"I haven't looked at that yet. But I can change the ocean floor as easily as dry land."

"OK, let's back up a step. What do we want our harbor to look like? The warehouses, the dock, the quays, the fort to protect the harbor mouth... and where would you put the castle?"

"Whoa, slow down! How about this?" I started changing the model using different shapes and locations. It ended up looking a lot like Port West Gate, only bigger. The castle was up against the crag cliffs, so it exposed nothing to the seaside to be exploited.

"OK, I like that layout, where do we put it?"

"The south tip of the Island." I raise the rest of the map and showed him where we could place it. "We'd keep the wall closed until we had everything built, with soldiers to guard it, and people living there." He nodded.

"Before we make a final decision, we'll let this stay up a day or two. We'll sleep on it and see if we want any changes."

***

After two days we had made no changes. "Are you ready to start?" I asked.

"No time like the present!"

"OK, the first thing we'll do is move down there. This will take a lot out of me. I'll need to rest and eat close to where I'm working. Let's get Beast and Harbinger ready, then we'll move the pavilion over." I closed the pavilion, and we went down to the stables to get Beast and Harbinger. We did not put on their armor as we would be underground the whole way.

We mounted and linked arms. I lowered us into the ground and we fast-traveled to a hillock on an open plain surrounded by forests.

"Welcome to Southland."

We dismounted, and I took out the pavilion book and lay it on the ground. I touched the book with the staff, "*Add another bed chamber and bathroom.*" The pavilion opened. I went inside to find there were now two bedchambers, with bathrooms attached to them.

We unsaddled the horses and let them run free and enjoy themselves.

I took him inside and showed him his bedchamber.

"Thank you, I appreciate the gesture."

"Well, it was that or listen to you complain about sleeping on the ground."

"I would not have complained, I'd have slept in the bedchamber over there." He laughed.

"I may not be back on time every day, don't get worried if I'm gone for a few days. As I said, this will take a lot out of me."

"OK, but don't push yourself, we have plenty of time."

"True, I will start by lowering the lake area first so the water won't flood everything." I sank into the earth and fast-traveled to the low place that would become our lake, then lowered the land quite a bit, thinking I could always raise it if it was too low.

I moved to the closest marsh lands to the lakebed, lowering a riverbed toward the new lakebed. Then I started raising the marsh lands. Water started moving right away, heading toward our new lakebed.

Once I completed raising each marshy area, I made a riverbed from the next marsh area and raised it. I spent all day repeating this process. At sundown I went back to the pavilion, ate and went down into the earth to recover. It took me two weeks to raise all the marshlands, and they were still draining, slowly filling our lake.

Before I started on anything else, I went back at night and lowered the Port West Gate Castle back into the ground. I left the harbor side walls and cannon emplacements, but everything else sank out of sight.

CHAPTER 29

I was now ready to add more rocky outcroppings to the existing crag barrier on our northern border, so I started at the western edge of the wall, working my way east. I added a 50-foot-thick, 80-foot-high barrier, leaving 10 feet between two rocky walls to mark the line along which I would split our new island off the main land mass. It took me three days to complete the barrier, forcing me to rest an additional day in the earth before I tried to finish the job.

The next morning, I started by moving the 10 feet of dirt between the new walls out of the way, leaving a channel into which the sea rushed Then I deepened the channel to 50 feet.

It took extreme concentration for me to order the newly formed island to move slowly away.

The runes on my hand and arms glowed, then moved up to my shoulders and across my chest and back. As I continued to exert force, the runes expanded, first onto my lower torso, then down my legs and feet. Eventually, they covered my neck, face and head. Still, I held fast to my efforts and all the runes began to pulse, lines appeared, like the outlines of armor. It felt like I was wearing armor, magic armor. My whole body was pulsing.

I found later the force had burned my clothes off, but I never felt the heat.

I don't know how long I held my concentration, but I could feel my consciousness traveling the length and breadth of the new island. I felt the island shudder and a moment later I felt it move, slowly at first but then like it was sliding across ice. I stopped pushing when the island was two miles offshore.

I thanked the earth and collapsed into exhaustion. When

I awoke, I was starving. I went up to the pavilion and redressed myself, then went to get something to eat.

Kade was at the table, "are you all right?"

"Yes, starving, but that happens when I exert a lot of magic. How long did I sleep?"

"You've been gone a week."

I sat and started eating, "a week?" I asked around a mouth-full of food. "That's the longest I've ever been out. Of course this is the first time I've moved an island." I ate two meals worth of food at one sitting then sat there resting. "Did you feel anything up here?"

"I felt a small shudder and heard a small rumble. Were you able to move it?"

"A little."

He looked at me a moment, "I'm not falling for that this time, how far did you move it, five miles?"

I smiled, "no, only two, I figured that was enough for our purposes."

He nodded, "plenty."

"The company should be back to Black Stag, or they will be shortly. Let's go check on things there before we do anything else."

We saddled the horses, before I could take the staff to close the pavilion, it closed at my thought. Then lifted up into my hand. I put it in my pouch and stood there thinking a moment. All the rune growth had changed me, made me more powerful. I didn't know how much, but it was significant.

We mounted and fast-traveled to just south of Black Stag Keep's pass where I donned the guise of the Mage Orcus. We rode in from there, Kade was recognized, and they passed us through at the gate.

The companies had arrived two days ago, were unloaded, and the new men were working with the veterans.

We found the sergeant major, "before you get too comfortable, there have been some changes."

"What kind of changes?"

"It seems we have made the king angry, enough that he has taken Port West Gate from Prince Kade. And as de Crypta is dead, I'm sure it won't be long before someone shows up here as the new owner."

He just looked at us, "about two years ago we had these two new officers. They were both crazy and always getting and trouble. Almost drove the captain crazy. Now I know what he felt like."

We chuckled. I could not resist, "It wasn't our fault, Sergeant Major."

"That was their story too. All right, where are we going?"

"I'll have three ships here in a few days. They will move us to our new lands in the south. Rest the companies a few days then we'll start loading."

"I'm not even going to ask. OK, we'll rest a day or two, then prepare to move by ship. How long a voyage?"

"A day, two at the most, barring foul weather. And when I said we were moving, I mean everyone, including farmers. But tell them they'll be moving onto new farms as nice as these, but bigger. Pass the word."

"Yes sir, everyone moves. Take everything with us."

"Exactly."

We went to the Keep and told the major-domo the same thing ... that we were moving in three or four days and to pack everything,

"Yes Masters," was all he said, and went to work.

Kade stayed at the Keep I made a quick trip to West Gate.

***

As Orcus, I went into Williamson's warehouse.

"Sir Mage," Arthur greeted me. "Please come into my office."

Once the door was closed, I said "I came by to warn you of some changes that will take place."

"Good or bad changes?"

"I'm not sure, maybe some of both. Prince Kade is no longer favored by the king, so he is no longer Duke of the Western District."

"Do we know who will become the new Duke or Earl?"

"We do not. But for your ears only, there has been another earthquake."

"We know, we felt it."

"Did you know that it has split off the Southern District from the Kingdom, and it is now an island two miles off the coast?"

"The whole Southern District?"

I nodded.

He stared at me, then smiled, "will you be building a harbor and warehouses?"

I smiled, "we'll be building a kingdom. Should I include a warehouse for you?"

"Most assuredly, what do you need from me?"

"Start with supplies for 1,000 people for two months, to be shipped to us as soon as you can put it together it. Then put a like amount together to ship to us in a month."

He was nodding and taking notes. "We also need a complete set of goods to set up farms. Everything from kitchenware to tools. I'll need ten sets of those, and will let you know more as we expand."

"I'll start on this straightaway."

I went down the dock to my warehouse where Mr. Hicks' office was located and gave him a similar set of orders.

I left him to be about his business, walked to the Inn and sat at a back table.

As I ate my bread and cheese, I listened to the local gossip. There was talk of a minor earthquake, and of the castle disappearing. They blamed the latter on the crazy old mage making some sort of magical mistake. There was talk of the Crown Prince's funeral, and a little of Prince Kade not coming back to Port West Gate.

I finished my meal, paid, and left. I dropped into the

ground flew back to Black Stag and slept in the earth to restore my strength.

***

Our ships arrived at Black Stag Cove the next day. Everyone rested there two days, then started loading the ships. It was all done in an orderly military fashion since the loading and organizing was left to Sergeant Major Miller.

Kade and I fast-traveled down to the southern tip of Southland and looked around at the lay of the land. I raised the usual tabletop relief map up, showing how the harbor, warehouses, town, castle, troop area, and farms could be laid out.

"What do you think?"

He looked at it for a bit, "It looks good on the model, let's see how it looks in the real world."

I nodded and turned, looking at the chosen site, then concentrating on what I wanted. I lowered the harbor, raising the surrounding lands. It all seemed much easier now, apparently taking no exertion at all. Somehow, moving the island had changed me and made me stronger. What would have taken me days before was done in an hour.

The harbor was 50 feet deep and stone lined. The castle was like the one I had raised at West Gate and the troop areas were similar to those at Black Stag, only bigger. A row of warehouses lined part of the harbor, adjacent to a main street that ran up from the harbor through where the town would continue to grow. We had plenty of room to move things around as needed.

The castle overlooked the harbor's mouth with cannon emplacements, for which I'd get a set of powerful guns later. I also put a Great Chain across the mouth of the harbor for added security, but then, just to be on the safe side, I placed an illusion over the harbor mouth that meant that when approaching from seaward It all looked like solid cliffs, with no opening.

The farms were well out of town and were fifty-acre plots with a house, and barn, like they were in Black Stag. Instead of fences or walls I put stone markers at each corner marking the fifty-acre plots. I pulled all the rocks out of the fields and used them in building our structures.

I put in drainage and sewer systems for the castle and the town, emptying into the sea down the coast away from the harbor. I placed wells throughout town, troop areas, harbor, and farms, and made sure the Castle had a safe freshwater cistern system fed from springs in the cliff at the land side.

I slowly opened the seawall and allowed the ocean to fill the harbor. Kade and I went up to the new royal gardens in the castle and looked out over our new kingdom. From here you could see out over the ocean south, east, and west. Looking north you could see to the horizon over our lands.

The freshwater lake was quite large, and now full. The overflow would empty into the harbor to keep the lake clean and flowing. If needed, I could raise an irrigation system for the farms. It was a beautiful sight.

"Perfect, or near to it," Kade said.

"Now we just need people."

Kade got a faraway look in his eyes, "we'll get them. There are always people looking to go elsewhere, seeking freedom, and a better way of life."

***

We flew back to Black Stag, then I rested in the earth for a while. But I didn't seem to need as much rest as I used to after shifting the earth.

I traveled to my herds of cattle and horses, thinking I'd like to take these back to Southland. But then a thought sprang to mind, a memory from the Hinterland mage I'd killed. There was a thing called a portal that was like a doorway between two places, and his memories said that only very powerful mages could open them.

"I wonder?" I concentrated on a mental image of the northern fields of Southland, and commanded, *Open!* Runes on my body glowed, and a circle of light started to appear before me. It grew until there was a circle twelve feet across in front of me, and I was looking at the Northern fields of Southland. I picked up a rock and tossed it through, and it bounced on the ground in Southland.

I shrugged my shoulders and stepped through. I felt no different, but I knew I was now in Southland. I stepped back through. *Close!* and the portal closed. I smiled at the thought. Apparently, I'M now a powerful mage!

I concentrated, felt for my cattle and horses and called them to me. Once they had all gathered, I opened the portal to Southland again and they all trotted through into Southland.

"I could be the biggest horse and cattle thief in the world!" I laughed. "OK, so maybe I'd buy most of them, I can afford them!"

I dropped into the earth and rested. Feeling the surrounding earth, then stretching my consciousness out, I felt, gold and silver, and coal and gems and earth oils.

It impressed me that there was so much silver around. It was all in grains like sand, but it was there. I called the silver to me. The silver sand started migrating toward me, my runes started glowing. The silver sand started to gather in a block before me, and I stopped when the block got to be the size of our Command Wagon. I did the same to the gold grains and nuggets, but that block stopped at about a quarter of the size of the silver.

I left the blocks and went to the coal deposits. I moved all the surface coal deposits underground. I put a few hands full in my pouch. I'd make some diamonds later.

I went back to the blocks of silver and gold, laid my hands on them and fast-traveled to the Southland castle. Under the castle I opened a vault, put the blocks in and went back to Black Stag. I ate in the mess hall with everyone else, then slept in the earth that night.

***

The first load of people and equipment left, heading for Southland. We left half of the mercenaries, and two Centuries at Black Stag to load the rest of the equipment and come with the next load.

Kade and I went on the lead ship. "Follow the coast south, Captain, I'll show you where the harbor is."

It took us a full day to get to Southland Harbor, where I raised the illusion and the three ships sailed in. Once docked, they started unloading our supplies, equipment, and people. I placed the illusion back in place, thinking we weren't ready for visitors yet.

The cooks went to the barracks kitchens and started getting ready to feed people. It was a simple, late meal. But we fed everyone.

By the end of the week everyone and everything had been moved from Black Stag to Southland.

While I waited, I created an "illusion stone" for our ships. While it was on board a ship, the crew could see through the illusion as they approached the harbor.

The soldiers had helped move all the farmers' tools, goods and livestock out to the farms. Allowing them to get to work on their new farms. They were assured that we would feed and support them until the first crops came in.

The servants had moved into the castle and started putting it into the condition they thought was appropriate for the new nation's rulers.

Our drover had come with us, and I had brought the cattle through a portal close to the freshwater lake. I made a mental note to get more cattle and increase our herd.

I went back to our old Black Stag Keep, then I lowered everything I had raised back into the ground, leaving nothing but the crumbled ruins of the original keep. Let the king fix it!

I went to West Gate Inn for a meal. This time in the guise of a common workman. The server came by, "food, ale," was all I said. I paid my coppers when she brought it back. The food was filling, which was about all I could say about it. I guess the higher tables got the better stuff!

It had been two months since Kade's fall from favor, but I heard no news about it, good or bad, from the inns or trading houses.

The newest talk was of the Hinterland Prince, who had decided he was not going to pay the ransom to free his father, who was being held in Vigil Castle. Instead, he had taken the opportunity to make himself King.

"That will get expensive for the young King, and I will ensure it does, I thought to myself.

I left the inn, dropped into the earth and started flying toward Hinterland's capital.

CHAPTER 30

I flew under, following the coast and found I could now fly faster and with less effort than before. As I traveled, the coastline changed from crags to cliffs, then to beaches. Even travelling at high speed, it took a long while to get to a large port. It was not the capital, so I continued up the coast. When I arrived at Hinterland's main city, it was what I would call a major port. I saw 20 or 30 ships loading and unloading cargo. There was also a large naval presence in port.

I flew under the city to the royal castle, finding it was a large sprawling thing built for show, not for war. I went up inside the walls of the castle, finding the prince (soon to be king) in a large dining hall eating with a group of his courtiers.

Maddie was not among them, so I moved through the walls looking for her. Finally, I found her in a small set of rooms in the royal wing, under guard. She did not look well... she had lost weight, and her posture was that of someone beaten down by circumstance. She sat looking out a window, eyes unfocused, and I wondered if they had drugged her. I moved to the other wall for a better view and that's when I saw she was with child.

"Well that complicates things, doesn't it?" I thought as I went back to the dining room. There were guards at the doors, and the doors were closed. I sealed the doors, so they could not be opened and then, in the guise of Orcus with my staff, I stepped out of the doors as if I had entered through them.

I stood there until I was noticed. "We were not to be disturbed! What is it, mage?" The prince-king demanded.

"They have sent me seeking information and clarification Your Highness."

He smiled because he thought he knew where this was going. "What information needs clarification?"

"The king in the south has heard you do not intend to honor the peace agreement, and you will not be ransoming your father."

"He has heard correctly. He may keep the old man and I will not be sending any ships for his ransom. I am now King of Hinterland."

I nodded, "and the king's daughter?"

"You may have her back; we never consummated the wedding vows. She was with child and I'll not raise a bastard!"

"The child is not a bastard, the princess was married when the child was conceived."

"I don't care, it's not mine, so your king can have her back. I can always put her on a ship if you'd like."

"Have her brought forth, then I shall decide." I released the door seal.

"Guard!" he called. The door opened and one came in.

"Yes, Sire?"

"Bring me the fouled princess," he chuckled.

"Yes Sire," he said and departed.

He continued eating and drinking and it was a while before the Maddie arrived. "And here she is, alive and well. Admittedly, more alive than well," he laughed.

I decided, not for the first time, that I really didn't like this guy.

Maddie stood at the door.

"Come in, princess, you have a visitor."

I turned, and bowed, "Princess."

She looked at me and nodded, "Sir Mage."

"Forgive me, but I must ask... the child you carry, who is the father?"

"Thankfully not his," she nodded disdainfully at the prince. "Although he has beaten me enough trying to make me lose it, so he could plant another. He would not touch me until I lost this child. The father is Earl Draugur de Crypta, my first husband."

My rage went cold instead of hot. "He beat you, trying to force a miscarriage?"

The princess looked at the prince-king, "he did."

"That's true," he interjected, "but in Hinterland husbands can beat their wives whenever, and for whatever, they wish to." I ignored him.

"Do you wish to go home, princess?"

She nodded, "yes, but to my brother, Prince Kade."

I turned back to the prince-king, "I agree, I shall return her to the Southern Kingdom."

"Good, be gone!"

I concentrated and opened a portal to the Royal Gardens in the Southland Castle. We could see Prince Kade on the other side as he stood there looking at us and frowning.

I stepped aside, "Princess, please tell your brother all that has happened to you. Tell him I will visit him after I conclude my business here." She nodded and stepped through the portal, and I closed it behind her.

The prince-king looked at me, and barked, "I said, be gone, mage!" I bowed and dropped through the floor.

"Yes, I will leave, but this will cost you dearly!"

These people were so greedy, I thought, that the easiest way to hurt them was to take their wealth, and then take their power away. Moving through the stones of the castle, I started on the top floor and took every piece of gold, piece of silver, every piece of jewelry, every gemstone I could find and dropped it in my magic pouch. Any large items made of gold or silver I took down to their treasury vault, which was the largest I had ever seen. I sealed the door and the moved the vault deeper into the earth, far away from what had been its opening.

I went under the harbor to one of the big first-rate ships-of-the-line. It only had a port watch on board, and those guarding it were regular navy sailors, not conscripts. Without mercy, I raised twenty stone dogs and sent them to kill everyone on board, ensuring that none escaped. All the bodies and blood were sent down into the earth. I left the dogs on guard to kill anyone who came on board.

I went to every warship in the harbor and silently took the gold or whatever valuables there were on board, moving it all into the hold of what had become MY new warship.

Now the real fun started. I fast-traveled to Vigil Castle and found King Manfred of Hinterland alone in his room. I opened the door and stepped in.

"One usually knocks before entering."

"I'll try to remember. I bring a message from your son."

"And what would that be?"

"He has made himself king. He will not pay your ransom, and he has sent the princess back home to her brother, so there is no marriage for peace."

He said nothing for a moment, then "now I know why some animals eat their young."

I nodded, "In this case I would agree."

"You are a mage?"

I nodded, "I am."

"What do you intend to do with me?"

"That depends on you. Would you like to go home and take vengeance on your offspring?"

He laughed, "I very much would!" He smiled evilly.

"He holds the capital, and its castle, where will you go?"

"The capital... you get me there, I'll take care of the rest."

"Any particular place?"

"The army fort."

I nodded and opened a portal to the fort. "Good hunting!" he walked through the portal and never looked back.

I fast-traveled back to my new warship, ordered its mooring lines to cast themselves off, and eased the ship away from the docks in the darkness. I asked the ocean to push the ship, and we cruised out of the harbor.

Once safely clear of the harbor I stopped the ship, then

moved back under the warships in the harbor and started fires on each of them. I asked the fires to burn the ships and anything they touched. The flames took off as if alive.

Then I went under the walls around the castle, collapsing them in several places and setting more fires. Once I had started fires in the powder magazines, it didn't take long for them to go up in mighty explosions. I asked the wind to blow over the fire to speed it on its way and it spread all over the city.

I went to the city livestock pen, opened a portal to the Southland and allowed hundreds of cattle, horses, sheep, goats and pigs to run through to get away from the fire and smoke. then I went to the royal stables and sent all the horses through another portal to Southland.

While the city burned, I went back under the castle to the treasury vault. I was thinking of moving it but had another thought. I opened a large vault, and opened my pavilion, I brought the huge treasury vault up against the pavilion-. I went inside the pavilion. I concentrated on what I wanted to happen. *Make the treasury vault part of the pavilion.* I went to the office and looked behind the tapestry. I smiled, there was a vault door there. I opened the door my new huge treasury vault full of valuables was now part of my pavilion.

I went outside and closed the pavilion book, and then the vault I had opened. I put the pavilion book away and flew under back to my new warship. I asked the ship to spread her sails, and as I sailed out of sight, the capital of Hinterland was completely in flames, and there was fighting in the streets.

***

I sailed south down the coast toward Southland, and when the other Hinterland port came into sight, I had the ship drop her sails, then anchor. I started fires on every navy ship there in the harbor, and while the sailors were fighting the fires, I stole all the gold chests from every ship and put them in the hold on my warship. I went to the powder magazines and moved all the casks of black powder into the hold of my ship. I had the wind pick up, and that spread the fires.

I went back to my ship, raised the anchor, and spread the sails. Looking aft, I could see the ships and the town burning. I continued on down the coast toward Southland.

I changed the pennant and mainsail to my Rampant Dragon sigil as I sailed at a leisurely pace back home. I had decided to give Maddie and Kade some time to talk. And that gave me time to consider what I, or we, were going to do about us and our child. Well, at the very least, I thought, I could make sure the child would be taken care of. Whether I could trust Maddie would take some serious consideration.

While I was sailing and thinking, I made the same improvements to this ship as I had my other ships, streamlining and cleaning the hull, improving the sail plan and removing some of the 120 guns to arm Southland Castle. This would become our most heavily armed merchantman. It took me a week to get to Southland, where I sailed into the harbor and docked.

Kade met me. "I suppose you just found this ship?"

"Oh, no! I stole this one fair and square. But they were busy with their other ships and didn't see me leave."

"Busy doing what?"

"Trying to put out the fires. And the crews were having a hard time getting help."

"And why was that?"

"Well, everyone else was busy trying to put out the fires in the city. And then there was all the fighting in the streets."

"I hate to ask, but why were they fighting?"

"Well, it seems the prince reneged on his deal to ransom his father and made himself king. Someone released the father and took him to the capital. Family fights can be so messy."

"You said someone released the father?"

"Yes, I heard a rumor that it was probably a mage — you know you can't trust them, right?"

"So I've heard."

"Anyway, as I was sailing away, Hinterland City and its harbor were in flames, and the army was fighting civilians in the streets. As I said, messy. The fire must have been bad, because the next port down the coast caught fire. too. Ships, city, everything."

"Yes, it's terrible how fire spreads. That should keep them busy for a while."

"That was my thinking, and if the prince survives, I'll pay him another visit, to make sure he does not."

"What do you intend to do with this ship?"

"Use some of the cannons for the castle, and use the rest to give us a heavily armed merchantman."

He nodded. "Will you be joining us for dinner?"

"Does she know where she is?"

"Yes, I told her that we were on an island, now the King-dom of Southland."

I nodded. "Then she knows I'm alive."

"She knows a mage did all of this," He pointed around, "and moved the island. She has not mentioned you, but I'm sure she suspects you are still alive. What other mage would work for free?"

I smiled, "there is that. But I don't think I'm ready for a meeting just yet."

"Don't judge her too harshly, Ghost. She acted the way she was taught. She just took it too far because she assumed you had the same motivations and were trying to get the best deal, just like she was."

I nodded, "soon, maybe, but not yet.

"On another subject, there is a full load of black pow-der in the hold, so take half for the castle. I'll be around." I dropped into the earth and then moved all the treasure chests and valuables from the ship's hold into the Royal Castle's treasury vault.

I traveled to the fields where the livestock had been transported, opened my pavilion, and sat down to a hot meal and cool wine.

***

The next day I was in the stables brushing Harbinger when Kade came in. "Your presence is requested, Sir Mage. By whatever name you wish to use ... her words, not mine." He was smiling.

I laughed, "will you go with me into the lion's den?"

"I will, but only to drag the body out. Other than that, you are on your own."

"I don't blame you, maybe I can do the same for you someday." We laughed.

We walked up to the Royal Garden balcony. Maddie was sitting looking out over the ocean. She heard us approach and turned, and I saw that she was looking a lot better than she did that night in the Hinterland castle. She stood up and you could plainly see she was with child.

"I need new clothes! Mine no longer fit, and I'm ugly!" Then she ran to the balcony and threw up. "And I have morning sickness, and it's all your fault!"

Before I thought better of it, I retorted, "if I recall, you were there, too."

"Uh-oh," Kade said.

She turned on me, "Oh, I suppose you think this is funny."

I backed up a step. "Not anymore."

She grabbed the chair, "Oh, I think I'm going to faint." I grabbed her as she started to fall, picked her up and held her and felt the runes on my body began to glow, then pulsate.

"Good Lord above!" said Kade.

I held her as she leaned her head into my chest and wept. I carried her to her bedchambers and sat down on the bed, still holding her. She was quiet now and my runes calmed down.

Kade nodded and left. I lay back with her, keeping her wrapped in my arms. She no longer wept, but slept peacefully.

It was midday before she woke.

"It's OK," I said, "I've got you. You fainted, you're all right." I felt her relax.

We lay still for a time. "I am so sorry, Ghost. I was a stupid, arrogant child, and I treated you terribly. I'll understand if you never trust me again, but I hope you can find it in your heart to forgive me. I need you... I can't do this by myself."

"I forgive you," I said gently. "And I'm not going anywhere. Well, except maybe to buy some clothes, but you have to come with me. I wouldn't know what to buy." She nodded smiling.

"I want to go to the capital, there is a lovely shop there that will have everything I need."

"We'll go anywhere you like." We lay there a while longer.

"That old mage, with the crazy eyes, he said he had killed you."

"He almost did, so it took me a while to heal, but I was not as dead as he believed."

"Is he dead? I didn't like him."

"If he's not dead, then I'm sadly mistaken. He won't be bothering us again."

CHAPTER 31

Kade declined Maddie's kind offer to come with us on our shopping expedition. Behind her back I was mouthing "please come! with praying hands.

He smiled, "no thank you. Buying women's clothes with my pregnant sister is not my idea of fun."

"I don't think it's anyone's idea of fun!" I muttered.

"What was that, dear?"

"I was agreeing with you, he should come."

"One day you'll wish you had."

"I'll risk it."

I opened a portal to the street where all the clothes shops were, and we stepped through as passersby stopped and stared. When I closed the portal, they moved on. I was wearing my light dragon armor without my helm, and with my real face. Ghost was now alive, having recovered from his fight with the "crazy old mage".

We went into the clothing store and Maddie looked at, and tried on, every dress in the shop. We, uh, I bought about half the dresses in the store. And of course, ladies do not carry money, as it would be unseemly. Now I knew why Kade had rabbited!

"Can we go to Vigil Castle?"

"When?"

"Now, of course!"

"Silly me." I opened a portal in the Great Hall, and we stepped through with all of Maddie's packages.

The kids screamed, "Aunt Maddie, Uncle Ghost!" Crown Prince Mathew and Emily came to see what all the excitement was about.

"Ghost?" asked Mathew.

"Your highness," I said, bowing.

"We thought you were dead."

"Close, but I got better!" The family gathered to hear the story and I gave them a cleaned version.

"So, Prince Manfred sent you back and rejected the ransom deal." Mathew asked Maddie.

"He did. He would not touch me except to beat me. Thankfully, the mage Orcus came to Hinterland and send me home to Kade."

"You know this Orcus, Ghost?"

I nodded, "I do, mild-mannered fellow."

"When we found King Manfred gone, we figured he had help to get away. We hear there is a war going on in Hinterland between father and son and the country is in ruin." I said nothing.

"The King is not happy he did not get his ships or any ransom, since the war cost a fortune. He levied a war tax of 50 percent from us when he returned to the capital. We are getting by, but it will be close for a long time."

"Maddie, you said you were staying with Kade... is he at West Gate? We had heard Kade was out of favor and had been sent away."

Maddie looked at me, "I didn't know. Kade said nothing about it."

I nodded, "the king blamed Kade for, well, several things. He exiled him, told him to make it on his own or not — he didn't care which."

Mathew was nodding, "Mother is still mad."

Then she started laughing. "What's so funny?" Mathew asked.

"Father sent Kade away to make it on his own. Well he did, and he is now King Kade of Southland. He has a powerful mage as his advisor, and friend. They also own a fleet of eleven, armed merchantmen trading ships. I would say they are doing quite well."

"Southland? I've never heard of Southland," Mathew said.

"It used to be called the Southern District. An earthquake split it off the mainland and made it an island two miles on the coast." Maddie answered.

Mathew started laughing, "father will lose his mind when he finds out. He'll want to tax Kade and take the island back under his control."

"Good luck with that," I said. "He kicked us out, and he doesn't get a second chance. He wanted to punish and embarrass Kade, to show him he needed The Crown. We'll we don't."

"How did you get a fleet of armed merchantmen?"

I shrugged my shoulders, "Hinterlanders attacked me so I took their ships. Hinterland's Prince beat my wife, so I burned their capital city to the ground, including their harbor and their navy's ships. They won't be bothering anyone for a while."

This was the first Maddie had heard of my retaliation.

No one, including Maddie, said anything, they just stared at me and I think my harshness shocked them. "As far as your sadly diminished treasury is concerned, let me go check something, excuse me for a while."

"Of course." Mathew said. I left the room, but before I dropped into the earth I went back to listen.

"That is an intense man." Mathew said.

"You have no idea," Maddie said, "father had better leave those two alone. It would cost him far more than he would ever gain. I learned that the hard way. Ghost does things out of love and friendship, but if you cross him, he can turn vicious and merciless."

"But you're OK now, right?" Emily asked.

"He has forgiven me, but it will take me a long time to earn his trust back."

I flew under toward the northern mountains. When I was close enough, I stretched my consciousness and called the silver grains to me. I stopped when the block was the size of a wagon. I then called the gold grains and nuggets. I waited until the gold block was the same size as the silver block before I stopped.

I laid my hands on the blocks and fast-traveled back to Vigil Castle's vault. I made it bigger and put the two blocks in the vault, but stopped when I realized that these massive metal blocks were not usable. Then, I smiled, touched the silver block and concentrated. Suddenly it collapsed into a huge pile of silver coins, each with the likeness of Princess Madison on one side and the shape of Southland on the other.

I did the same thing to the gold, forming each coin with the likeness of King Kade on one side and Southland on the reverse.

"That should cover them for a while!" I walked back into the family area, where everyone was still sitting and talking. They turned to me as I entered, "it was as I thought. Your lands contain some silver and gold ores."

"How long will it take to get it out?" Mathew asked.

I shrugged my shoulders, "A few minutes at most."

"Ghost!" Maddie said smiling.

"It's in your treasury vault. You should go look. There should be enough to hold you for a while." We walked down to the vault and Mathew unlocked the door, opened it and looked in. Emily saw inside the vault and began to cry and hugged Maddie.

We walked into the vault with lit lanterns. They stared at the piles of coins. Mathew picked one up looking at it and laughed.

"A gift from Southland," I said.

Maddie looked at the coins smiling. "Poke the bear much?"

"Not me, that's Kade, I'm the sensible one."

"You are both crazy, but you are the worst. It's a good thing you have each other. And it's a good thing I have both of you." She hugged me.

"Yes," Mathew said flipping a coin, "I believe this will

hold us for a while."

***

Crown Prince Mathew's words turned out to be prophetic. A month later Kade started receiving messages from King John, ordering him to present himself at Court. Kade replied:

"No thank you. I Abdicate. You told me to make it on my own, or not, and you did not care which. I made it and I have court duties of my own to attend to."-King Kade I, King of Southland.

I didn't deliver the letter, but sent it back by a messenger from West Gate.

I foresaw trouble coming and advised Arthur Williamson to move all his businesses and cash from Port West Gate to Southland. I moved the blocks of silver and gold into the Southland Treasury Vault and turned them into Kade and Maddie coins.

Arthur and Mr. Hicks had opened trading agreements with Hinterland. They were also in search of other nations to trade with.

I went to the slave pens in West Gate and bought all the slaves that had a trade to offer or were farmers. I opened a portal and took them through to Southland. We put them in a warehouse temporarily until we could get farms opened or a place for them to live while they served. They were all working toward freedom.

Kade sent letters to the third sons of our former kingdom inviting them to come serve in our army. They were asked to swear fealty to King Kade with the promise that, once their service was complete, they would be awarded lands to start their own houses.

We didn't mention that our officers would have to be trained by Sergeant Major Miller and then serve with the mercenary companies as enlisted men before earning their commission. They would have to work for the lands they got.

The four Centuries had completed their training and augmented the castle and harbor guards. Top-Sergeant Cooper was appointed as their master sergeant.

Things had been relatively quiet. Maddie's belly was getting bigger, but she had no more morning sickness. She turned to writing letters to third daughters, recruiting ladies-in-waiting for her court.

Hinterland's civil war was still going, but had turned into a stalemate, with neither side garnering enough support for a final victory

Kade handed me a letter at breakfast, from his father. Once you got past all the flowery words, it boiled down to a declaration of war. They were seizing all our assets in the kingdom, would take any of our ships wherever they found them. And they were blockading our harbor.

I looked out to sea, and saw that there was indeed a ship cruising just offshore.

"I'll be right back." I dropped through the floor and flew under to their ship. I took all their black powder, even what they had loaded in their cannons, brought it all back and put it in our powder magazines. I then raised rocks up under their ship, lifting it up out of the water holding it in place. I then went back to breakfast.

"That should keep them busy." I said.

"What did you do, dear?" Maddie asked, buttering her toast.

"I stole all of their black powder, including what they had loaded in their cannons. And then ran their ship aground," I said smiling.

Kade laughed, shaking his head.

"I think I'll take a message to the king of my own. Nothing dangerous, just a warning. Would you like to send a letter?"

"No, but no killing... yet," Kade said.

"No killing... yet." I answered.

"Can you take one to mother for me?" Maddie asked.

"Of course."

***

I left Maddie's letter on the queen's desk. I would wait until early morning before I acted, so I slept deep in the earth.

It was about two in the morning when I put my plan into action. I slowly lowered all the castle wall down into the earth, making all the walls and watch towers only three feet off the ground. I left the main gate alone so traffic could still flow. Then I drained the moat and raised the bottom so there was only flat ground outside the walls.

I followed the river from the capital to the coast where it met the ocean and raised a reef blocking ship's passage, but allowing the river to still flow. Then I went back to the castle and waited.

Soon, there was lots of shouting and running around., and the king and queen were up and walking the walls.

"I told you to leave them alone, but you wouldn't listen! How do you plan to fix this, now that we are all but defenseless?" The queen demanded. The king said nothing, just turned and went back inside. That should keep them occupied for a while. Since I was here, I went down to the slave pens to see what was available.

I entered the slave market in the guise of Orcus and said, "I would like to see the Slave Master." I handed the flunky a Southland gold coin, since I thought I'd start them in circulation.

He bowed, "a moment, sir."

He returned with the Slave Master. "My name is Orcus," I said and handed him five Southland golds. "I wish to buy slaves. I need craftsmen, house servants, farmers, anyone with a skill. Family units are better. I'm not looking for concubines, no castoffs or troublemakers."

He bowed, "of course sir, this way and I will have the best brought in for your inspection."

He did as I asked, and I bought one hundred slaves, including a dressmaker, and her family who were there because they had defaulted on a debt.

When he had shown me all he had, he approached me. "Sir, that is all the common slaves I have that fit your request. But I have another that you may be interested in."

"How so?"

"Three ships were taken, two guarding the third. When they took the ships, their cargo was rich. They were also carrying the niece, so she says, of a foreign king. I have sold all the captured soldiers and sailors except the lady and her four ladies. I must say she is beautiful, as are her ladies."

"You did not try ransom her?"

"In truth I tried, but no answer ever came. I've had her for six months. You are more well-traveled than I, perhaps you could ransom her where I could not?" He was telling me the truth, as far as it went.

"I will see her, then decide."

"We must go to another house where they are kept, as they are ladies."

I nodded, "lead on." They took me to a nice house in a good section of the city. We went inside and they served me wine. The ladies we brought before me. They were all pretty women and the niece was the prettiest of them.

"Has my uncle, the king, sent you to ransom us?"

I shook my head, "He has not, Lady. I am here on my behalf."

"You will buy us to ransom?"

"Perhaps."

I looked at the Slave Master, "A moment." I opened a portal to Southland Castle. Maddie was there and I motioned to her to come. "Talk to them, see if they really are royals." She nodded and went over to them.

I waited while the women had their heads together talking, and after a few moments she came back to me and whispered, "buy them."

"Slave Master, give me a total price for all I have bought

today plus these five women."

"50,000 golds," he said and Maddie laughed.

I opened a portal, "good luck!" I said, and Maddie began to step through.

"25,000." He said

"I'll give you 8,000 for all."

"fifteen."

"Twelve, and the portal is closing." I stepped through. The portal started closing.

"Done, 12,000," he shouted.

"And all the ladies' clothes," Maddie added.

"And their clothes," he said.

"Done," I said. I paid with Hinterland bills. When the Slave Master was satisfied, I sent the ladies, and their clothes, through the portal to where Maddie stood.

The Slave Master and I returned to the market, where my other slaves were waiting. We gathered them in one place, and I opened a portal to a warehouse in Southland Harbor where they would be taken care of. I followed the last ones through.

CHAPTER 32

Once I had our new people seen to, I went up to the castle and found Maddie and Kade on the balcony drinking wine.

"Who are our guests?" I asked.

"I'm not sure. They are royals, but how high born is uncertain. She said she was a niece, but I believe she's really the daughter of King Fredrico of Castillia."

"And that would make her?"

"Princess Martina Castile."

I looked at Kade, "well, King Kade, what will you do with your guest?"

"Me?"

"Oh yes, this is one of those royal-only problems that you get to deal with. I just build things, and, OK, steal things... and kill people. Anyway, you get the idea."

"Speak of the devil," Maddie said.

Turning I saw that Princess Martina and her ladies were approaching.

"Princess Martina, may I present King Kade of Southland and his sister Princess Madison."

Before she remembered who she was supposed to be, she curtsied, "Your Highness."

Kade nodded, "Princess Martina, welcome to Southland."

Kade turned to me, "Sir Mage, perhaps we could sup in your pavilion?"

I smiled, "Of course, Sire." I lay the pavilion book down and opened it. Once it had finished opening, to the party's considerable surprise, we went inside. Kade took the head of the table, as he was acting host.

"How very nice, dear," Maddie said, giving me the "we'll

talk later" look. I chuckled.

Food appeared that was suitable for Princess Martina and her ladies and we spent a pleasant evening talking. They were indeed from Castillia and she was indeed the king's daughter. She said they had made her a niece to keep the ransom lower, and not to be used against her father.

"King Kade, will you ransom me to my father?"

"No, Princess, you may leave anytime you are ready-. Send your father a message so he may send a ship to get you."

"Could you order your mage to open one of those portals to send us home? I do not wish to spend all that time cramped in a ship. Then my father will buy the mage from you."

Kade's eyes went hard. "The mage is my brother, and not for sale at any price. And if he chooses to open a portal that will be his choice." He looked at me, "do with her as you will, brother." He stood and stalked out of the pavilion.

I stood, "ladies I believe dinner is over." They stood in silence, shocked at Kade's reaction, and left my pavilion. Once we were all outside, I closed it and put it away. I searched my gathered memories, and found that the alchemist had once been to Castillia, so I could open a portal to there.

I stepped to the balcony away from them, concentrated on Castillia and gathered my strength. My runes began to glow, and when I felt ready, I opened a portal straight into King Fredrico's throne room. That was actually pure luck but it made me look good. Inside, guards were drawing swords.

I stepped aside, "ladies, you may go."

"Our clothes?" one asked. I concentrated and their trunks came up through the floor and through the portal. The ladies walked through, the last one turned after she was through the portal.

"What boon would you ask of my father?" It was now clear that the woman who had said she was Princess Martina was a double. Now the real princess spoke, while the others went to their knees behind her.

"Nothing... You have offended my brother, and his hospitality." I closed the portal.

***

After a week, I let the blockade ship back down into the water and they set sail for home right away.

Our first of the third sons appeared and began training with the mercenary companies. Two more showed up a month later. The Sergeant Major put them to work straight away and so far, to their credit, they were sticking with the training.

Our town was growing, as were the number of farms. Now we were only buying slaves that were farmers and those with families if we could get them. We now had 50 active farms and they should all be self-supporting by next year.

We had also brought in hog farmers and a few more drovers for our cattle. I was going to Hinterland once a week and buying young cows to increase our herds. We now had over a 1,000 head.

Kade had been working with the mercenaries to keep busy and active. I brought Crown Prince Mathew and family in for a feast to give everyone a break. Maddie also needed some female company. Kade and Mathew rode over much of the area looking over things and talking.

Over dinner Mathew asked, "Ghost, will you come back and build more farms for us at the price Maddie quoted?"

I smiled, "I take it people are moving out to the farms."

"There is a waiting list to go out on them. I could fill 20 farmsteads tomorrow."

"I'll make you a deal, I'll come build 20 farmsteads for nothing, if Emily stays with Maddie until after the birth."

"I would do that, anyway."

"Quiet woman, men are bargaining here!" Matthew said. Everyone laughed.

After breakfast the next morning I opened a portal to Vigil Castle, and Mathew and I went through. I raised 10 farms on the West Road, and 10 more on the South Road.

"I started one time to raise a small fort on your East Road about ten miles out," I told Matthew. "It would be an early warning outpost and help to keep bandits under control. Would that be something you'd like me to do?"

"I like it! Make it big enough for two squads of troops to stay there full time."

"I can do that, what about on the North Road? The south and west are secure."

"Yes, do that too, that will make the farmers feel even more safe." It took me half a day to raise all the farms and the two forts. The two forts also had stables for all their horses, wells, and storage to hold in a siege until help came from the castle. I also raised ten miles of paved road going west, as I had done in the other directions.

Once I finished my work, I told Mathew we'd see him in a week and headed home. But curiosity got the better of me, and I fast-traveled to the Capital Castle. Workmen were around it digging a new moat and they were using logs to build a palisade. Well, at least the king was putting people to work, but I wondered if he was paying them.

I fast-traveled to the coast where I had blocked the river. They were digging a canal down to go around my blockade. My curiosity satisfied; I went home.

***

It was all rather anticlimactic when it happened. I had brought in a mid-wife for the birth, but they were only in the royal suites for three hours when they came out with a baby boy. I guess royals did things differently! I acted suitably impressed. Everyone survived and was healthy, which was a very good thing. I must admit my son was perfect — just like his father.

He was crying when they handed him to me, and I held him in my arms close to my chest. All the runes on my body lit up and he stopped crying and was peaceful. My runes stayed lit for a while then went out. When I handed him back, I noticed a rune on the center of his chest. No one said anything, so I didn't.

The mid-wife stayed with us for a while. I took Emily and children home.

Time seemed to fly by. The boy, who we named Maximilian and called Max, seemed to grow daily. Maybe it was because I had never been around babies before, but I thought he seemed particularly inquisitive. He wanted to see and touch everything, but Maddie said that was natural.

We were at our normal breakfast, when my hand started tingling. This time it was different. I sensed I was being called, maybe summoned would be a better word. All the runes on my body began to glow. Kade and Maddie stared at me, Max laughed because he liked the lights.

"I have to go, I'm being summoned. I'll be back when I can."

"How long will you be gone?" Kade asked.

"I don't know. This has never happened before."

"This is a mage calling?" Maddie asked.

"Yes, I'll return when I can." I kissed her and Max, then clasped wrists with Kade. "Watch over them until I return."

"You know I will." I nodded.

I sank into the earth and fast-traveled to the Capital City graveyard. I flew into the crypt that was calling me, but could see nothing. There was no one around the chapel, so I emerged there and went inside. On impulse, I took a large purse of gold out of my pouch and put it in the collection box.

I looked toward the crucifix at the front and bowed. "I am healed, and doing well, thank you for the water and bandage." I walked through the chapel and down the side steps to the crypts. The doors were still open and the stone knights stood silent watch at the outer doors.

When I approach they came to life. I held up my hand. "I have been called." They stopped, stepped aside, and the doors opened. I entered, and the doors closed behind me. The room had not changed. The rotting corpse sat on his dais watching me as I entered.

"Ah, the thief returns," he said in his hollow voice.

"Not by choice, I can assure you."

"Much of life is not by choice."

"True, but I never thought to see this place again."

"And I see nothing else."

He seemed to want to talk, so I encouraged him. "How did you wind up in this place, and in this condition?"

"Arrogance... arrogance pure and simple." I waited for him to say more.

"I was an artisan, a maker of jewelry. Then I discovered I had a talent for making my jewelry finer, more exquisite. I learned the art of runes, arcane runes. My work became true works of art, and I became jealous of them, no one deserved them but me... until I realized that they possessed me rather than me possessing them."

"I sold some minor works to live. Even my minor works were grand. After years, my age caught up with me. I lost my finesse of hand and eye. I sought a way to keep my youth and youthful skills. Nothing I did seemed to work.

One day a powerful mage sought me out and commissioned an exquisite, complicated piece. I bargained with him, saying I would make his piece if in exchange he would conjure me my youth so that I would stay young. He agreed. He worked his spell, and I became young again." The corpse laughed at the memory.

"I made his arcane piece, and it was my best work, the best I had ever created. It was a set of rings and a bracelet, much like the one I gave you. When he came to collect his piece, I was so jealous of it I would not give it to him. I had my payment, what could he do, how do you take back a conjuring? He became furious, shouting that he had kept his part of the bargain and I must keep mine.

"I laughed at him, his body runes began to glow, and he

attacked me, planning to take my work. He cast his spells, his lightning, his fire, his ice. My creation took them all and protected me. He saw he could not hurt me, so he stopped."

"You have your payment, of youth, I give you what your greed has purchased. You shall never die and cast another conjuring."

"I was overjoyed — youthfulness, forever." The corpse's laughter became hysterical.

"Not quite, as you can see. I am still alive, after a fashion, but my youth has failed once again. But my time was not wasted. I figured out a way to get my youth back. The artifact you wear contains youth from those you have taken. You will give it back to me, and I will become young again."

I looked at my hand. "When you have your youth back, can you make me another one?"

"Yes, I know the secret now. Return it to me and we shall both remain young."

I nodded and walked toward him, and he came down from the dais. I held my hand out toward him and he reached for it but just before he touched me, I grabbed his wrist, pulling and spinning him around. My arm encircled the top of his head as I drew my knife and with a slash cut his head off.

The head laughed hysterically, "you can't kill me!"

The stone knights burst into the room but my stone dogs came up through the floor and attacked them. I dropped into the earth taking the head and body with me. Lightning bolts, fireballs, and ice shards hit me and my runes were ablaze protecting me. I could not kill him, so in desperation I commanded, *Teach me!*

The head shrieked and vibrated as the body convulsed. He fought like nothing I have ever faced. "No!!!" he screamed. There was an explosion in my mind, and his memories hit me. His insanity hit me; his skills hit me. It was too much, all at one time. I tried to hold on, but it was all too much to absorb. As darkness began to take me, I saw someone else in the background, but I could not hold on. Darkness...

I awoke with the lifeless severed head still clutched in my arms, the lifeless body not far away.

"You survived."

I slowly turned my head to see who spoke. "I'm not so sure that I did."

He chuckled. "And your mind is intact, it seems."

"How long was I out?"

"A little over a month."

"A month?"

He nodded.

"Who are you, anyway?"

"Oh, I'm not really here, I left this surprise for greedy guts if he ever tried to break my spell. Which I knew he would try someday."

"You're the mage he cheated."

He nodded.

"Is there anything I can do for you?"

He smiled, "you've already done it. A word of warning … be careful of greed." Then he faded away.

I left the skull and body where they were and came up to find that the stone knights and dogs had gone back to earth. I walked over the chest behind the dais and didn't even open it before I pushed it down into the earth. I'm a little greedy, but I'm not crazy. Besides, I can now make my own arcane artifact whenever I want one.

I concentrated on my hand and lifted the ring-bracelet away from my bone and up through my skin. I took it off and set it aside. I looked at my hands and arms. I didn't see any runes. I reached down and touched the ground and it felt solid.

But then I concentrated, then pushed, and my hand sank into the earth. I reached down and grabbed the chest and pulled it back up. I put my ring-bracelet back on; it sank back into my skin and around my bones. I pushed the chest back down into the earth.

If I've been gone a month, and I saw no reason for the

specter to lie, Maddie would be wild with worry — and plenty mad. But after facing an insane undead mage corpse, she should be a piece of cake.

I opened a portal home and stepped through, laughing, to the rest of my life.

OTHER BOOKS BY JAMES HADDOCK

The Derelict Duty

Prologue:

The Blaring klaxon jolted me out of a sound sleep. I threw my covers off and was halfway to my Vac-suit locker before I was fully awake. It felt like I had just fallen to sleep having just finished a long EVA shift. It would be just like Dad to have an emergency drill after an EVA shift to see if I had recharged my suit. I had, I always did, both Mom and Dad were hard taskmasters when it came to ship, and personal safety. Vac-suit recharging was top of the personal safety list. If you can't breathe, you die, easy to remember.

Donning a Vac-suit was second nature for me, after 16 years of drills and practice exercises. Having literally been doing this all my life, but I loved life on our Rock-Tug. I was reaching for the comms when I felt the ship shutter. "That can't be good," I said to myself.

Mom's voice came over ship-wide, "This is not a drill, this is not a drill, meteor strike, hull breach in Engineering". Mom's voice was just as calm as if she was asking, what's for lunch. This was a way of life for us, we trained and practiced so that when the reality of working in "The Belt" happened you didn't panic, you just did your job. You didn't have to think, you knew what you needed to do, and you did it.

I keyed my comms, "Roger, hull breach in Engineering, where do you need me Mom?" "Get to Engineering and help your Father, I'm on the Bridge trying to get us in the shadow of a bigger rock for some protection." Mom answered. My adrenalin was spiking but Mom's calm voice, helped to keep me calm.

I sealed my helmet and left my cabin heading for Engineering. The klaxon had faded into the background, my breathing was louder than it was. I kept telling myself "Stay calm, just do your job, stay calm."

I had just reached Engineering, when the Tug was rocked by a succession of impacts each one harder that the last. The hatch to Engineering was closed and the indicator light was flashing red, telling me there was hard vacuum on the other side. I switched my comms to voice activated, "Dad? I'm at the hatch to Engineering it's in lockdown, I can't override it from here." "Dad? Dad?, Dad respond!

"Mom, Dad is not answering, and Engineering is sealed, you are going to have to evac the air from the rest of the ship, so I can open the hatch." Mom's steady voice replied, "Understood, emergency air evac in 10 seconds."

Those were the longest 10 seconds of my short life. The hatch indicator light finally turned green and the hatch door opened. The Engineering compartment was clear. No smoke, no fire, some sparks and lots of blinking red lights. I looked over to the Engineering station console, there sat Dad. He had not had his Vac-suit on when the hull was breached.

Hard Vacuum does terrible things to the human body. I suddenly realized that I had not heard Dad on comms the whole time, just Mom. She probably knew what had happened but was sending help in the hope that Dad was all right and that maybe the comms were down.

I heard Mom in the background declaring an emergency and calling on the radio for help. Her voice still calm somehow, "Mayday, mayday, this is the Rock Tug Taurus, Mayday, we have taken multiple meteor strikes, have multiple hull breaches, please respond."

"Come on Nic, think! What do I need to do?" I asked myself. I closed the hatch to Engineering, to seal the vacuum from the rest of the ship. I turned and started back toward the bridge. There was an impact, a light flared, and sparks; time seemed to slow, there was no sound, we were still in a vacuum, just shuttering vibrations and sparks. Holes seemed to appear in the overhead and then the deck, it was so surreal.

The meteors were punching holes through our ship like a machine punching holes on an assembly line. "Meteor storm"

Duty Calls

Duty Calls continues the story of Nic, Mal, Jazz and Jade as they fight to hold what belongs to them. The Corporations are becoming more aggressive in their effort to steal their inventions. Our four friends are matching the corporate's aggression blow for blow. The fight has already turned deadly, and the Corporation has shown they aren't afraid to spill blood. Nic has shown restraint, but the gloves are about to come off. They've gone after his family and that's the one thing he will not tolerate.

From Mist and Steam

Searching the battlefield after a major battle Sgt. Eli finds a dead Union Army messenger. In the messenger's bag is a message saying the South had surrendered, the war was over. Along with the Union Messenger was a dead Union Captain carrying his discharge papers, and eight thousand dollars.

Sgt. Eli decides now is a good time to seek other opportunities, away from the stink of war. While buying supplies from his friend the quartermaster, he is advised to go to St. Louis. Those opportunities may lie there and a crowd to get lost in. Sgt. Eli, becomes Capt. Myers, a discharged Union Cavalry Officer, and strikes out for St. Louis.

The war has caused hard times and there are those who will kill you for the shirt you are wearing. Capt. Myers plans on keeping his shirt, and four years of hard fighting has given him the tools to do so. Realizing he must look the part of a well-to-do gentleman, he buys gentleman clothes, and acts the part. People ask fewer questions of a gentleman.

What he isn't prepared for is meeting an intelligent Lady, Miss Abigale Campbell. Her Father has died, leaving the family owned shipping business, with generation steam-powered riverboats. They have dreams of building steam-powered airships, but because she is a woman, there are those who stand against them. Capt. Myers' fighting is not over, it seems business is war. They decide to become partners, and with his warfighting experience, and her brains the world is not as intimidating as it once seemed.

Hand Made Mage

Ghost, a young Criminal Guild thief, is ordered to rob the ancient crypt of a long dead Duke. He is caught grave robbing by an undead insane Mage with a twisted sense of humor. The Mage burns a set of rune engraved rings into Ghost's hand, and fingers. Unknown to Ghost, these rings allow him to manipulate the four elements — earth, wind, fire, and water.

When he returns to the Guild to report his failure, everyone thinks he has riches from the crypt, and they want them. While being held captive, Ghost meets Prince Kade, the fourth son of the King, who has troubles of his own. Ghost uses his newfound powers to escape from the Guild, saving the Prince in the process.

Spies from a foreign kingdom are trying to kill Prince Kade, and Ghost must keep them both alive, while helping the prince raise an army to stop an invasion. Ghost finds out trust too soon given is unwise and dangerous. He is learning people will do anything for gold and power. As Ghost's power grows, his enemies learn he is a far more deadly enemy than any they have ever faced.

Mage Throne Prophecy

A routine physical shows Captain Ross Mitchell has a flesh-eating virus that specifically targets the brain. Prognosis says he'll be a vegetable by week's end. Having survived numerous incursions in combat around the world, Ross decides he's not going out like that. He drives a rented corvette into a cliff face at over 200 MPH. The fiery impact catapults him toward the afterlife.

Instead of finding the afterlife, he finds himself in a different body with an old man stabbing him in his chest. He fights free, killing the old man before passing out. He wakes to find he's now in the body of Prince Aaron, the 15-year-old second son of the King. In this medieval world, the Royals are Mages. The old man who was trying to kill him was a Mage "Vampire". Instead of blood, the old Mage was trying to steal Ross/Aaron's power, knowledge, and in this case, his body. When Ross/Aaron killed the old Mage, his vampire power was transferred to him.

He now has the memories, knowledge, and powers of the old Mage. Ross/Aaron must navigate this new environment of court intrigue with care. His older brother, the Crown Prince, hates him. His older sister has no use for him. The King sees him as an asset to be used, agreeing to marry him to a neighboring Kingdom for an alliance. Before the marriage takes place, the castle is attacked.

Someone is trying to kill him but is finding it most difficult. Where Mages fight with Magic, Ross/Aaron fights with magic and steel. It's hard to cast a spell with a knife through your skull or your throat cut. As Ross/Aaron travels with his fiancée toward her home for the marriage to take place, they are attacked at every turn. Someone doesn't want this wedding to happen. Ross/Aaron has had enough of people trying to kill him. With Aaron's knowledge, and Ross' training, they take the offensive. The Kingdom will never be the same.

Wizard's Alley

Scraps, a gutter child, is sitting in his hiding place in a back alley, waiting for the cold thunderstorm to pass. Suddenly, lightning strikes in front of him, and then a second time. The two lightning bolts become men—two wizards— one from the Red Order, the other from the Blue.

The Red Wizard, chanting his curses, throws lightning bolts and fireballs. The Blue Wizard, singing his spells, throws lightning bolts and ice shards. So intense is their fighting, they become lightning rods. It seemed as if God Himself cast His lightning bolt, striking the ground between them and consuming both wizards in its white blaze. Scraps watched as the lightning bolt gouged its way across the alley, striking him.

Rain on his face awakens Scraps. The only thing left of the fighting wizards is a smoking crater and their scattered artifacts. He feels compelled to gather their possessions and hide them and himself. The dispersed items glowed red or blue, and he notices that he now has a magenta aura. Magenta, a combination of both red and blue, but more powerful than either.

Scraps then does what he has done all his life to survive. He hides. And unknowingly, he has become the catalyst for change in the Kingdom.

Cast Down World

In the summer of 2257, the asteroid Wormwood was closing in to strike Earth a glancing blow. Even a glancing blow would be catastrophic. Earth's governments and militaries united to try to shift Wormwood's path. Earth launched every nuclear missile she had and succeeded in changing its path, just enough to miss her surface. In doing so, shards from the asteroid, caused by the nuclear blasts, struck the earth. In those shards were spores that caused a change in all forms of life. Wormwood also changed Earth's magnetic field, affecting weather patterns and causing earthquakes and tidal waves.

The devastation caused society's collapse. Only the strongest survived the Great Dying. In the years that followed, mutations began to appear in animals and people. It was a time of lawlessness, where the only law was the one you could enforce. Cities and larger towns became walled city-forts. Some chose to live outside the city-forts as ranchers, farmers, and scavengers. They enforced the law with violence, and the law of the old west returned. Out of this came the Peacekeepers, modeled after the legendary Texas Rangers. They were empowered by the city-forts to be judge, jury, and executioner. They were a group of hard men: hated, feared, and respected.

This is the story of Price—a human mutation, raised in the frontier wilderness—who becomes a PK Scout.

———————

Printed in Great Britain
by Amazon

18133686R00181